Doyle Mysteries

The Scent Of Murder

Duane Wurst

ISBN-13: 978-0-9883947-5-9

Text and cover design by Duane Wurst, Berne Studio
Cover images © Duane Wurst

Printed in the United States of America

Acknowledgments

This novel is dedicated to my wife, Sharon. She is an avid reader and we are both fans of Cozy Mysteries. This is the first of the Doyle Series of Mysteries and I am grateful to Sharon for being at my side.

Thank you Sharon... I love you!

Visit my website at:
www.DuaneWurst.com

Recipes from this novel will be available on my new website.

Chapter 1

Doyle Prepares for Farewell

Ten Years Ago

Detective Albert Doyle walked into Detroit Police headquarters expecting criticism from his commander for not solving the Jerry Commelda case. His partner, Detective Lester Thornson, was at his desk waiting for Doyle's arrival. Doyle never reached Lester's desk.

The commanding officer yelled, "Doyle, get your ass over here, NOW!"

Doyle didn't like the ominous tone of his voice. He and Lester were investigating the murder of Jerry Commelda, a mob-connected business owner killed outside his downtown apartment. The case remains at a standstill, and the brass is putting pressure on them to find the killer.

"What's the problem, Sir?" Doyle asked.

"Lieutenant Edward Souther, of Major Crimes, wants you to call him... now. He said You're not to tell anyone, especially your partner. Here's his number... he expects a call immediately, so use my phone."

Doyle took the slip of paper, called, and said, "Lieutenant, this is Doyle... Yes, sir, I'll be there in five minutes... I have told no one, Sir."

Doyle rushed to the elevator and found the small, unmarked office on the third floor. Before he could knock, a voice yelled, "Come in, Doyle, the door is open."

Three men stood next to an old metal desk. The lone black officer approached Doyle with an extended hand. "I'm Lieutenant Souther, and I'm in charge of this operation. Please sit down; this will take a while."

Doyle sat on the grubby faux leather chair next to the desk. "Someone should let my partner know I'm being detained. Lester will wonder what happened."

"Don't worry about Lester. He's got a new partner and is on a different case." Pointing to the slim white officer, the Lieutenant said, "Your new partner is Kevin Stall. He's also from the Major Crimes Division. You're on the Commelda investigation, but everyone is being told that you both are being assigned a fresh case."

"What the hell is this all about?" Doyle demanded.

"We believe the commanding officer is a mole. I can't give you a name, but we've suspected him of leaking to the mob several times, and now we have recent evidence he's trying to interfere with your investigation. We want you to follow the leads we've dug up, because we're setting a trap to catch the commander and the officers helping him."

"I don't like this one bit. Do you have any idea what my partner will think? If he asks, I must tell him something. God, man... I can't screw him like that... he deserves better."

"Look," Lieutenant Souther said, "you have a choice. Tell him and you're out of a job, or don't tell him and we'll catch the killer and the corrupt cops. It's as simple as that."

Kevin Stall approached Doyle and whispered, "Doyle, it will work out. I couldn't tell my partner either, so we're in the same boat. Let's do the job, and then we can clear the air with our partners."

Doyle left Lieutenant Souther's office and returned to Homicide. Someone had already cleared Lester's desk; apparently, they had moved him to his new partner's desk. Doyle checked his phone. There were three messages from Lester. Doyle ignored them.

Homicide Detective Albert Doyle and his partner, Kevin Stall, parked in front of the Bangles Starlight Lounge, on Eight Mile Road. The two detectives received a tip from Major Crimes that Jerry Commelda's killer would be at the bar this morning. The tip came from Eddie Sutter, another suspect in the investigation.

Doyle was on the phone with headquarters. "Lieutenant, when will backup be here? According to Eddie, our man will be here any minute."

"They are on their way, don't worry... we have you covered."

Kevin yelled, "What about the mole? Does he have anyone in the area? We don't want a run in with some corrupt cops."

The Lieutenant said, "Tell Kevin we're watching the mole like a hawk; you shouldn't have any problems."

Doyle and Stall couldn't wait for back-up. The killer drove into the parking lot, got out of his car, and rushed through the front door. Doyle told his commander, and the commander gave him the OK to apprehend the man.

Kevin approached from the back of the bar as Doyle entered the front door. The bar was dark with a heavy scent of stale beer. Doyle saw his man standing next to the heavy oak bar. Holding his gun and ready to shoot, Doyle told the man to put his hands up, which he did. Suddenly, Doyle saw a flash and felt blood running down his back and leg. The gunshot was silent but painful; his hands grasped at the exit wound in his abdomen as he dropped to his knees. The wounded detective watched his partner apprehend the killer; his face hit the beer soaked wooden floor. Doyle knew it was over and drifted into darkness, laughing at the situation... he thought, *Twenty years on the force... ending in a grubby bar on Eight Mile Road.*

The Present

A Doyle Company Suburban wove its way through the streets of Detroit toward Greektown. Its driver exited Gratiot and made two left turns, south on Beaubien Street and left into a narrow alley. Mr. Doyle's restaurant faces Macomb Street, but he prefers to enter through the kitchen.

The Suburban stopped, and the driver, dressed in a crisp black suit with a Doyle's emblem on the jacket, jumped out and opened the back door.

Albert Doyle, a sixty-three-year-old gentleman with a full head of gray-brown hair with white accents, stepped out of the vehicle, pulling two shopping bags from the back seat.

He turned to the driver. "James, if you like, you can stay here until we leave for Pigeon at three. I would like to arrive at my new home in Sand Point before dark."

"Thank you, sir... I would love to stay for your farewell party."

James walked with Doyle to the back entrance of the restaurant. He put his card into the security pad and punched in a series of numbers. The door unlatched, and he pulled the massive door open. The aroma of gourmet delights flooded the alley.

"Smells good, Sir."

"It always smells good, James."

Doyle passed through the doors and set his bags on a small workstation. Felix, the head cook, approached him and with a pained smile he said, "Al, this is a very sad day. You will leave us, and we will miss you."

"I'll be back whenever I'm in Detroit. This was my first Doyle's restaurant, and it will forever be my favorite. Don't worry, Felix, I'll keep in contact."

"Yes, but I will miss working with you. We have worked together for ten wonderful years. It makes me sad, Sir." The chef turned away.

He may have had a tear of sadness in his eye, or perhaps it was from the onion he was holding.

Doyle is a self-taught master chef. Ten years ago he began a business venture that resulted in six Detroit area Doyle's restaurants and a nationwide chain of twenty-six Doyle's Pubs. Last week he signed a deal with a large holding company, and today he passes the keys to his business to the new owners. On his last day in Detroit, Doyle will celebrate his retirement with former employees and friends.

He chatted with the prep-cooks as he tasted the items being prepared for his party. Since opening the restaurants, he'd gained fifty pounds. At five-eleven and two-hundred-thirty pounds, he is not fat, but stocky. His doctor insists he lose weight, but when your business is food, it's hard to avoid the temptations.

2007 Was A Very Bad Year

Before Doyle reached the dining room, he heard someone pounding on the back door. He checked the security camera and recognized his old friend and former partner, Detective Lester Thornson, with another man at his side.

He opened the doors and said, "Lester, you old son of a bitch, you're early but come on in." It surprised Doyle to see Lester since the two hadn't talked since he left the homicide department.

"Doyle, this is my partner Jim Lee. I know we're early, but we're on the job and can't come later this afternoon."

Doyle burst out laughing. "It's been a long time, Lester. I assume you didn't want to miss the champagne and hors d'oeuvres?"

"No, I came so you could meet my partner, and to wish you a happy future," Lester had a serious tone in his voice. Detective Lee could feel the tension between his partner and Doyle.

"I was just heading to the dining room, so come along and we can talk. I need to make sure everything is perfect before the guests arrive, but it's essential we have this conversation."

Doyle opened the swinging doors to the dining room, where soft lighting bounced off the stark white walls and glass covered and stainless steel tables with matching leather chairs. The walls showcased massive photographs featuring scenes from Greektown's past. The room had a *casual industrial* look, a stark contrast to what you would expect in a hundred-year-old historical building.

"Lester, I missed seeing you when I left the force in 2007. I realize we had problems, but I always hoped you would come around and allow me to explain what happened."

"Yes, there was a big problem; I allowed my feelings to control my actions. We were friends, and I thought you were making a mistake when you sued the city for what happened. It took years to realize you had made the correct decision."

Doyle handed Lester a cup of coffee, and Jim requested water. The three men sat at a table.

"Damn it, Lester, you had ten years to tell me that. What the hell took so long?"

"I tried a dozen times. I even wrote you a letter, but it didn't happen. When I learned you were leaving, I knew I had to talk with you and make things right between us."

Lester put his coffee down, and with teary eyes he said, "Doyle, please forgive me for being a stupid bastard. I shouldn't have doubted your motives, and I'm sorry."

Doyle stood and stepped forward with his arms stretched out. They hugged for a moment, then Doyle asked, "Jim Lee, how do you put up with such a stubborn partner?"

Jim laughed and watched the tension dissolve between his partner and Doyle. The two men shook hands, and Jim replied, "I don't. We argue like an old married couple, then I tell him what a wonderful detective he is, and he forgives me."

"Lester, you've trained your junior detective well."

Lester smiled and sat back down. After taking a sip of coffee, he asked, "Are we good, Doyle?" It surprised him how forgiving his former partner was. Doyle's time away from the force had changed him. The aggressive partner, who drank in excess, is now at peace.

Doyle smiled. "We're good."

Jim asked, "Mr. Doyle…"

Doyle interrupted, "Jim, it's Al or Doyle. My dad was the only Mister in my family."

Jim continued, "Doyle, Lester tried to explain what happened ten years ago, but I want to hear your version. Was it as bad as Lester said it was?"

Before Doyle spoke, a restaurant staff worker interrupted. "Sir, can I finish putting out the hors d'oeuvres? I don't want to interrupt you, gentlemen."

"Yes, Carl, everything looks wonderful, and you won't be interrupting." Carl turned to Jim and asked, "Can I get you something else to drink, sir? Perhaps tea or a soda?"

"Tea would be nice. Hot if you have it." Jim smiled at the attendant.

"Yes, sir."

As the staff worked, Doyle turned to Jim and said, "Now back to your question. Yes, it was bad!"

Lester sat back in his chair, his arms crossed in front of him. "Doyle, I need to hear this too. The only version I got was the official department story and the gossip spread among the detectives."

"OK, but this may take a while. You know how long winded I can be, Lester."

"I sure do. All those stakeout hours we spent in the car with you talking and talking… on… and… on."

"You did your share of talking about your lovely wife Alice and your little girl, and I am glad Amber and her girlfriend recovered from that nasty shooting at King High School."

"Thank you, but go on with the story," Lester suggested.

"In 2005, Lester became my junior homicide detective. He came up through the ranks and studied hard to pass all the tests. We had a good working relationship and solved our share of cases.

Toward the end of 2006, we were working on the Jerry Commelda case. Jerry died in a drive-by shooting; He was walking along the sidewalk in front of his apartment and someone with an automatic rifle killed him. At first, it looked like a random killing, but we discovered Jerry was a business owner with potential mob connections.

The deeper our investigation took us into Jerry's work, the more we suspected his company was a front for a money laundering scheme, and we discovered mob ties in Detroit, Chicago and Canada.

Out of the blue, I got ordered to meet with Internal Affairs. They wanted me to come alone and bring my file on Jerry's killing. I didn't like it, but I followed orders. When I got to the meeting, two suits from Major Crimes were also there.

They assigned me a new partner, who was a Major Crimes officer. They said I couldn't tell anyone. I wanted to tell you, but I couldn't. I became part of an ongoing internal investigation involving a commanding officer and two other detectives.

Major Crimes also provided two leads to follow. Jerry was not only into money laundering; he was up to his armpits in trafficking underage girls. I wanted to tell you what was going on, Lester, and God knows I tried to give you hints, but you got the idea I wanted you off the case and built a wall between us.

Lester got up and stood with his hands on the back of the chair. "The commander told me you asked for a new partner, and he said it was your personal request. You can understand why I got pissed, and every time I tried to talk to you, you skipped out and avoided me. Dammit, Doyle, you made me feel like shit!"

"The whole fucking affair made me feel like shit too. I hated the situation they put me in and I wanted out, but I couldn't refuse to work with them because they said my job was on the line."

Jim Lee interrupted by saying, "Guys, let's get on with the story. You can bitch at each other later; right now I want to hear how Doyle got shot."

Lester sat down, and Doyle continued with his tale. "My new partner, Kevin Stall, and I followed the trail and ended up with a solid lead on the shooter. He went by the name of Eddie Sutter and was a suspect in two shootings. We dug deep and found out where he was hanging out."

When we brought him in, he admitted they had asked him to kill Jerry, but he didn't want to get involved in human trafficking. He said he could lead us to the man who tried to hire him and the man who killed Jerry, provided we gave him protection and immunity. We struck a deal and got the information we needed.

Kevin and I planned to bring the killer in for interrogation. The man who hired him would also be brought into the station. We would let them know we had the other in custody, so we could work them against each other.

We planned to collar the shooter at his local bar, and Internal Affairs arranged for backup. We kept waiting and called twice for our backup. I decided there wasn't time to wait any longer, so when the suspect walked into the bar on Eight Mile Road, I gave Kevin the signal and I entered the bar's front entrance while Kevin entered the back door.

I opened the door, took one step into the bar and felt a sharp pain in my back and collapsed. I remember seeing three men running out of the bar, stepping over my lifeless body, as my world grew dark.

The next memory I have is that of a lovely nurse pushing an over-sized needle into my arm. She said I had been in a coma for three weeks and was lucky to be alive. I looked at the tubes running into my body and asked her how this is lucky?

I spent the next week trying to find someone who knew what had happened. Kevin disappeared, and when I called Major Crimes and Internal Affairs, they wouldn't take my call. The commander stopped in, but he wouldn't talk about the shooting.

The union rep came in and suggested I plan for my retirement. I was being forced out of the department. You can imagine how frustrated I was. I got pissed and made a call to my lawyer, who connected me with another lawyer who gathered evidence and sued the City of Detroit and the Detroit Police Department.

We discovered Major Crimes and Internal Affairs both knew there was a leak about our sting operation, but they didn't let us know. They were more interested in catching the crooked detectives and the commanding officer than they were in keeping us safe.

I didn't want a lawsuit, but what choice did I have? I was in a hospital bed in a serious condition, so my lawyers took the lead. When they offered a proposed settlement, it shocked me when Detroit offered two million dollars if I left the force and kept silent. All I had to do was sign a non-disclosure agreement, and they wanted to sweep everything under the rug.

I wanted justice, and getting money wasn't my goal. I told my lawyer there was no way I could screw the Detroit and the police department. My lawyers insisted, and they said if I didn't sign the settlement, the department was ready to make me the scapegoat. By my agreeing to the deal, the crooked detectives and commander would get the axe. No one got charged with a crime except the shooter, who pleaded guilty to accidental discharge of a firearm resulting in death. He would get five to ten years. The man who shot me went free.

Lester took a deep breath. "Doyle, that clears up a lot of the mystery. Will you get into trouble for telling us this?"

"Today I don't care what the Detroit Police Department says. I used the money they gave me to build my first restaurant, and the next year I built two more Doyle's Eateries. Today I'm selling over thirty restaurants, making a huge profit, and I will live up north for the rest of my life."

Lester broke out laughing. "Like hell, Doyle. I know you better. You and Detective Maxwell have been working together on cases ever since you left the force. You can't keep your nose out of homicide affairs. The boys in homicide agree... you're like a bloodhound, sniffing out every murder that comes up in this city."

Doyle smiled. "Lester, you're still full of shit, but I love you. You know me too well, so tell me what case you're working on today?"

Jim pulled his chair back from the table and stood. "Lester and I are the lead detectives on a series of killings; that's why we can't stay longer. Doyle, thank you for setting the record straight. I understand why Lester felt hurt, and I appreciate the position you were in, but please don't let the next ten years slip away without keeping in touch with us."

"Thanks, Jim. I'll keep in touch. In fact, Lester, the two of you are always welcome to visit my cottage in Sand Point. It's on Lake Huron, and there's plenty of room. I understand the Caseville Festivals are a lot of fun, so you could bring the family up and spend a week or two."

"Sounds good. You know my address; send me a reminder. Good luck with the retirement thing."

Chapter 2

Mrs. Hoffstarter Arrives

Lester and Jim Lee left through the kitchen as Mrs. Hoffstarter and her guest, an attractive middle-aged woman, walked into the dining room. Doyle gave Mrs. Hoffstarter a big hug.

"Trudy, I'm so glad you could make it to my party. I see you found a friend to drive you here?"

"Yes, Anne Horton is my helper. She drove my car, and we didn't even get lost. Anne, dear, this gentleman is Albert Doyle, my good friend and new next-door neighbor."

Anne shook hands with Doyle and helped Trudy with her coat and purse. The two women sat at a table with Doyle.

Trudy, a slender woman in her late eighties, knew Doyle from his detective years. She was a psychiatrist working with the Detroit Police Department, both as a therapist to police officers and as a consultant on murder cases.

Doyle called a server to the table and asked Trudy and Anne what they wanted to drink. Anne requested black coffee, and Trudy said, "Ice tea with lemon, please."

She looked around and realized they were the first guests to arrive. "Oh heavens, Doyle, are we too early?"

"No, everyone else is late. Please excuse me for a moment; I need to check with the staff. I have a few more details to take care of."

Doyle went into the kitchen, leaving the two women to sip on their drinks. A server brought a tray of appetizers and asked if they wanted one. Anne was eager to try the assorted treats and placed several on a plate.

"Trudy," she said. "This is a beautiful restaurant, and Mr. Doyle is a handsome man. Is he married?"

"Anne, hands off. He's not married anymore, and I'm sure he isn't looking for another wife."

"I was just wondering. Is he gay?"

"Heavens no! He got burned by his first wife and now he's more interested in his business than women."

"That must change. Without a woman, he will be lonely living in that enormous house. To think, a single man in a home with five bedrooms, six baths, and two kitchens. And who will clean that place?" Anne grew silent as she considered the question she had asked.

"Trudy, tell him I want the job. I can clean once a week for him, like I do for you. I bet he keeps a clean house, so it wouldn't take a lot of work."

Trudy turned to her friend and replied, "You want to get closer to him, don't you? Are you turning into a gold digger?"

"No! I only want to help Mr. Doyle enjoy his retirement." Anne said with a huge smile.

Before Doyle returned from the kitchen, the two women set out in search of the restroom. When they returned, they discovered the dining room filled with police detectives standing around two tables and restaurant employees milling around the hors d'oeuvres table, while other guests walked around the room with drinks in their hands. Soft music played in the background.

Doyle took a microphone and welcomed everyone. He asked that they enjoy themselves as he mingled to greet each of them.

Maxwell Brown approached Doyle. He gripped his arm and said, "We have a special gift for you, but it can wait. First, I have to ask if Lester was here earlier? We urged him to make things right before you leave."

"We talked, and everything is fine. In fact, I invited him and his family to spend a couple of weeks at the cottage next summer." It was a relief for Doyle to have settled the rift with his former partner. For the last ten years it troubled him, and he wanted to clear the air many times, only he didn't know how and kept procrastinating.

Maxwell beamed, "That's great, Doyle. When you have a minute, the guys want to present you with a going away gift."

"Why not now?" asked Doyle.

"No. It will be better later. After you've visited everyone."

Doyle became curious, but agreed. He shook hands and chatted with the other detectives and visited his many other guests.

There was a constant stream of guests coming and going. Doyle was getting tired, but he didn't want to miss anyone. Having his friends attend this party meant the world to him. He hoped his son might make the trip to see him, but that was a long shot.

Roger is forty and resembles his father; tall, solid build with streaks of gray hair. Unlike his dad, Roger is bitter. He blames his dad for his problems and seldom visits him. When the two visits, Roger spends the time complaining about the past.

It's better that Roger didn't come today, thought Doyle. *This way, he can't ruin my party.*

One person Doyle doesn't expect at his farewell party is his ex-wife, Nancy. They divorced when Roger was five years old. It was not a friendly divorce because Nancy did everything she could to make Doyle's life miserable, including filing and winning total custody of Roger. Doyle was a patrolman in downtown Detroit and had depression... exacerbated by his heavy drinking.

The divorce was a wake up call, and Mrs. Hoffstarter's counseling became his salvation. Trudy helped Doyle realize that losing his father was at the crux of his problems. Awareness of the past led Doyle out of the darkness of his depression, allowing him to face the future; a future filled with adventure, self-fulfillment, and friends. Today's party is about Doyle's friends.

Meeting Copper

Doyle's return to Mrs. Hoffstarter's table, to spend more time with her and Anne, pleased her. After a long visit, she wanted to start for home, and he asked if she would join him for breakfast.

"You're my neighbor now, and it's just a short walk across your driveway. Besides, I'm sure you're eager to see what the contractors did to my cottage. I haven't seen the finished results, but it's a big change from how Cora Torengia decorated," Doyle explained.

Mrs. Hoffstarter smiled at the idea. "I would love to. But please, not too early because at my age it takes longer to get ready."

Doyle helped her with her coat and suggested they meet mid-morning. "How about ten o'clock?" he asked.

"It's a date. She kissed his cheek and walked out with Anne."

Anne turned back and said, "It was nice to meet you, and I hope to get to know you better soon."

Doyle smiled. "Thank you, Anne."

As the guests left, Max approached Doyle and reminded him about the special gift the detectives wanted to present him.

Doyle took Max's arm and said. "I told you, *no gifts*, so this better be something special, since you've teased me with it all afternoon. You know I wanted this party to be a gift to you guys."

"Doyle, you know how we always told you how much you're like a bloodhound, the way you don't let the scent of a killer get away from you?"

"Yes, so what did you get? A nose plug?"

"Bring him in, guys!" yelled Max.

Doyle became speechless when a beautiful copper brown/black bloodhound walked into the dining room, followed by a dog handler from the Detroit Police Canine Unit. The dog walked up to Doyle, sat down, and sniffed the air. His droopy eyes met Doyle's eyes, and Doyle swore he smiled at him.

Max put his arm over Doyle's shoulder and said, "On behalf of the Detroit Homicide Division, I want to present a friend you will love for many years." Max turned to the dog handler and said, "Carol, could you give Doyle the details on Copper."

In a soft voice, Carol said, "We call him Copper; you can change it, but he won't like it one bit. Copper is a two-year-old trained search dog. I have to tell you they cut Copper from the program because he is the most stubborn bloodhound we've ever seen. He has one of the best noses, but he also has a mind of his own, hates changes, and thinks he knows everything."

Doyle laughed. "A match made in heaven."

"That's how we saw it, Doyle," Max said. "We also have several bags of his favorite food, so you don't have to pick any up on your way to your new home in Pigeon."

Doyle thanked Max and the other detectives, shaking their hands. After becoming friends with Copper, he asked his driver to take the bloodhound to the kitchen. "You can give him some of his food to eat and put the rest in the Limo."

Last Guest

After the last guest left, Doyle prepared for his trip north. He asked the chef to prepare a takeout basket for him so he'd have one less thing to worry about when he got home.

The chef laughed as Doyle explained he didn't know what would be in his refrigerator. "The dog's food could be the only food in the house. It's not proper for a renowned chef like me to be eating dog food."

Chef Fritz asked what kind of food he wanted, and Doyle suggested a variety. "I'm cooking breakfast for a friend tomorrow, and I would appreciate any food you could spare."

"I'll make a box and give it to your driver," said Fritz.

Doyle returned to the dining room where he heard a woman's

voice ask, "Am I too late, Al?"

Doyle recognized the voice. It was his older sister, Samantha. "Never, Sam... you're never too late."

He reached his arms around the large woman and hugged her. "I thought you said you couldn't come today?"

"I changed my appointments so I wouldn't miss the party. Then I forgot about it. You know my memory is getting bad. They tell me it comes with age; I hate when doctors say that."

"Sam, you're only ten years older than I am." Doyle's sister was an attractive, tall woman with gray hair. "You look like Mom, and seeing you makes me miss her so much."

"It's been eight years since she went to be with Dad," Sam sighed. "She never lost her memory, so I wonder if I got my poor memory from Dad?"

Doyle was in deep thought and didn't respond to her question. "I'm glad Mom was here when I opened this restaurant. Remember how proud she was? To think, one of her children followed her into the business and in the same location as her restaurant."

Doyle built his first restaurant in the building where his mother had run her business many years ago. Doyle and his sister, along with their older brothers, Matthew and Taylor, spent many hours working in the restaurant. Both brothers died in the Korean war, two weeks apart.

"I remember your grand opening, Al. It's my short-term memory that's getting bad. Did Roger show up?"

Doyle was silent for a moment. With sadness he said, "No, Roger didn't come. I sent him an invitation, but I didn't expect he would respond. The last time we talked, he got mad at me because I was spending all his inheritance on my stupid restaurants."

"His inheritance?"

"His mother told him he would be my only benefactor. She told him to get chummy with me so I don't get upset with him and leave him out of the will. Sam, it upsets me how his mother has turned him against me."

Sam could feel the anger in Doyle's voice and wanted to calm him down. Nothing upset him more than talking about his ex-wife.

"Doyle, it won't help to get upset. Remember when Mom said, *It is what it is?* You can't change her or Roger. Every time I talk to Roger, he spends most of his time complaining about you. The two of you are too much alike. You're both stubborn, and you both expect the other guy to back down first. I keep telling him that his mother brainwashed him, but he won't listen."

Sam hugged her little brother. "I'm sorry the two of you can't be closer. That ex-wife of yours sure did a number on him. It's too bad he doesn't see it."

"Speaking of children, how is Laurie? The last time I saw her was a year ago. She stopped in to tell me she was moving to California."

Sam sighed, "Well, she never made it there, and I had to send her money to come home. She's working in a nursing home now and doing much better."

"That's good. I take it she's accepted that she will never be a big star in Hollywood?"

"Yes, but she still wants to do theater... only her expectations have lowered. It's too bad, but like I tell her, not everyone can make it into the big time. She's been accepting acting jobs in Detroit, and she's doing well."

"Let me know when she's in a theatrical production. I would love to come down and see her." Doyle said. He reached into his pocket and pulled out two business cards. "Give her my card and tell her to call me and keep one for yourself. I have lots of room in Sand Point, so whenever you want a vacation, the two of you are welcome to come up to the cottage."

James, Doyle's driver, walked from the kitchen and interrupted the conversation when he asked, "Are you almost ready to go, Sir? You said you wanted to get home tonight before seven."

Doyle looked at his watch. "God, it's getting late, Sam." He turned to James and said, "Yes, I'll be ready in a minute. Is everything in the limo?"

"Yes, sir. All I need is you and that new dog of yours."

Sam looked surprised. "Dog? I didn't know you had a dog."

"It was a gift from the guys in homicide; a bloodhound named Copper; he's a friendly dog, but he'll be a lot of work."

"Good," said Sam as she put her coat on. "Friends are always a lot of work, but they're worth it."

"It's the same with our family, Sam., so remember to call me. I want to spend more time with you, and my new home is only a few hours north."

Sam gave Doyle a hug and kissed his cheek. "I will." She looked at James and whispered, "Drive carefully; your passenger is a special man."

"Yes, he is, and I will drive with care," James said.

Doyle accompanied Sam to the front door and entered the kitchen to say his goodbyes to the staff. He looked around the kitchen one more time; the memories of the last ten years inundated his mind. It saddened him to be leaving, but losing the burden of managing a large corporation will be a welcome relief. His doctor advised that he slowed down ... or else. Doyle dismissed his doctor's orders; however, today he believes he's made the right decision and is looking forward to an adventure-filled future.

With James holding the kitchen exit open, Doyle walked Copper into the alley. The back door of the Suburban was open, and Doyle persuaded Copper to sit on the seat. Doyle slid into the seat next to the bloodhound, held the leash, smiled and said, "James, let's go home."

Chapter 3

A New Home For Doyle and Copper

Doyle watched the city of Detroit pass by his car window. Driving north on M-53, they were leaving the hustle of the city, and he could feel the tension in his shoulders lessen. He chuckled at the sight of Copper with his nose pressed against the window and his eyes following the fast moving landscape. Doyle didn't know what was going through the bloodhound's mind, but he could imagine how puzzled the dog must be, leaving his kennel behind and driving away with a new master.

Doyle put his head back and closed his eyes. It was a long day, and he grew tired. In a few minutes, there was a soft sound of snoring. Copper looked up at Doyle and turned so that he was facing him. It looked like he wanted to lick his new master's face, but he put his head down into Doyle's lap and closed his eyes.

James glanced in his rear-view mirror and smiled when he saw Doyle. He turned off the radio and his cell phone so there would be no interruptions, and he put his headphones on. As he drove toward Pigeon, James listened to his favorite audiobook.

The Suburban wound its way north on M-53. In Bad Axe, James took the shortcut to M-142 and drove toward Pigeon, then north to Crescent Beach Road. When he pulled into Doyle's driveway, Copper looked out the window and gave a low bark.

James opened the garage door and parked next to Doyle's new

Buick. As the garage door closed, Doyle stirred, looked out the window, and realized where he was. He asked, "How the hell did we get here so fast, James?"

James laughed and replied, "Sir, you had a two-hour nap. I could see the day's events had caught up with you, so I let you sleep. Copper enjoyed a long nap too."

Doyle looked down at a large wet spot on his pants where Copper had been sleeping. "Well, Copper, I guess you have a drooling problem, so if you ruined these pants, I'm taking it out of your food allowance." Copper had a puzzled expression and made a low growl.

James opened the back door, allowing Doyle to step out of the vehicle. He reached into the back seat and took hold of Copper's leash and led him into the backyard to do his business. James then led him into the house.

Doyle went through the items in the back of the Suburban, pulling out several boxes and suitcases filled with clothing. The moving crew already brought most of his possessions to his new home in Sand Point.

James and Doyle carried everything from the car into the house, setting the boxes on the kitchen counter. Doyle opened the refrigerator and discovered it was full of food. He had trouble making room for the items Fritz had packed for him.

James noticed the overloaded refrigerated and burst out laughing. "I thought you said you wouldn't have anything to eat but dog food."

"Well, James, Copper has expensive tastes, so perhaps I was right. Don't you think he'll love those porterhouse steaks and that rib roast?"

"I'm sure he will, sir... I'm sure he will..." replied James.

When everything was in its proper place, Doyle gave James the grand tour. There were five massive bedrooms and six baths on three floors. The home had a modern cottage look with decor that reflected the cottage setting. On one wall was a huge copper sculpture depicting five sailboats racing across the water.

"This is nice, sir. I take it you've always wanted to live here?" James asked.

"No. Last month my friend Trudy, who lives next door, asked if I wanted to come up and look at the house. The previous owner needed to make a quick sale because of legal problems, and Trudy said it was a good price and a magnificent home, so I made an offer and here I am. This is the second time I've been in the house. The first time was to tell my builder, decorator, and landscaping contractors what changes I wanted. We put in a new kitchen downstairs, and I had all the rooms painted. The woman who owned the house had dark, dreary walls, and since my home in Palmer Park was dark and dreary, I wanted a change. In fact, I let all the furniture go with the sale of my Detroit home."

"I'm sure you'll enjoy living here. My friends tell me Caseville is a great party town in the summer, and if you buy a boat, you'll be able to fish every day," James said as he looked out the enormous windows facing the beach and Lake Huron.

The sun was getting ready to set, and the colors bouncing across the lake were fantastic. The two men sat on the deck and enjoyed the sunset until the giant fireball slipped below the horizon.

"This is nice, Sir. I wish I didn't have to, but I should get back to Detroit. I start my new business in the morning, so I shouldn't be late. If I am, I'll have to reprimand myself."

Doyle shook James' hand and thanked him for ten years of service. "I hope everything works out with your new business. Knowing you as I do, I shouldn't worry."

Doyle waved his hand as James drove off. He shut the garage door and returned to the house. Copper found a glorious spot in front of the unlit fireplace, and he knew what the rug was for. Doyle bent down, turned the gas fireplace on, and sat in a comfortable chair next to Copper.

The two enjoyed the fireplace until both became hungry. "Well,

Copper, what are you hungry for?" Doyle asked.

He found the bag of dog food next to the counter and grabbed a bowl from the cupboard. "I'll get you a real dog dish tomorrow," he said as he filled the bowl with dry food. He grabbed another bowl and filled it with water.

Copper enjoyed the food, but when he saw Doyle eating leftover food from the party, he drooled on the floor. Doyle laughed and warned, "Watch it, Copper, you have your own food; this is mine. I've lived alone too long to share my things."

Looking at the drool on his new floor, Doyle realized Copper would be a messy dog, but he was getting attached to his new companion and wouldn't let a little mess come between them... for now, that is.

First Morning In Sand Point

Doyle had a restless night, and he wasn't sure why he kept tossing and turning. The bed was the softness he liked, and the room felt warm and comfortable. At three in the morning, while he was in the bathroom, he realized how quiet it was. *Deadly quiet*, he thought. *Where are the fire trucks, cop cars, gunshots, and screaming neighbors?* He asked himself.

When Doyle decided to spend his retirement years in the resort community of Sand Point, he didn't realize how secluded he would be. He spent his childhood in a small apartment in Greektown, above his mother's Greek restaurant, and grew accustomed to the sounds of the city, and now he must accept the silence of a lakeside cottage.

The only sounds Doyle heard during the night were Copper's snores and grunts and an owl or some other noisy animal. As he lay in bed at six a.m., thinking about getting up, he felt two paws stepping on the edge of his bed. He reached for the bedside light, and when his eyes adjusted, he realized he was face-to-face with Copper.

"What do you want?" He asked in a gruff voice.

Copper's tail wagged violently, and Doyle could see the leash hanging from his mouth.

"Now? You want to go out now?" Doyle asked.

Copper dropped the leash on the bed and started for the door. He turned around, ran back to Doyle and tugged on his bedspread. Doyle laughed, sat up, and pulled his slippers on. He attached the leash to his collar and said, "They trained you well in Detroit, didn't they?"

As Copper pulled him from the bedroom, Doyle grabbed his robe and threw it over his broad shoulders. "Hold up; it's cold out there, and I don't want to get sick."

Copper stopped and waited for him to finish getting dressed, and when Doyle was ready, the bloodhound rushed to the side door, pulling Doyle behind him.

Doyle stood shivering as Copper did his business on the lawn. Copper's nose sniffed the air, and Doyle realized he had to get him inside before he demanded to follow the scent. "Come on, Copper, I'll take you for a walk on the beach after breakfast. Let's go get food; you must be hungry, so come on."

Doyle put food and water out for Copper while he checked his phone for messages. There were a few congratulatory messages from past employees, but none of the messages required his attention. As he sat at the massive counter, looked out the windows and watched a distant ship.

Doyle sipped coffee and considered the day's events. His friend, Trudy Hoffstarter, will be over for brunch at ten, and that means cooking something special for a special lady. Doyle decided the most urgent task involved his new roommate, Copper.

When his contractor, Waters and Sons, remodeled the cottage, Copper was not a consideration. Now, however, the bloodhound is a major part of Doyle's future, so he found Water's business card and dialed the builder's phone number.

"Richard, this is Albert Doyle."

"How do you like the work my boys did?"

"So far I love the work, but something came up and I need a huge favor. My so-called friends at Detroit Homicide gave me a bloodhound as a goodbye gift, and I need modifications to my home A.S.A.P."

Doyle listened as Richard told a long story about a friend who owned a bloodhound.

Doyle was in a hurry so he interrupted the builder with, "Yes, Richard, drooling is a problem with bloodhounds... Yes I understand... Richard, can you install a doggy door on the north wall and add a fenced-in area, about eight by twelve next to the east deck and wall? I read that they have artificial grass for dogs... see if you can find some of that."

The contractor said he would schedule the job for next Monday; however, when Doyle offered a bonus to start the job Friday, Richard agreed and said. "We'll be there tomorrow, but if we work over the weekend and it will cost you overtime pay for my workers."

Doyle told him he would pay whatever it takes. The builder established his reputation on prompt service for the well-to-do homeowner, and for Doyle the added cost was not a problem since he had more money than he could ever spend. However, it was important that Copper had free access to the outdoors when nature called, without having to beg.

Copper was sitting at Doyle's feet listening to the conversation, so Doyle reached out and patted him on the head and behind the ears. "So, Copper, did you hear all about your new escape hatch? It will make our lives easier, but now we have to get rid of that drooling thing you have going on there." He took a napkin from the counter and mopped up the floor while Copper continued drooling and wagging his tail.

Doyle checked his watch and realized he had less than two hours before Trudy would walk over for breakfast. He was looking forward to preparing brunch for her, but first he needed to know where everything was. His longtime employees moved his belongings to the new home and purchased food for the refrigerators and two large freezers. Unfortunately, they didn't leave a map telling him where they put things. After a thorough search, he found the ingredients he needed for a spinach and ham quiche.

Doyle was a perfectionist and moved items from the upstairs refrigerator to a walk-in freezer downstairs. They overstocked his kitchen, and he wanted nothing to spoil.

It will take time figuring out what food I have and more time to eat it all, he thought. *Perhaps I can throw a big party or find a needy family to feed for a month.*

Doyle gathered the ingredients to make a Greek quiche crust and filling. The recipe was one of his mother's favorite and he often offered it in his restaurants. Once he had the crust formed, he prepared the ingredients, added the beaten eggs, and set the oven timer. He knew he could shower and get dressed before the timer went off.

As Doyle walked out of the bedroom, the timer buzzed. He laughed because Copper was sitting in front of the oven listening to the buzzing noise.

"See, Copper, I have the magic touch."

He took the quiche out and placed it on a cooling rack. "Doesn't that look good?"

Copper watched Doyle's every move, and his tail looked like a conductor's wand. After making a pot of coffee and setting out a bowl of fresh fruit, Doyle organized beautiful white plates on the dining table with his personalized silverware and cloth napkins. He then waited for his guest of honor to arrive.

Copper heard Trudy coming up the steps and ran to the door, followed by Doyle, who shoved Copper aside with his foot. "Let me greet her first, Copper," he insisted as he opened the door.

Trudy was radiant in brown slacks and a lovely peach blouse, with an off white cardigan. Doyle grinned and said, "You look beautiful as usual, Trudy. Come in and meet my new friend, Copper, but be careful, he's an equal opportunity drooler."

Trudy reached down and stroked Copper's nose as his tail went into overdrive. Doyle laughed because he knew the bloodhound approved of her. If it ever came to the dog or his friend, she would win because there was more history between them.

"If you like, I can give you some pointers on how to reduce the drooling. My husband and I had many dogs in our younger years, so I learned a few tricks."

"Wonderful, we can discuss them later. First, I want to show you what my decorator did to the house, and then we can get down to brunch." As they walked through the house, Doyle noticed his contractor walking across the deck.

Trudy asked, "Isn't that Mr. Waters, your contractor?"

"Yes, and I need to talk to him for a minute," Doyle said as he walked toward the dining room sliding door. He stepped onto the side deck and talked with the contractor. Mr. Waters took out his measuring tape and did a layout of the area, while Doyle stepped back into the house.

"Didn't you finish the remodeling?"

"Yes, I did, but now I have to make accommodations for Copper. I'm adding a doggy door and outdoor pen so he can go outside whenever he wants. It'll be a self-serve pit stop."

"What a wonderful idea, but keep it clean, or Copper won't want to use it."

Doyle laughed at her comment. "That reminds me, do you think your housekeeper, Anne, would work here one day a week?"

"She will love the job because she has a crush on you. Somewhere in my purse I have her number," Trudy said as she searched her small black purse. "Here it is. Just call her and she'll tell you what days she has available, but please be careful Doyle, Anne can be both charming and manipulative."

"Trudy, I'm a big boy and I'm sure I can handle myself around her."

"Just remember I warned you." Trudy laughed and suggested they begin brunch.

Chapter 4

Scouting The Village

Trudy complimented Doyle on the Greek quiche and fruit he prepared for their brunch. As she sipped her coffee, she brought up a question she wanted to ask after he announced the purchase of the house in Sand Point, making him her new neighbor.

"Doyle, you could have moved anywhere in the world, but you moved to Sand Point. Please tell me why." Not that Trudy didn't want Doyle as a neighbor; instead, she suspected he may want more from her than she could give. At one time, Doyle was her patient, and they became friends... just friends. *He is young enough to be my son,* she considered. *In fact, I often view him as the son I never had.*

"Trudy, when you said this house was on the market, I believed you wanted me to move here to be your neighbor and... perhaps something more. You said this would be a great place to retire, and I trusted your opinion, so if I'm not happy here, it will be your fault!" He let out a huge laugh and grinned at the shocked look on her face. "I'm joking, Trudy; let me explain why I moved here."

"You know I am from Detroit's Greektown neighborhood; however, I never told you my father is from Caseville and he moved to Detroit during the Second World War. He wanted to go to Europe to fight, but he failed the physical, and once he was in Detroit, he stayed. He found a room in Greektown and soon met Mom. The rest is history, and history is why I moved to Sand Point. As we get older, we want to learn about our roots."

"Dad talked about my grandfather, *the fisherman*. My great grandpa came here from Canada in the 1800s and ran a fishing boat out of Caseville and Bay Port. I want to learn more about him and my great grandma, and I feel like Huron County is my home. It is where I belong and where I want to spend the rest of my time. Having a beautiful neighbor like you is a wee bit of Irish luck."

Doyle's explanation relieved Trudy; however, she didn't find humor in his joke, but she overlooked the issue because he was a good friend. "You will love Sand Point, even if the winters are cold and quiet."

"Trudy, how long did it take you to adapt to the silence?" Doyle asked.

"I never found it a problem because I lived in a secluded subdivision outside Pontiac, and we had the cottage here for many years. What took the greatest effort was getting used to the solitude after my husband died. As you know, my family avoids visiting, but I thank God for my new friends. Which reminds me, Colton and Lacie are coming over tomorrow for lunch, and I would love to have you there to meet them."

"Isn't Colton the teenager who witnessed the killing here last month, and Lacie is his girlfriend?"

"Yes, they are my good friends; lovely youngsters, and I'm sure you will enjoy their company. They have a half day at school, so I invited them for lunch around noon."

"If you like them, I am sure I will also, and yes... I would be most happy to come to lunch, provided you allow me to use your grill and cook the meal." Doyle insisted.

"That was my plan." Trudy said with a smile. "Now tell me what your plans are for this afternoon? Long naps, watching television or do you have a good book to read?"

"None of the above, my dear. Copper and I are going for a walk on the beach, and then we'll drive around town. I'm interested in researching my grandfathers, so I'll be visiting the area museums."

Trudy smiled. "The Caseville Historical Society is a wonderful group; I attend many of their events. Several years ago, they remodeled the Maccabee Hall, and today they use it as a museum. I would suggest starting there."

Doyle found a small map of Huron County, and Trudy marked points of interest. She spent many summers in the area before moving to Sand Point and has vast knowledge of the community.

"If you visit these locations, you will have discovered the county," Trudy said.

"Perhaps, but I think I should also visit the area restaurants and bars, because it's the people who make a community."

"You'll find several types of residents here: farmers, locals, and newcomers. You'll be the latter, so be careful. Farmers and locals won't trust you, and the other newcomers will want to enlist you in their plans to take over the area. They want Sand Point to be like the communities they came from."

Doyle laughed and promised he would be careful. "I won't get involved in any evil plots to overthrow those in control, Trudy."

"Good... now I need to get home, because Anne is coming this afternoon and I want to clean the house before she gets here. It's silly to clean before my cleaner arrives, but there are things I don't want her to do, like my laundry. The woman doesn't sort clothing, and she's ruined some of my nicest outfits."

Doyle walked her to the side door and asked if she wanted him to walk with her. She declined his offer, so he stood and watched until she was out of his sight, and then he grabbed Copper's leash and attached it to his collar.

Copper was more interested in being outdoors than doing his business, so Doyle walked down to the beach. The two of them walked along the edge of the lake. A cool breeze blew from the north, but the sun was shining enough to make it a beautiful day.

When they returned to the house, Copper ran into the woods.

He pulled Doyle behind him and then stopped next to a dead deer lying on a pile of oak leaves. The odor of rotting flesh turned Doyle's stomach, but it was the scent that brought Copper here.

As he walked around the carcass, Doyle noticed an arrow in the animal's chest. "Copper, I thought it was illegal to hunt here," he said. "You know what this means? I have my first murder case in Sand Point. *The case of the dead deer in the woods!*"

Doyle laughed as he dragged Copper away from the deer carcass. Copper didn't want to lose the deer's scent, and Doyle didn't want Copper bringing the scent home, so he pulled the bloodhound back to the cottage.

Doyle brushed Copper off before letting him into the house. He hung the leash next to the door and looked for a telephone book. There was a county directory on the kitchen counter. He found the number for the sheriff's department in Bad Axe and dialed it.

A young sounding woman politely answered, "Sheriff's department, how may I help you?"

"Hello, my name is Albert Doyle. I live on Sand Point, and I would like to report that my dog found a dead deer in the woods, near my home."

"Yes, sir. There are dead deer in the woods, so how can I help you?"

"Someone shot the deer with an arrow in a residential community. Isn't that against the law, and shouldn't someone remove the carcass?"

"I can report the deer, but we have no one who removes dead animals from the woods. If it were in the center of the street, I could find someone who might move it."

Doyle could tell the young woman was laughing at him, and it infuriated him. "Since I don't appreciate the carcass so close to my home, perhaps I should ask someone to move it onto the road, so you can remove it."

"Sir, that is not a good idea. Give me your number and I'll ask the sheriff if we can help you."

Doyle gave her his number, but imagined her throwing it into the trash. "Copper, you may smell that dead deer all winter unless I pay to have someone remove it."

Caseville Exploration

Doyle spent several hours working around the cottage, organizing his belongings, setting up his office, and moving furniture. He liked what the decorator did with the main room, but he didn't like where the decorator put his favorite recliner. The light gray leather chair was the only piece of furniture, other than his mother's oak desk, that Doyle brought with him from Detroit. It was clear the decorator didn't appreciate the recliner's finer points and put it in an out-of-site corner. Doyle moved the recliner closer to the center of the room, next to an end table. He sat down, got up again, and kept pulling the chair until it was in the perfect spot to watch the lake, a task which took several attempts. The last location was perfect; he could see the sunrise and sunset, and anyone walking along the beach.

"Copper, come look at my new favorite spot."

Copper walked into the room, looked around, sniffed the chair and gave Doyle a scowled look.

"What's the matter? Perhaps you don't have good taste either. Or is it you want a rug here?" Doyle pointed to the empty spot next to the recliner. "Let me see what I can find." He walked around the house, searching every room until he found a yellow and orange oval rug. It wasn't the best color for the off white and gray front room but was a good size and fit nicely next to Doyle's chair. Copper circled the rug and laid down... now satisfied with the view.

After having a light lunch, Doyle grabbed his coat and Copper's leash. He was ready to explore the community for the first time. He came to Sand Point to meet the interior decorator and his contractor at the cottage, but he didn't drive around the village. In fact, Doyle never visited Caseville, Pigeon, or Sand Point as an adult. When he was ten, his mom and dad drove the family up north to attend his grandfather's funeral, where he met two cousins and a great aunt. His grandmother died before Doyle's birth, so he never met her.

Following the map Trudy made for him, Doyle drove to town, stopping first at the cemetery along M-25. He didn't have time to study the monuments, but he drove through the cemetery anyway. It surprised him how large it was and how far back the dates went. There were many pioneers who died during the 1800s. He decided he would return soon to find his grandparents' graves to see how their gravestones had withstood the elements. *Perhaps I can have a new one made*, he thought.

Doyle drove along the shoreline, taking the back road into town. He passed the Island Bar and Grill, which was open with only three cars parked in the lot. It appeared to be a large establishment, again something to visit later.

As he drove through town, he made mental notes of restaurants, bars and businesses he wanted to visit, but today his mission was to visit the museum. He followed Trudy's directions and parked in front of the two story wooden building. There was an open sign on the porch and two cars parked in front. He parked his Buick next to a red pickup truck.

It took a moment for his eyes to adjust from the bright afternoon sun to the darkness of the museum. Once he could see, he wandered around the building, excited to see a variety of artifacts. A tall and trim middle-aged woman with short gray hair smiled and approached.

"I haven't seen you here before, so welcome to the Caseville Museum. My name is Barbara Cummings. I'm a board member of the society. Are you visiting the area today?"

"Yes, but I moved here yesterday. I'm living in Sand Point, next door to Mrs. Trudy Hoffstarter."

Barbara smiled and said, "Trudy is such a wonderful person.

We go to the same church, and I'm on two committees with her. It's incredible how quick her mind is for someone of her age. I swear she runs circles around me."

"Oh, I doubt that," Doyle said as he picked up a book on the history of Caseville. "I moved here because my father's family was from this area. Patrick Doyle was my great grandfather. He settled in the village after the civil war. Dad said he was a commercial fisherman and came from Ireland, through Canada. Grandpa was born around 1889 and worked with his father. He took over the fishing boat when Patrick Doyle retired. My dad wanted nothing to do with commercial fishing, and he ended up in Detroit. That's where I am from."

"Impressive family heritage. We have a great deal of information here on the early days of Caseville; perhaps you'll find something about your grandparents," Barbara said as she followed Doyle around the museum. "There is also a museum in Pigeon. They have more historical documents and old newspapers going back to the late 1800s."

Doyle found her well versed in Caseville's history, and he asked several questions regarding the historical objects on display. Barbara asked him if his wife was also interested in history, and Doyle responded with, "No, my ex-wife wouldn't be interested in anything relating to this kind of history. The only history she cares about is our past marriage, which she won't let me forget."

Barbara tried hard not to laugh, but she couldn't, and Doyle burst out laughing with her. His face turned red, and he said, "I'm so sorry. I shouldn't be talking about my ex-wife like that. I take it you're married?" he asked.

"Yes, I'm married, and he loves history. Barry will be around later this afternoon. We both taught school in Saginaw, and we retired here nine years ago. If you would like to join our group, we meet once a month — the third Thursday of the month at ten a.m."

"Barbara, I might join your group since I'm looking for projects I can get involved in, and this sounds promising."

The prospect of another member lifted Barbara's spirits. She stood in the doorway and watched Doyle drive off, then she called her husband. "Barry, guess what! I think we have another potential member. His name is Albert Doyle, and he moved here from Detroit."

Barry asked what Doyle had done before retiring, and Barbara said she forgot to ask. "We can ask him at the next society meeting, if he shows up. He told me his great grandfather was a commercial fisherman here, and he seems to be very intelligent. I think he has money because he purchased the Torengia cottage next to Trudy Hoffstarter."

Barry whistled, "That must have cost him a fortune. Of course, there was the murder there last month, so old Cora might have been eager to get rid of the place."

Chapter 5

Time In The Village

Several yellow Caseville School buses, filled with smiling students, drove through the village, forcing Doyle to wait at the corner of Main Street. After the buses passed, he turned onto M-25 and drove through the heart of the village and then across the Pigeon River. He kept track of the businesses; many were closed for the winter. Driving past the entrance to the County Park, he noticed an outdoor amphitheater and a drive leading to the beach. He turned left at the now closed Dairy Queen and headed north. There were no swimmers on the beautiful beach.

"I guess early November isn't the best time to go swimming, is it, Copper?" he asked. Copper looked at him and then turned to watch the seagulls flying over the beach. His tail wagged, and Doyle knew the bloodhound wanted out. "Sorry, pal, I don't have time to chase seagulls. We'll be home soon, and then we can walk down to the beach." Copper seemed to understand because he settled down and watched the seagulls.

Doyle studied Trudy's map. As he returned to M-25 and drove south, noticed a church outreach hall and thrift shop with an open sign on the door, and checked it out. He walked into the building where a young woman stood behind the counter with two preschool children at her side. Doyle approached and noticed a large handwritten sign advertising a Thanksgiving dinner for anyone who didn't have a place to go for the holiday.

"It's a grand project. Me and my kids will be there. You can come to the dinner too." The young woman said as her youngest child played with a one armed grubby doll.

"I would like to speak to the person in charge of the dinner," requested Doyle.

"I'll get her," she said as she walked into a small office. A tall. Well groomed woman of forty followed her out. "This is Marge, our manager."

Doyle put his hand out and said, "My name is Albert Doyle, and I would like to help at your Thanksgiving dinner. I sold my restaurants in Detroit, and now I want to help my new neighbors. I live in Sand Point and have lots of time to offer."

"Well, Mr. Doyle, that's kind of you. How would you like to help? We can always use cooks and servers at the meal, or perhaps you would like to donate to our group. Cash is one of our favorite donations," Marge said with a chuckle.

Doyle took out his billfold and removed a check. "If you have an ink pen, I can give you a check today."

"Oh, wonderful," Marge said, as she handed him a pen.

Doyle wrote a check to the church and handed it to Marge. "You can use this for food, but I would also like to help cook and serve the meal. I am a master chef and would love to help."

Marge looked at the check and gasped, "My God! Is this a mistake? You wrote this check for two thousand dollars."

"No mistake, but I wouldn't spend it all on one meal. I would suggest you make it stretch."

Doyle and Marge set up a time for him to stop by and help prepare for the dinner. Doyle left with a wonderful feeling. *I'll enjoy living here*, he thought.

He returned to the car and took Copper out for a walk. Copper was thankful and did his business while Doyle used a plastic bag to gather the evidence. Together they drove toward the chamber office and parked in front of the small building.

A balding middle-aged gentleman sat working behind a desk. Upon seeing Doyle, he said, "Good afternoon and welcome to Caseville. I'm Roger Harding, the Caseville Chamber representative. We have several flyers, and I would be glad to answer your questions," Roger said, pointing to a rack of flyers.

"Thank you, Roger. I moved here from Detroit, and I'm checking out my new hometown." Doyle picked up flyers and a new map. "I understand your Cheeseburger Festival is popular."

"It is. We had over two-hundred-thousand visitors for the festival. It's our most popular event. We have many festivals throughout the year. Something for everyone... that's our goal," boasted Roger. "May I ask your name?"

"Doyle, Albert Doyle. I'm a retired homicide detective from Detroit and the former owner of the Doyle chain of restaurants. I purchased Mrs. Alberto Torengia's home in Sand Point."

Roger became excited and jumped out of his chair and walked toward Doyle with his hand extended. "It's an honor to meet you. I've visited your Greektown restaurant many times after attending the Tigers games. A wonderful experience, but it surprised me to read about your retirement... and to think, you're moving to our little village," Roger was almost giddy with excitement. "Will this be a summer home?"

"No, it's my year-round home. My grandfather was from Caseville, and I'm trying to find my roots."

Roger smiled and asked, "Have you visited the museum yet. It's a wonderful resource."

"Yes, I visited the museum, where I met Barbara Cummings, a pleasant woman. I may become involved with the Historical Society."

Roger gave Doyle more information and flyers about the Village, festivals and events from other towns in the area.

"If you would like to join our chamber, we are always looking for fresh blood. Here is our meeting schedule, and remember, you're always welcome to attend even if you don't become a member."

Doyle left the chamber office and walked around town looking for a newspaper rack. He stopped at the gas station south of town. He didn't need gas, but he figured they would have the Metro newspaper. Doyle didn't transfer his home delivery subscription; instead, he purchased the online version, and hated it. *There's something about holding the paper in your hands. My computer doesn't feel like a newspaper*, he thought.

The woman behind the counter gave Doyle the newspaper subscription telephone number and said they deliver the paper four times a week in Sand Point. Doyle reminded the clerk that they publish the paper every day in Detroit. She smiled and replied, "Yes, and we have the paper here every day, home delivery is only available Tuesday, Thursday, Friday and Sunday morning. It's a cost savings for the newspaper."

When Doyle pulled into his driveway, the Waters and Sons Construction truck sat on the side of the road, and he saw a small loader digging the footings for Copper's outdoor patio. "Look, Copper, they're building your bathroom." The new construction didn't impress Copper. He has the whole yard and beach to do his business; it is beyond his comprehension why he needs a small caged-in room.

Before it got late, Doyle called the Metro Times and set up home delivery. He realized it was getting close to dinnertime, so he telephoned Trudy to see if she wanted to go out to eat, or he could bring over a meal. She decided she would enjoy eating at Lefty's Diner.

Doyle told her he would pick her up in an hour. He remembered driving past the diner and figured he wouldn't have to change into something dressy. Copper was standing at the large window overlooking the patio. He kept his eyes on the men and machines working there. Doyle laughed, because Copper's tail wasn't wagging and he had a concerned look on his face. Copper put his head down on his paws and moaned. It became obvious to Doyle that Copper dislikes change.

Doyle and Trudy arrived at Lefty's Diner before the dinner rush. There were only two other patrons. Trudy selected a booth, and the server gave them a menu and ice water.

The young woman who waited on them impressed Doyle. She would be a welcome addition to his staff in Detroit. Then he thought, *Don't dwell on the past... It's over.. You are not a restaurant owner anymore.*

Doyle studied the diner with its bright colors, black ceiling and vintage signs and pictures on the walls. It had a unique decor with a Key West feel.

He asked Trudy what she suggested, and she said, "I often have the Mexican steak or chicken fajitas, and sometimes I have a chili footlong, and their onion rings are homemade and the best!"

By the time Doyle and Trudy finished their meal, the diner was overflowing with families. "Why so many customers?" he asked.

Trudy laughed. "It's Caseville, and these people are retired. We hate to cook, so we come to Lefty's or one of the other restaurants, and many local families who are too busy to cook often eat out. If you become a regular customer, you will see the same faces every day."

As Trudy finished her statement, Barbara walked in with a man who Doyle assumed was her husband, Barry. Barbara approached Doyle and said, "I see you found our favorite diner." She extended her arms toward Trudy and hugged her. "Doyle, I want you to meet my husband, Barry. He's the president of the Museum Society."

Barry shook Doyle's hand and made small talk about the area. He welcomed Doyle to the next meeting and then led his wife to a table where they sat with several other people.

Driving back to the cottage, Doyle said, "Trudy, this is a small town, isn't it?"

"During the winter, yes. Everyone knows everyone else, and they all want to know your business. There's also a lot of back stabbing and status climbing. Be careful who you make friends with and tell no one those things you don't want the whole town to know. They are all into caring and sharing."

"You mean gossip?" asked Doyle.

"That's what you call it in the city; here we call it caring and sharing." Trudy said with a big grin.

"OK, caring and sharing."

Back To The Dead Deer

The sound of the construction crew woke Doyle at six in the morning. He wanted to go back to sleep, but Copper was ready to go outside, so Doyle dressed in blue jeans and a Detroit Tigers sweatshirt.

Copper watched him and knew when he was ready to go. Together they walked out the side door. Doyle avoided going near the construction crew, and he could tell Copper appreciated the consideration. Together, they made their way down to the beach. Copper wanted to return to the dead deer, and it took considerable effort to keep his nose away from the carcass. After half an hour of walking, both were ready to return home. As they walked, Doyle noticed a familiar face jogging along the edge of the lake. It was Barry Cummings.

Barry yelled, "Hey neighbor, is that your bloodhound?"

"Yes, his name is Copper. He's a new member of my family; I think he's a keeper."

The two men stopped in front of Doyle's cottage and talked about the weather, fishing, and the coming winter. Barry asked what the builders were doing, and Doyle said, "It's a new room for Copper because royalty always gets their own wing of the castle."

Barry was at a loss for words, so he told Doyle he had to get back home. "I'm working at the museum this afternoon, so if you get a chance, stop in. Remember, we meet on the morning of the third Thursday of the month... that's next week; we'd love to see you there."

"Perhaps, but I have a lot planned, so it might not fit into my schedule," Doyle said. He then pulled Copper up toward the cottage. Before they got into the house, Copper broke away and ran into the woods. Doyle knew what he wanted, so he ran after him. "Copper, no! You don't need to smell that dead deer again. Damn! I've got to get rid of that deer." He caught Copper and dragged him home, scolding him all the way.

With copper in the house, Doyle went outside to talk with Richard and his son. The two had finished pouring the concrete and were standing next to their loader.

Doyle walked up to them and said, "Richard, I need help."

"Sure, Doyle, what is it?"

Doyle told him about the deer and asked if there was anyone who could remove it. He mentioned it is upsetting Copper, and by spring the carcass will be overly ripe.

Richard laughed at Doyle's situation. "Pal, I'll remove it for you. I own some woods where I can dump it. I'll just add it to your bill."

"Wonderful, Richard... you're a lifesaver." Doyle said. He then asked, "Do either of you want ice tea or a cola?"

"No, we should get back to work before the cement dries. I need to finish troweling and set the poles for the fence and roof. We should finish this job tomorrow afternoon. I hate working on a weekend, but you wanted it done, and I can use the extra cash."

Chapter 6

Lunch With Colton and Lacie

After spending the morning sorting through a mountain of paperwork, he realized how late it was getting to be so he placed the ingredients for the lunch he'd offered to cook for Trudy's friends in a brown grocery bag then walked across the driveway to Trudy's house.

"Trudy, I'm late," Doyle exclaimed.

"Yes, I see. The kids should be here any minute. Will you be able to have lunch done in time?" Trudy asked with a chuckle.

"Don't tease me. You know I always get my meals on the table in record time. It's the hallmark of my success."

Within minutes of Doyle's arrival, Colton and Lacie rang Trudy's doorbell. Trudy opened the door to greet them. "Well… come on in, you two." She held the door open as her guests entered. "I want you to meet Al Doyle, my new next-door neighbor."

Doyle studied the two teenagers. Colton looked to be almost six feet tall, with brown hair, deep blue eyes, and a dark complexion, while Lacie was about five feet tall with blond hair and blue eyes. The couple smiled at Doyle, who extended his hand. Colton grasped and gave Doyle a hearty handshake.

Doyle turned to Lacie and said, "Trudy told me all about you two. I've known Trudy for almost forty years; she is one of my best friends."

"When did you move to Sand Point?" Lacie asked.

"Trudy called me last month after they arrested Mrs. Torengia's grandson for murder and drug dealing, and she mentioned Cora listed her home with a Realtor. Mrs. Torengia needed the cash, and I wanted a new house so it was a win-win for both of us."

Colton laughed, "I might have had something to do with her grandson's arrest."

"Oh, I heard all about that. You impressed my friends at the Detroit Police Department. Anyway, I am now Trudy's neighbor, and it is a pleasure to meet the two of you. Trudy deserves to have such caring friends."

"We're also pleased to meet you, Mr. Doyle," said Lacie.

"Please call me Doyle or Al," Doyle added. "Now, let me get cooking. I'll prepare lunch for the four of us; I hope you like Greek cheeseburgers."

Lacie and Colton laughed. "We sure do," said Colton. "You know we have a local festival to honor the cheeseburger."

"I heard all about the festival today at the Chamber of Commerce office. I've never attended the festival. The one time I was in Caseville, I was ten years old, and we weren't here for a festival; it was Grandpa's funeral," Doyle said as he took the ingredients from the brown bag and arranged them on the kitchen island.

"If you'll excuse me, I have a meal to prepare," Doyle said.

Lacie and Trudy walked to the large windows overlooking Lake Huron while Colton sat at the kitchen table to watch Doyle prepare lunch.

Doyle told Colton about the chain of restaurants he operated after he left the Detroit Police force. Colton read a newspaper article about the Detroit area restaurants, but it surprised him to hear Doyle also owned a large chain of *Doyle's Pubs* nationwide.

"I decided I was ready to retire, so I sold them all for a tidy profit, and here I am."

Colton couldn't believe an ex-police detective could become so successful. "Where did you learn to cook?"

"My mom owned a small Greek restaurant in Greektown. She insisted that all her children should know how to cook. Besides, we were cheap labor. Since we lived above the restaurant, it was a part of our lives, and cooking became second nature. After I left the Detroit Police, I received a large settlement, and I used that money to start my business."

"Congratulations. I hope you enjoy your new home, and I would love to sign you up for newspaper service, and my company also specializes in security systems for the home and business." Colton advised.

Doyle burst into a hearty laugh. "Smart and ambitious — an impressive combination, Colton."

"Thanks. I better find Lacie."

"Colton, I'm right here," Lacie said from behind him. "I was listening to the two of you."

Colton stood and offered Lacie a chair, just as Trudy walked into the room and asked, "Doyle, do you have drinks ready for our guests?"

Doyle reached into the huge refrigerator and pulled out a pitcher of iced tea. "I sure do. Colton, would you grab some tall glasses and ice? I have to run these Greek burgers to the patio. The grill is hot and ready."

Colton poured four glasses of tea and walked to the patio to watch the burgers with Doyle.

Trudy smiled. "Lacie, I think your boyfriend likes Doyle."

"Police officers and detectives impress Colton. He dreams about being a detective, yet he doesn't want to be a police officer. It may be one reason he started the security company."

Colton and Doyle returned from the grill with a platter of burgers and potato wedges.

"Lacie, look at these burgers. This man knows how to cook, and he has fantastic stories about crime in Detroit," Colton reported. "I'm impressed."

"Well, you haven't tasted my Greek burgers yet," Doyle replied.

The four diners gathered around the kitchen table as Doyle finished preparing the meal. He placed the burgers on warmed buns, sprinkled feta cheese on the meat, and added sliced red onions and a slice of tomato. On top of this, he poured a mixture he called Tzatziki sauce, a cucumber/yogurt sauce with sliced onions. He drizzled olive oil over the potatoes and added garlic and grated cheese. On the side was a small Greek salad with sliced olives.

After taking a bite of the burger, Lacie exclaimed, "Oh my God, Doyle! Enter this hamburger in Caseville's cheeseburger contest next summer. This is fantastic, and I bet you could win."

Everyone agreed with Lacie. A lively conversation continued during and after lunch. The topic centered on the abuse of Jenny Stillmore, a girl at school. The teens witnessed Jenny being abused and were looking for ways they could help Jenny get out of the relationship.

"Don't get involved," Doyle said. "You said you reported the abuse, you tried to get her help, and she knows you care. If you continue to interfere, you will only get hurt. Trust me, domestic violence is a delicate matter. There are reasons Jenny continues this relationship, and you cannot change her; she must make the change.

As Colton and Lacie prepared to return home, Doyle offered Colton his card and said, "Please, if you ever need help, call me. I have many connections and would be glad to assist you. Also, I already called the Metro Newspaper for home delivery. I presume you'll be delivering my Sunday paper."

Colton and Lacie thanked Doyle for the splendid meal, and Colton reminded Trudy that they would pick her up for Thanksgiving dinner next Thursday. Colton asked Doyle if he would like to join them for dinner, but he declined.

"It would be lover to join your family dinner, but I am helping to prepare Thanksgiving dinner at the Church Outreach Hall. It's my opportunity to give back to my new neighbors."

Lacie replied, "What a wonderful gesture. Perhaps we can get together some other time. Come on, Colton, you have a business meeting this afternoon."

As the teens walked to their vehicle, Doyle turned to Trudy and said, "You have a knack for making friends with the nicest people. Those two are a fine example of the upcoming generation. I wish my son were like Colton."

"He is special," agreed Trudy as she shut the door. "Anne should be here soon, so don't worry about cleaning the kitchen."

"Good, I was hoping to talk to her, and I will be careful."

"I know it sounds foolish, but Anne is pushy and not afraid to say what she's thinking. She's not married now, and I know she would love to snag a wealthy man... like you."

Trudy heard Anne's car in the driveway and said, "Speaking of our she-devil, she's here now."

Doyle opened the door, and Anne flew into the room. Anne wore tight jeans and a plunging V-neck top that showed off her ample bosom. "Mr. Doyle, it's nice to see you."

She turned to Trudy and asked, "Trudy, how are you feeling today?"

"I am feeling good, Anne. We had lunch with Colton and Lacie, which was very enjoyable."

Doyle was eager to talk to Anne about a job. He also realized Copper would be ready for a pit stop outside, so he interrupted the two women and said, "Anne, could you clean house for me once a week? I'll pay you the same rate as Trudy."

"I would love to help you, and I have Tuesday mornings open. It takes four hours a week, but I don't do windows, except for you. I'll do whatever you desire." She cooed.

"Light cleaning is enough. So, I'll see you Tuesday morning. I'll have a key made for you in case I'm out. I'm glad you can help me, but now I have to go. Copper must be ready to explode."

"Copper?" asked Anne. "You have a roommate?"

"Yes, he's a bloodhound. Don't worry, he's trained and friendly."

Anne smiled. "Al, I love animals, and I'm looking forward to seeing more of you. I'll be there at eight on Tuesday morning. OK?"

Doyle said yes, gathered his cooking supplies, and said good-bye.

Copper Likes Smoked Salmon

Doyle walked across the driveway, and Copper greeted him as he opened the side door. He had his leash in his mouth, and his tail was wagging.

"How do you always know when I'm at the door, Copper?"

Copper didn't answer; he looked Doyle in the eye and growled. Doyle was learning Copper's sign language, so he connected his leash and walked him out the side door. As they approached the patio, it surprised Doyle to see that the builders had almost finished the fence and roof of Copper's new outdoor room.

"Look at that, Copper." Doyle walked toward the fenced in patio. "The contractor installed artificial grass, and there's a water outlet that looks like a fire hydrant with a garden hose. Tell me how much you like this room, Copper!"

Copper walked away... unimpressed. He did his business on the lawn, and bolted towards the woods, followed by his leash.

"No... come back here." Doyle yelled.

Copper couldn't find his dead deer, and he wasn't happy. He howled and kept his nose in the leaves where the dead animal had been.

"There you are. Hah ha! Now you can find something else to play with... preferably something living."

On the way back to the house, Doyle stopped to talk with Richard. "Nice job with the patio and the deer! Will you finish Copper's patio this afternoon?"

"No, I'll be back on Saturday to finish the roof, and your dog can use the room Sunday morning. I installed the doggy door, but I still have to calk around it, and I want to tighten the roof. We don't want it flying off in the middle of a storm, do we?"

"No, that would be a problem." Doyle walked around the fenced in area and opened the gate. "Can I walk on the grass now?" He asked.

"Yes, it's done, but I should give you some cleaning tips. Your dog's solid waste will stay on top so you can pick it up like you do on the lawn, and his pee will drain through the fake grass. You can use the hose to wash the grass down, and I'll leave you some special cleaner that will take care of any odors. I found the plans online and got overnight delivery of the artificial grass. I think you'll like it."

Richard's work impressed Doyle. "If you bring me the bill tomorrow, I'll have a check for you."

Richard smiled and assured him the bill would be ready. "It's my pleasure, but I have to ask you something. This is the first addition like this I've done, and I want to take photographs and post them on my Facebook page because I'm sure other dog owners would love this kind of doggy patio."

"No problem, Richard, but please don't post my name with the photographs. I don't want a bunch of people stopping by to look at my property."

"I won't tell anyone, but in a few days everyone in the community will know. That's what Caseville and Sand Point are famous for... gossip! It spreads like wildfire, and it can burn people, too."

Doyle was eager to continue exploring his new community, so he loaded Copper into the Buick, and took out the map that Trudy had given him the other day. "Where to first, Copper? We have all afternoon."

Copper didn't offer an opinion; he sat on the front seat looking out the window. Every time a deer went by, he growled and sniffed the air. *I wonder if he's still looking for his dead deer?* Doyle asked himself.

Today, Doyle turned south and drove toward Bay Port. As he entered the small village, he checked the map to find the Fish Company. "Copper, do you want fish?" he asked. Copper didn't respond.

Bay Port is a small town with a big history. Commercial fishing and a sandy beach have always made the town famous. A railroad magnate from Saginaw built a fantastic hotel with indoor plumbing and electricity. The famous hotel was a destination for droves of sightseers. The railroad featured excursions to the hotel with low cost packaged deals. Unfortunately, the lake receded, and the beach turned into a marsh. No one wanted to vacation in the swamp, so they tore the hotel apart and auctioned the pieces to area homeowners.

Doyle climbed the steps of the Bay Port Fish Company and walked into the historic building. The aroma of the fish market reminded him of Eastern Market in Detroit. He often arrived at the market early enough to get the freshest fish. Today he wanted information and whitefish. A middle-aged woman wearing a sweatshirt, jeans, and a soiled apron covered in fish scales, stood behind the counter. Her name tag said *Nancy*.

Doyle studied the fresh fish in the display case and ordered whitefish; three pounds of fresh fillets and one whole fish... smoked. "Nancy, do you know anything about the history of the fish company?" he asked.

"No... I'm sorry... I only work here. There is a museum south of town, and I know the Pigeon Museum has a lot of information about Bay Port. Perhaps they can help you," the clerk offered as she weighed the whitefish.

"Before you put that in a bag, add a fillet of smoked salmon and cut off some for my bloodhound. He's in the car."

"Sure," Nancy said as she put a small piece of salmon into another bag. "You know once he eats this he'll be begging you to bring him back."

"Good, that will be a great excuse to come back." Doyle laughed and walked to his vehicle. He could see Copper's nose twitch as he laid the bag on the seat. The bloodhound's drooling convinced Doyle to hurry, even though they trained him to wait for a snack. "Here, eat this and stop making the seat wet."

Copper loved the smoked fish, and as he drove, Doyle kept snacking on his fish... sharing with Copper, who was getting hooked on the new treat.

Doyle drove to Pigeon, a small farming village seven miles south of Caseville. He took a few minutes to find the Depot Museum, and because it was after three o'clock; they were closed. He tried looking through the windows to no avail.

Instead of heading back to Sand Point, he stopped into Main Street Cafe for a cup of coffee. Angie, a polite young server, took his order and asked if he was new to the area. Doyle told her where he was from and why he had moved from Detroit to this area.

A large man with a full white beard overheard Doyle talking, and he approached him with an extended hand.

"Hi there, mister. I'm Bobby Engelmart. I overheard you say you were a retired police officer. Well... I was a county deputy until I retired, and then I was the part time Pigeon Village police officer. Are you a new resident, vacationing, or just visiting?"

"I moved here. I was a Detroit Homicide Detective for almost thirty years and then a chef for ten years. Now, I'm just retired."

"That's nice. Is your wife retired too?" Bobby didn't let Doyle answer before he asked more questions. "Where did you say you live now? In Pigeon, or in the area?"

"No, yes and yes," quipped Doyle.

"Well... OK, then. I welcome you to our town, and if you ever have a problem, I'll be around."

"Thank you," said Doyle. "I should go; my bloodhound is in my vehicle, and he needs a walk." Doyle didn't want to give Bobby any more information. He paid his bill, gave the server a nice tip, and started toward the exit. Bobby called behind him, "Don't forget to pick up after that bloodhound of yours. We like to keep our village clean, you know."

Chapter 7

Doyle Meets Sandra

Doyle asked Trudy to come over for dinner, but she wasn't feeling well, so he spent Friday evening eating baked whitefish with vegetables, garlic mashed potatoes, a Greek salad, and a chilled glass of Chardonnay. Copper had leftover chicken breast and water.

After dinner, he watched a beautiful sunset and later sat in front of the fireplace, reading the newspaper he picked up at the corner party store while listening to classical music on his built in sound system. Copper laid on the rug, occasionally walking over to the new *doggy door*. He wanted to know what it was for, but Doyle wouldn't open it because the builder advised him to wait until Sunday.

He put the paper down and thought about the past week. When he left Detroit, he didn't know what to expect, but he knew he could handle any situation. What he didn't prepare for was the loneliness. In Detroit, Doyle always had people around him. He thrived on the action and adventure of city life.

Doyle had many friends, but they were business friends. His boyhood friend and fellow police officer had passed a few years ago, and it had been almost a year since he had had a serious relationship with a woman. Here in Sand Point, Copper and Trudy are his only friends, and adventure equals a walk on the beach. *Perhaps I made a mistake moving here*, he thought.

"Copper, do you like it here? Or would you rather be back in

Detroit?" Doyle didn't expect the bloodhound to answer, but Copper stood and walked over to him. He laid his head on Doyle's lap and grunted. Doyle thought, *Not a yes, nor a no... perhaps a little gas from dinner?* He sniffed the air. *Yes... it's gas.* Doyle chuckled at the doggy gas Copper released. *I guess we'll stay, but we need to make more friends.*

Doyle woke early and took Copper out for his morning business. There was a light snow covering the beach, and the water was choppy as if a storm might be approaching. It didn't take the bloodhound long, and Doyle obliged by running back to the cottage.

"Just imagine how cold it will be in January, Copper," Doyle said as he scooped dried food into his bowl. "I still have to pick up a better dish for you. Want to go to Bad Axe today?" There was no answer, just a crunching sound. "I understand there is a Walmart there."

Doyle prepared a small pot of coffee, and while it was brewing, he dropped a bagel in the toaster and arranged cream cheese and butter on the table. He wished he had a newspaper but knew it wouldn't arrive until Sunday morning. Instead, he turned on the television in the living room and listened to the morning news while he read the online version of the newspaper on his cell phone.

Copper walked by the big screen, looked at the image, and then sat by the patio door and watched Richard Waters and his son. They arrived early to finish the new outdoor room in the backyard, and Copper grew curious. *That strange little door is just his size, and he wants to know what it's for.*

After he finished breakfast, Doyle called the Pigeon Museum. A recorded message announced the museum would open at ten. He planned to be there when they opened because he had a feeling that today would be the start of something special.

Sandra Is Beautiful

Pigeon is a small village seven miles south of Caseville. With a history that goes back to the 1880s, Pigeon has always been a booming farming community. Today, like most small towns, the retail stores struggle to stay open. Bad Axe, the county seat fifteen miles east of Pigeon, has a Walmart and several other retail chain stores. In years past, a shopping trip to the big city meant a drive to Pigeon. Today, people will drive for over an hour to do their shopping.

Doyle parked in front of the Pigeon Museum Research Center. The museum opens at ten; he was fifteen minutes early. "Copper, let's go for a walk," he said. Doyle did not know how long he would be at the museum, and he didn't want Copper to have an accident in the Buick... not that he thought he would.

As he returned, he saw a woman with brown hair streaked with gray stop in front of the building. She was in her late fifties and a very attractive woman. He watched as she gathered her leather purse and briefcase and walked toward the museum door, unlocked the door and walked in.

"Copper," he whispered. "Nice looking woman, isn't she?"

Copper looked up at him, and Doyle swore he smiled. "I agree. Finish up so I can talk to her."

With Copper in the vehicle, Doyle walked into the museum.

"Hi, my name is Sandra Breeman. If you have questions, I can try to help you. We have books on the history of the area, obituary records, old postcards and photographs covering the Western Thumb Region."

Doyle smiled and said, "Thank you, Sandra. My name is Al Doyle, and I moved to Sand Point a few days ago. Detroit is my hometown, but my dad's family settled in Caseville in the late 1860s. I'm trying to trace their history, and I could use any help you offer. I'm new to genealogy."

Sandra picked up a book about the history of Caseville and handed it to Doyle. "We could start here, and we also have newspapers from the late 1890s, which might have information. One good place to look is in the obituaries. We may find the location of your grandparents' gravesites."

Sandra's professionalism impressed Doyle. "Are you a trained historian?" he asked.

She laughed. "No, but I love history. I've researched my family and my former husband's, but I'm an amateur. All the *Friends of the Museum* group are interested in preserving our history, so we volunteer to work here throughout the year."

Holding the book, Doyle walked around the building, studying the large historical photographs. "These are impressive. Do you have any fishing boats? My grandpa was a commercial fisherman, first in Caseville... then in Bay Port."

"Not on display. There are photographs in the scrapbooks and on our computer database. I'm sure we could find one or two."

While Sandra looked for the photographs, Doyle sat at a table and studied the book on Caseville. He saw several references to his grandfather and asked Sandra if she had paper so he could make notes.

Sandra returned with a spiral notebook. "Here, you can have this one. She set the notebook down. I also found pictures of some early fishing boats in Caseville. There is a list in this article. Do you know the name of your grandfather's boat?"

"Gee... no. I never met my grandfather, and my dad didn't share with us. Dad refused to follow Grandpa into the fishing business, and they didn't talk for many years."

Doyle was enjoying his visit. He found traces of his family, and Sandra made him feel welcome. He wanted to ask her out for coffee, but he was unsure of himself and didn't want to seem too eager.

Doyle showed Sandra the book on Caseville and said, "This one book is excellent. Could I borrow it? I can return it in a few days. I want to scan the information and pictures."

"I wish I could, but we have a rule against lending to anyone other than members."

"OK... How do I become a member?" Doyle asked.

"Are you serious? I mean... we need more members, but it should be something you want to do, not just a way to borrow a book."

Doyle smiled. "Yes... I'm sure. I have nothing to keep me busy, and I need a hobby. That's why I moved up here... to find my roots, so how do I join?"

Before Doyle finished his question, Sandra handed him a form to fill out. "I need this information and then the twenty dollars membership fee."

Doyle filled out the form and took several flyers filled with information about the group. He then reached into his billfold for money, but took out a check and handed Sandra the check for one thousand dollars.

Sandra laughed. "Are you serious? It's only twenty dollars, or a hundred for a lifetime membership, and you don't have to impress me with your money."

"I'm not trying to impress you. I want to become a lifetime member, and I figured this would cover it, provided I live another fifty years."

Sandra accepted the check, and after looking at her phone she said, "It's noon, and I usually go to Main Street for lunch. Would you like to join me?"

It relieved Doyle that she asked. "Yes, I was thinking of asking you, but I didn't want to be too bold."

"Wonderful, we can talk more over a good meal. Do you think your bloodhound will be OK in the car?"

"Yes, provided I take him for a walk first. Why don't I do that while you lock up here, then I'll meet you in the restaurant?"

Making Friends In Pigeon

Sandra found a cozy table along the south wall of the cafe and ordered coffee for herself.

"There will be two of us, but I'm not sure what he'll be drinking," she told Angie, the server.

Doyle walked into the cafe and spotted Sandra. He hurried to her table and joined her. Angie brought Sandra's coffee and smiled at Doyle. "Mr. Doyle, it's nice to see you back again. Will you be having coffee too?" she asked.

"Yes, and a glass of ice water, please. I was lucky today, Angie. Sandra was working at the museum, and I'm finding everything I needed."

"That's nice. I'll be back in a minute with your coffee," she said after handing the couple a menu.

Sandra smiled. "Angie is a sweet girl. I know her parents and her grandmother. I take it you came in here yesterday after you found the museum closed?"

"Yes, and I'm glad I came back today. Now tell me what you suggest for lunch."

"I like their homemade potato chips, and I enjoy them with a sandwich."

They both ordered fish sandwiches with the homemade chips. The two were becoming friends, with Sandra enjoying Doyle's humor and Doyle realizing Sandra is a delightful conversationalist.

Their conversation soon revolved around family. Sandra didn't ask about Doyle's divorce, but her ears perked up when he talked about his ex-wife.

"I was a young Detroit patrolman, and I took my job home with me. I'm someone who becomes engrossed in his work, and my wife wanted a full-time husband. Our son was five years old, and she got full custody... while I ended up paying child support and alimony." Doyle explained.

"I'm sorry; that must have been difficult for you. How is your relationship with your son now?"

"He hated me when he was young because his mother poisoned him against me. Today our conversations turn into arguments, but he still wants me to make him rich by leaving everything I have to him. Before I moved here, he criticized me for spending *his* money on a stupid cottage."

Angie brought their lunch, and both Doyle and Sandy admitted the homemade potato chips were excellent. In between bites, Doyle asked Sandy about her family.

"My husband and I grew up as next-door neighbors. Being in the country, we lived a half mile apart. The year after we graduated from high school, we married and ended up with two strong and independent sons, who look just like their dad. My husband, Mike, died of lung cancer five years ago, so I transferred the farm to the boys, Ronald and Raymond. We set up a trust so they work the farm as partners and, upon my death, they own the farm, but they must make payments for the land while I'm living."

"It sounds like you get along with your sons. Congratulations."

Sandra's smile became solemn. "Yes, I get along with each of my sons; however, they fight with each other. I hate when they try to place me between them. I won't let them do that because they have no right to expect me to interfere with their business. They are adults and they need to behave like adults, not little boys."

After lunch, Doyle asked Sandra if he could call her so they could plan an outing. She responded with, "If you mean a date, yes, but I'm not looking for anything beyond having a friend, and as a friend I would like you to call me Sandy, like most of my close friends."

"Agreed! Being new to the community, I need a friend. I consider myself a social person, and it's not fun throwing a party for just me and my bloodhound."

Sandy laughed and exchanged her cell phone number with Doyle. Before leaving, he let Copper out of the car, and Sandy gave him a big hug. She fell in love with Copper and said, "I can't wait to introduce you to my cat, Casey."

Doyle smiled all the way home, and Copper sensed his joy. He stopped for the Saturday newspaper and some fresh milk at the Sand Point Market. As he paid the cashier, he heard a familiar voice say, "Doyle, I see you're out and about. Don't you love Caseville?"

It was the man from the Chamber office, and Doyle wasn't sure of his name. "Yes, I love it here. I was in Pigeon all day at the museum, and I had a wonderful time... Roger." Doyle remembered the name at the last moment.

Roger smiled. "Then you met Sandy today. She works at the museum on Saturdays. Beautiful woman, isn't she?"

"Yes... exquisite." Doyle finished paying and walked over to Roger. "How long have you known Sandy?"

"We go way back. She and Mike were a year ahead of me and my wife in school. We were all devastated when Mike died, leaving her and the boys to fend for themselves, but I guess we all have to go sometime... right?"

"Right, better later than sooner, though." Doyle said in all seriousness. He often thought about death, but hated to dwell on it.

"Well... have a good evening. Have you selected a church up here to attend? My family goes to the Methodist church in town, but we don't have a shortage of churches, so you can take your pick," Roger said as he got in line to pay for his purchases. "I have to get my weekly lottery tickets; one of these days I'll win the big prize."

"Good luck with that; I'll see you around, Roger." Doyle left the party store realizing that he would have to adapt to the fact that everyone knows everyone else in Huron County. He got into the Buick, and Copper begged to see what was in the bag.

"It's just a newspaper and some milk. I'll buy you a treat tomorrow." Doyle said as he headed home. A frown formed on Copper's face, and he turned to watch the other cars and drivers in the parking lot.

Chapter 8

Colton Finds Jenny and asks for help.

Doyle was fast asleep when Copper put his paws across his chest and licked his face.

"What do you want?" He asked, half awake. Since there was no answer, Doyle looked at the alarm clock, which read three fifteen. He then heard his cell phone ringing and realized why Copper had woken him.

Doyle reached across the bed and checked the phone. The number wasn't familiar, but he felt a need to answer.

"Hello, Doyle speaking."

Doyle recognized the voice of the young man he had met at Trudy's home on Saturday. "Mr. Doyle, it's Colton Blackwell, and I apologize for disturbing your sleep, but I'm at a house six houses east of you. Could you come here? I found Jenny, the girl we told you about, at Trudy's, and she's dead."

Colton's statement shocked Doyle, and he responded with, "How did she die?"

"In a hot tub."

"Did you call the police?"

"Yes, I called them, but I could use moral support. The police will be here soon, and I don't want to create more problems for myself by saying something stupid."

"Colton, I'll be there as soon as I can get dressed and make coffee."

Doyle hung up and said, "Thank you for waking me, Copper; that was Colton." Doyle grabbed his jeans and a sweatshirt. After using the bathroom, he made a small pot of coffee, which he put in an insulated mug, and since it was dark and he wasn't familiar with the neighborhood yet, he drove the short distance.

Colton's Jeep sat next to the road with its lights out. Doyle parked behind it and walked up the driveway, where he saw the young man on his knees, looking at the girl in a red dress laying on the steps of the hot-tub. The water had turned bright red from her blood, and the girl's wrists appeared cut and covered with blood. The scene reminded Doyle of the many crime scenes he had witnessed in Detroit.

Doyle stood silent as Colton whispered, "I'm so sorry, Jenny. Did someone do this to you, or did you want to end your pain?" He wiped the tears from his eyes and added, "I promise, if someone did this to you, I'll try to find out who. You didn't deserve to die."

Doyle kneeled down and put his hand on Colton's shoulder. The young man looked into Doyle's caring eyes as Doyle asked, "Son, did you feel her answer? Some detectives believe they can. I never had that experience, but I always ask the victim what happened."

"I sensed her telling me someone else did this to her." Colton said through his tears.

"That will be the question we need to answer."

Looking over the crime scene, Doyle asked, "Did you take a photograph?"

"No, it never crossed my mind. Do you think I should?"

"Yes, take a couple from this angle and then from over there. Be sure you disturb nothing."

After Colton finished taking the pictures, Doyle suggested they stand next to their vehicles. "The police will be here soon," he said. "In fact, I see flashing lights through the trees now."

A Huron County patrol car approached and parked in front of the Jeep. A middle-aged county deputy and his younger assistant walked up to Colton and asked, "Where is she?"

Colton knew the officer and pointed to the hot tub. The deputy told Colton and Doyle to stay put while they investigated. Doyle watched as they walked toward Jenny. Another vehicle approached. Colton said it was his dad. "I asked him to finish my paper route, since I'll be here a while."

Colton introduced his dad, Adam, to Doyle. As the two men shook hands, a state trooper drove up and stood by his patrol car waiting to talk with them. Colton kept his eyes on the officers and told Doyle the trooper's name was Steve Lithkowski.

Colton's dad drove off with the Jeep to finish the route. He left Colton's car with him. As soon as Adam left, Trooper Steve approached. Doyle walked up to the trooper before the trooper could say anything and extended his hand. With a voice of authority, Doyle said, "Trooper, my name is Albert Doyle, a retired Detroit homicide detective. I am here at the request of my friend, Colton. After calling the police, he remembered I lived just a few houses west of here and felt a need to have someone of knowledge help him during this horrible time. I'm sure you understand?"

"Yes, I understand, but I need to speak with Colton alone. Colton, come with me so we can talk in the patrol car."

Doyle stepped closer to Trooper Steve, and with his face inches away he said, "Officer, you will not interview Mr. Blackwell without an adult, such as myself or his parent, in his presence. Is that understood?"

The trooper stepped back with a look of rage filling his gaunt face. He returned to his patrol car and used the phone. Doyle and Colton watched as he argued with someone, perhaps his commander.

When he returned, he apologized to Doyle and asked them both to accompany him to the patrol car to talk.

Colton explained what happened, and he mentioned he had witnessed Jenny's boyfriend, Luke, abuse her in and out of school.

The trooper took notes and asked Colton why he had asked Mr.

Doyle for help.

"Colton, you don't have to answer that question," Doyle advised.

"Oh, Trooper Steve knows why I asked you to help. The trooper has a problem with teenagers because he thinks all of us are guilty of something. Perhaps he is projecting his own personal experiences as a youth onto us," Colton said with a chuckle.

"Smartass," quipped the trooper.

"That's enough, trooper. You needn't call my friend vulgar names," responded Doyle.

After they cleared the scene and loaded Jenny's body into the ambulance, the EMS workers drove away. Deputy Ned approached Colton. "Ned, this is Albert Doyle. He's a retired Detroit detective and a good friend of mine."

Doyle smiled at hearing Colton's description. "Yes, a good friend."

He shook Ned's hand and complimented him on his good work. Doyle told the deputy he never expected a murder on Sand Point.

"Who said anything about murder?" asked Ned.

With great skill, Doyle pumped the deputy for information. "Well, aren't all deaths considered murder until proven otherwise? I mean, a young girl in her prime, what evidence is there that she would kill herself?"

"Her Facebook page. She posted a goodbye note," said Ned. After he said that, he realized that he might have said too much. "But that's for Sheriff McNabb and the coroner to decide. I just gather the evidence."

After Ned and his partner left, Doyle and Colton stood next to the Jeep talking. Colton thanked Doyle for helping. "I know you didn't want to get involved in a murder/suicide, but I trust your opinions, and I know I can learn from you."

"So, why not become a police officer?" asked Doyle.

"No... I want to run my security business. If a mystery crosses my path, all the better. I seem to have a knack for stumbling into mysteries."

"It's not luck or a knack... you're observant. You saw the lights on at this house and knew they shouldn't have been on. Anyone else would have missed that clue. Colton, you have a nose for mysteries."

As Doyle got into his car, he smiled. *Living here might be more fun than I expected*, he thought.

Party Planner

Doyle awoke after eight on Sunday morning, eager to read his morning newspaper, listen to the news report on Jenny's death, and see how Copper likes his new doggy door and outdoor rest area.

The first task was to let Copper use the door. No luck! Doyle opened the door, and Copper brought the leash to him. Doyle then tried pushing the bloodhound out the door, but Copper resisted... holding his ground by spreading his front legs and digging his paws into the floor... refusing to budge an inch.

"What's your problem, Copper? I paid a fortune for this door and outdoor room, and you *WILL* use it!" Doyle insisted. *But how do I get him to do that?*

Copper needed to go out *NOW*, so Doyle connected the leash and took him out. Doyle opened the outside gate to the fenced-in room and dragged Copper into the dog area. He kneeled down and patted the imitation grass. "It's all yours, Copper. Now isn't this nice? Look, a fire hydrant to pee on and grass just like the lawn outside. Go ahead; it's OK to do your business in here."

Copper wouldn't soil the hydrant or artificial grass, and Doyle didn't know what to do. Realizing he was losing the battle, he relented. "OK, outside we go, but you will go in here someday" Copper was too busy relieving himself to hear Doyle.

Doyle read the newspaper that Colton had delivered earlier, and while he and Copper ate breakfast, he listened to the local news to hear what they reported about the death on Sand Point last night. Unlike Detroit, Huron County has few major crimes, so when there is a murder or robbery, it's big news. The reporting of Jenny's death was very subdued because the police ruled it a suicide. Out of respect for the family, they often say, "The deceased person died *suddenly* or *unexpectedly*." Most of the residents know the code words, so it seems odd to hide the truth.

By noon, Doyle became bored and drove into Caseville. He discovered that on a cold Sunday in November, there were few locals and fewer visitors milling around the souvenir shops, antique stores, bookstore, and assorted gift shops. The gas station was busy, a few shoppers were at the local hardware, and several cars parked in front of the grocery store. The bar called The Blue Water Inn looked like it was hopping, so it won out. Doyle parked along the street and told Copper he wouldn't be long.

"I want to catch a little of that small town gossip," he told Copper.

Doyle discovered that there was a traveling pool tournament taking place at the Blue Water Inn. As soon as he opened the door and walked in, he felt the eyes of everyone in the bar turn toward him. A low murmur of voices asking who he was almost drowned out the country music blaring on the jukebox.

He walked up to the bar, found an empty stool and ordered a diet coke, not because that's what wanted to drink, but because it was neat and easy to order.

The bartender brought his drink and said, "You're the retired police officer from Detroit, aren't you? Didn't you help young Colton kid... the teenager who delivers newspapers?"

Doyle laughed. "And how did you hear about this?"

"Oh, I'm sorry. I'm Will Braunson. My brother, Deputy Chad, assisted Deputy Ned Wooddell this morning. My brother said you talked to them. So, do you believe Jenny killed herself? Ned says Colton told his girlfriend someone murdered her."

"I'm not sure. It surprises me how small this community is."

Will looked puzzled. "Small? Are you making fun of us?"

"No, I've lived in downtown Detroit all my life, but now I live here, and I find it charming that everyone cares about each other so much."

"We sure do, and welcome to The Blue Water," Will said as he walked away.

An older man dressed in an old black suit was sitting on the stool next to Doyle. He was deep in thought and appeared inebriated. The man stood and wove his way to the men's room. A few minutes later he returned with the front of his pants wet. *God, I hope that's not me in thirty years.*

With that image in his mind, he finished his drink and prepared to go home to figure out how to coax Copper into using his new outdoor room. He reached the exit when Roger, and perhaps his wife, entered the bar.

"Doyle, it appears you're finding all the popular hangouts. This is my wife, Mindy. Mindy, this is Albert Doyle. He owned the restaurant in Greektown that you liked."

"Yes... with the same name as yours! That's clever, isn't it, Roger?" Mindy didn't wait for an answer; she noticed a friend and rushed to give her a hug.

"Well, I better go. I hope you come to the Caseville Chamber meeting. Remember, every second Tuesday of each month at six-thirty," Roger said, and then he joined Mindy by the pool table. It was clear they knew several of the team members.

Doyle left the bar and looked across the street. There was a park with a statue. *I must check that out soon,* he mused as he opened the Buick's door. Copper was eager to see him, but he didn't act like he needed to go out, so Doyle drove toward Sand Point.

"Copper, living here will take getting used to. Have you noticed how strange these folks are?" Copper looked out the window and growled. He didn't agree; he saw another dog across the street.

After taking Copper out for a walk, Doyle called Sandy. He needed to talk to someone *sane*. Their conversation lasted well over an hour, and Sandy understood his feeling of isolation.

"You're going through a big change; it'll take time to adjust. You'll love Sand Point if you give it time. And trust me, not everyone is insane here. Just a little *off,* if you understand what I mean."

Doyle laughed. "I do. Would it help if I gave a party for some people I've met? I have a place in my home for entertaining, and I'm always more comfortable when I'm hosting. I miss being in control."

"Well, I, for one, would love to see your new home and taste your cooking, so yes, it would be a good idea. When do you want to have the party? Remember... Thanksgiving is just two weeks away, so it's before or after."

"Would next weekend be too soon?" Doyle asked. "That way I can use up the excess food I have in the refrigerator and freezer."

Sandy considered for a moment. "Saturday is out, too much going on, and Sunday afternoon everyone will be busy. The best day might be Tuesday; there are no meetings Tuesday evening."

"Great! Let's make it at six p.m. a week from Tuesday. I'll serve a buffet of Greek food, and we can call it a *Get To Know You Party*. I would love it if you could handle the invitations. Perhaps keep it to four or five couples plus you and me?"

"It sounds wonderful, Al," said Sandy. "I'll stop at noon to help, and I'll tell the guests to be there at five for cocktails."

"Perfect! My outlook on living here has improved already; thank you."

"My pleasure, but I have to get going. I'm working at the hospital in Pigeon in the morning and then I'm at the community center for a few hours."

"Have fun... bye.."

Copper displayed a grin on his face and a sparkle in his eyes, just like Doyle.

Chapter 9

Cops and Robbers

Copper poked his nose into Doyle's bedroom at three in the morning to make sure he was sleeping. When he heard the low rumble of snoring, he returned to the kitchen and walked up to the small doggy door. His nose twitched as he inspected around the door, and then he poked his head into the opening. The door magically opened, and Copper walked into the outdoor area. He looked back at the door and returned to the house.

After several trips back and forth, the bloodhound knew he wouldn't get trapped outside. He walked to the rug next to Doyle's gray leather recliner and picked up his favorite chew bone. With the bone in his mouth, he walked outside and lay in the center of the room. He played for an hour and then fell asleep. When the sun rose, he realized where he was and hurried back to the house just as Doyle walked into the kitchen. Doyle met Copper at the counter, and Copper had the leash in his mouth. Doyle knew what that meant.

"Copper, you need to use your new outdoor room," Doyle said as he led the dog to the doggy door. Copper placed his front paws in a *no-way-in-hell* stance and refused to go through the small door. Again, Doyle relented and took Copper outside to do his business. As they walked past the fenced in dog area, Doyle saw Copper's dog bone laying on the imitation grass.

"You scoundrel, you were in the room last night, weren't you? Do you see that? It's your dog bone." Doyle forced Copper to see into the room. "Why are you doing this?"

Doyle felt betrayed, and Copper knew it. He stood with his tail between his legs and a sad expression on his droopy face. "What am I going to do with you?" asked Doyle.

He opened the outside door and led Copper into the room. Doyle removed the leash and left Copper alone in the area. Following the instructions he found on the Internet, Doyle walked into the yard and picked up sticks and branches and some of Copper's waste. The Internet suggested putting the sticks where you want the dog to pee and rubbing the dog's waste into the artificial grass. This will let the dog know he can do his business there.

After following the instructions, Doyle left the room and locked the small door, leaving Copper alone in the outdoor room. After a few minutes, Copper was scratching at the door. Doyle looked out and saw he had used the room, so he let Copper back into the house and congratulated him. Dog and master were both proud of their accomplishments.

Doyle cleaned up after Copper. When he returned, he gave the bloodhound a special treat and spent an hour brushing and grooming him.

"Copper, I'm so glad that nonsense is over. If you keep using the new room, I promise I'll take you for a walk every day, unless it's too nasty outside." Copper rubbed against Doyle's leg and then laid down on the rug, looking out toward the beach.

Doyle spent the day working on the internet. Sandy gave him a list of websites where he could find records from the past. He found grave and obituary information and also a record of his grandfather's boat trip from England to Canada and a marriage license.

Late afternoon, the doorbell buzzed, startling both Doyle and Copper.

Doyle opened the door. "Colton, how can I help you?"

Colton explained, "Doyle, Sheriff McNabb asked Seth and me

to set up security cameras and watch out for the burglars who have been breaking into the homes on The Point. We would like to place two cameras on your mailbox."

Doyle agreed and walked to the street with Colton. "Seth, this is Mr. Doyle."

The technology Seth was using fascinated Doyle, and the two talked for a few minutes about the security camera Seth would install.

Doyle watched as Seth set two cameras on his mailbox. One will look east for vehicles coming into Sand Point, and the other a mile down the road in the opposite direction. Turning to Colton, he said, "When do you think these robbers will strike?"

"If they stay on the same schedule, they will break into another home tomorrow morning. That's why we're setting the cameras up tonight."

Colton studied the two camera views and suggested that they may only need one other camera. "The third camera should be west of here."

Seth thought for a moment and agreed. "Well, that will save us a lot of time and energy. Mr. Doyle, you have the perfect location."

Doyle laughed. "I moved here because of the location, but I was looking forward to a nice quiet retirement at my lake cottage. Instead, I'm greeted with a dead girl in the hot tub, and now a security trap to catch home burglars. It's just like being back on the force in Detroit, only with a beautiful lake view."

"Welcome to The Point, Mr. Doyle," laughed Seth. "If you spend time around us, you'll run into all kinds of tense situations."

Doyle laughed and then turned serious. "Just make sure the two of you avoid contact with the robbers. Watch them, then call the police. When I was on the police force, we always waited for backup before we approached a dangerous situation. The one time I didn't wait, I almost died."

Colton told Doyle that the police would be in the area all morning. "They're part of the trap, and we will be careful."

Doyle had difficulty sleeping because he kept thinking of the teenagers looking for the burglars. At five in the morning he heard something outside, so he walked to the side door and looked out. The moon was almost full, but it was still difficult to see. Colton parked his Jeep in front of his driveway, hidden by some pine trees, then Seth came walking along the trees separating Doyle's home from his neighbors. He stopped and stood next to a large pine tree and unzipped his jeans to pee.

Doyle wanted to yell when he saw an older man walk up behind him. The large man put his finger into Seth's back. The teenager put his hands up, thinking it was a real gun pointed at his back. Seth said something, and the man let him finish peeing.

Doyle grabbed a fry pan and a roll of duck take from the kitchen. Without making a sound, he opened the side door and, in his slippers, he walked to where the burglar was holding Seth. Doyle cracked the pan on the back of the burglar's head, and the man dropped to his knees and went limp.

Seth turned around as the robber hit the ground. There stood Mr. Doyle with a huge grin on his face and a cast iron fry pan in his hand.

"Here, hold my fry pan while I duct tape his hands and mouth. We don't want him to wake up yelling to his friends," Doyle whispered.

Seth watched as Doyle worked. "You weren't afraid he would shoot me in the back?"

"No. I figured his finger would only shoot blanks," Doyle said. "Besides, I'm an expert with a fry pan."

Doyle bent down and grabbed the man's limp arm. "Let's pull him to the Jeep. I don't want to stand out here because they might come looking for him."

Colton almost lost it when he saw Doyle and Seth pulling a body up to the road.

Seth had a huge smile on his face as they laid the robber's body next to the Jeep. Doyle saw a car with its headlight off, approaching from the other direction. It was Deputy Ned, and behind him were two other county deputies.

Ned walked toward the Jeep. When he saw the man taped up, laying on the road, he turned to Doyle and said in a whisper, "What the hell?"

"Fry pan." Doyle said. "I hit him with one because he had my friend, Seth, hogtied."

"And what was Seth doing?" Ned asked, almost laughing.

"Peeing on my trees. That's what he was doing!" said Doyle.

To avoid laughing, Ned turned to the other officers. "OK, men. Let's go into the house and round up the robbers."

The police officers, with their hands next to their guns, walked up to the door. It took less than five minutes for the officers to escort two men from the house. As they did, Colton turned his headlights on so he could see the action.

Doyle yelled to Ned. "The one we caught is awake now. I'm sure he wants to ride with his buddies."

Ned walked over to the Jeep. Doyle and Seth helped the man get onto his feet. The deputy laughed when he saw the robber's hands taped behind him with duct tape.

"Nice handcuffs, Doyle."

"I learned that trick when I was a homicide detective in Detroit," Doyle said.

"Impressive," said the Deputy, as he ripped the tape from the robber's mouth.

Colton and Seth cringed. They could almost feel the man's beard and lips ripping off with the tape.

"Hurts, doesn't it?" Ned asked the robber. He read the man his rights and led him toward the patrol car. When the robbers were all loaded into the cars, he walked back to the Jeep.

"Well, thank you for your help, men. Colton, I'll let you know what we find, but I'm sure these men are the robbers we've been looking for. Deputy Mike and Chad will search the home for prints, photograph the damage, and then take your statements. I'm taking these three crooks to Bad Axe."

"Ned. I think I recognized the youngest robber with the long hair. He's a substitute driver for the newspaper; I recall one of the other drivers saying he got the job because his girlfriend works in the circulation office. If that's true, they would have access to the list of customers who leave for the winter."

"Good lead," Ned said. "I'll look into it. "Well, thanks again. And Mr. Doyle, welcome to the neighborhood."

It only took a few minutes for Deputy Chad to take statements from Colton, Seth, and Doyle.

After he recorded Colton's, he said, "We're done here for now. If the sheriff needs more, he'll contact you. Now I have to help Deputy Mike finish up the robbery scene."

Doyle picked up his fry pan and said he was heading home. "I've got to get my beauty sleep, and I'm sure you boys need to finish their newspaper deliveries."

"We sure do," replied Colton. "Before you go, thank you for saving Seth."

"No problem. I had more fun than I deserved tonight."

It's A DATE

Doyle met Sandy at the Pigeon Museum Research Center in Pigeon early Wednesday morning. The center isn't open on Wednes-days, but Sandy agreed to open the building for a personal visit. They planned to spend the morning going through obituary notices in the newspapers and museum files. Doyle hoped to get more information about his great-grandfather, the commercial fisherman, and Sandy wanted to help him.

Doyle told her about his experience Tuesday morning, and it surprised Sandy to learn about the robberies. "Why haven't they notified us about these robbers? God, my house could have been on their list."

"I'm sure the police wanted to avoid adverse publicity for the community, and the robbers only broke into the homes of people they knew were away for the winter," Doyle explained. He also told Sandy about the fry pan he used on one robber who tried to capture Seth when he was peeing on his trees.

"You know, Al, your eyes twinkle when you talk about the adventure you had. I feel you enjoy being a detective," she said.

"I did, and I do. Having Colton and Seth around has been fun. I hope they don't get into trouble trying to solve Jenny's death."

Sandy asked if he had decided on a menu for the party they were throwing next week, and he said, "Yes and no. I'm doing a Mediterranean buffet with a wine bar. I'm not sure what I will cook. It'll be a small group, so I was thinking of two entrees, a potato, two vegetable dishes and salads, and garlic breadsticks. Dessert will be my famous pumpkin roll with homemade ice cream."

"You know you're making me hungry. Was that your plan?" Sandy asked.

"No, but we could go out for lunch. Any suggestions were we should go?"

"How about The Other Place? They have good food, and they serve drinks."

"What other place are you talking about?"

Sandy laughed. "The restaurant's name is *The Other Place*. Look," she said, pointing out the window, "It's right across the street."

"Strange name for a restaurant," Doyle said as he helped Sandy with her coat. "Couldn't they have picked something besides that?"

"I think it's kind of cute, and the name piqued your interest, didn't it?"

"I guess, but I might just like that other place better. You know the one not across the street, but down the road."

"Oh, that's the owner's other place, El Rio. It's a Mexican restaurant. Both have good food, but I'm not in the mood for Mexican today."

The conversation continued as they walked across the street. They liked the food and joked with the staff about the name. After lunch, Sandy asked if he would like to join her on Saturday evening. "I'm going to a theatrical production in Port Austin. It's a Mark Twain comedy called *Is He Dead?* A few of my friends are members of the Community Players, and it's always a fun time. We'll go out with them after the play for a few drinks... if you like."

"Wonderful. What time should I pick you up, and do I need a new tux?"

Sandy laughed. "The play begins at seven, and you can dress casually. You would be out of place in a tux. A sport coat would be nice, but it's not mandatory."

Doyle suggested having dinner in Caseville before the play, and then they could drive to Port Austin. "I'll pick you up at five, if that's ok?"

"I'll give you directions to my house. Why don't you stop in at four thirty and I'll give you the grand tour, and we can eat in Port Austin? It's not a fancy place, but they have home cooking, and I'm sure some actors will eat there before the performance."

When they reached the parking lot of the museum, Doyle gave Sandy a quick hug and kissed her cheek. "Thank you for being my friend, Sandy."

"I'm the thankful one, Al. I'll see you Saturday."

As Doyle drove home, his phone rang. It was Colton again. He wanted advice about how to continue his investigation into Jenny's death. Doyle said he would be home all afternoon.

From school, Colton headed straight for his meeting with Doyle. As he drove past the Washingham home, he could see police tape laying on the ground. They removed the robbers' van, but the sheriff's men didn't do a great job of clearing the crime scene.

He turned into Doyle's driveway and parked next to his beautiful black Buick Enclave. He rang the doorbell, and Doyle, dressed in a Tiger's sweatshirt and jeans, greeted him. Colton could tell his clothes were not from Walmart. *Perhaps he shops at a designer store in Detroit*, he considered.

"Colton, come on in. I saw you admiring my new Buick. I purchased it when I moved up from Detroit. It's the first personal car I've owned in many years."

"It's a beautiful vehicle; makes my Jeep look old," Colton said with embarrassment in his voice.

"Your Jeep looks fine. Do you drink coffee? I made a fresh pot, and you're welcome to a cup, and I also have cookies. It's a new recipe I wanted to try."

Colton accepted a cup of coffee and took one cookie. His eyes kept wandering around Doyle's beautiful home. It was like Mrs. Hoffstarter's home, but Doyle's had more masculine features. The large kitchen featured a counter with several leather chairs.

Colton sat in one and felt at home. "This is nice, Doyle. It reminds me of a man-cave; like the one Dad and I created in our garage. I use ours as the office for our new security business."

"Thank you. Every day the place gets a little closer to what I want. I had a large home in Detroit, but most of the furniture was old and dark. This house is modern and needed what they call *cottage accents*."

Doyle looked around the room. "Now I sound like a decorator. To be honest, I had someone else do this. I'm creative in the kitchen, but not at decorating a home. I know what I like, and I conveyed that to the professional decorator, who knew how to achieve it."

"It looks great," Colton said as he took another cookie. "I have a copy of Jenny's diary. After Jenny's sister loaned me the diary, I made copies and highlighted areas I found interesting and relevant."

Doyle picked up the pages and read. As he read, Colton walked to the large picture windows and admired the view of Lake Huron. While standing by the windows, he felt something rub against his legs.

It was a rusty bloodhound with brown and black markings, sniffing his leg and watching his every move with great curiosity.

"What's your dog's name?" Colton asked.

"Copper," replied Doyle. "He's a bloodhound, and he needs to smell everything, so take care."

Colton sat down on the plush yellow and orange rug and played with Copper. Doyle walked into the room and sat in his large leather chair. "I can tell Copper likes you since he often stays away when strangers visit."

"What do you think of Jenny's diary?"

"It's obvious she was being abused. But I wonder if there was another abuser. The way she talks about Luke and at other times about, *Him*. As if there were another man involved," Doyle observed.

"That's what I felt when I read it, and from what the police say, Luke has a good alibi."

"You said his parents gave him an alibi. I'm sure they would lie to protect him."

Colton thought for a moment and said, "The police seem to believe his parents."

"Yes, but they are not looking for a killer. The police assumed suicide all along."

Colton thought about what Doyle said as he scratched Copper behind the ears.

Doyle laughed as he watched Colton. "You keep that up, and Copper will be your friend forever."

"I hope so," said Colton. "If Luke didn't kill Jenny, who did?"

"That's the million dollar question. Let's go over what we have for clues." Doyle walked back to the counter, and Colton followed him. On the counter were five-by-seven prints of the photographs Colton took at the crime scene.

It was hard to look at them as the memories rushed back into Colton's mind. Doyle took a black marker and wrote on a large white sheet of paper. He wrote Jenny's name over her photograph. Then he wrote Luke's name next to hers and *his* next to his name.

"We know Luke was abusing Jenny. Have you ever seen Jenny with someone else?" asked Doyle.

"No. According to her diary, he had been her boyfriend for the past two years, but that's as far back as the diary goes. She could have had a boyfriend before, but how would we know that?" Colton asked. "How can we investigate this?"

Doyle thought for a moment, sipped coffee, and took a bite of his cookie. He said, "If we were the police, we would talk to her parents and all of her friends. Since we aren't the police, here's what we'll do. I will investigate Jenny and Luke's families. I can get information from the police and public records."

"What should I do?" Colton asked.

"I want you to talk to the students at the school. Find anyone who knows if Jenny had other boyfriends before Luke. Be careful, Colton. You don't want Luke to become aware you're snooping around," Doyle warned.

Copper put his paws on Colton's knees and looked at him with his big droopy eyes. It was as if he were repeating Doyle's warning.

Chapter 10

Helping Colton

Friday morning, Colton called Doyle to let him know what had happened with his investigation. "It didn't go well," Colton explained he was in a fight at school with Luke.

"I didn't start the fight. Luke found out we were asking questions, and he went into a rage and came at me with a knife. I tried to defend myself, but he told the teacher I started it, and now we are both suspended from school for two weeks."

Doyle could tell his young friend was almost in tears and suggested he come over to talk. Colton said he had a Black Friday advertisement section to deliver to the stores early Saturday afternoon and agreed to stop in after he finished. "I'll see you around two, if that's OK with you."

"Two will be fine. Colton, please don't worry... I believe you, and I'm sure we can get you out of this mess," Doyle said.

When Colton finished his Saturday store drops, he drove to Sand Point, pulled his Jeep into Doyle's driveway, and walked to the side door. As he stood on the beautiful deck, Colton looked out across Lake Huron and watched a freighter making its way down to Detroit.

Doyle opened the door and suggested he come in before the storm hits. "You won't have a nice evening for driving tonight," he said.

"I'm just glad I have a four-wheel-drive Jeep, and a shovel." Colton walked into the kitchen and bent down to pet Copper. The bloodhound was eager to have his ears scratched, and Colton obliged.

Doyle offered Colton a flavored coffee, which he accepted. As the two men talked about the case, Colton kept his eyes on the lake. In the distance, he could see dark streaks of snow squalls, and he kept thinking of the SS Edmund Fitzgerald and how it sank during a November snowstorm.

"Your mind is a thousand miles away, Colton. Did you hear anything I said?"

"Sorry, Doyle, I find it relaxing here, and I was thinking of the freighters I saw heading to Detroit."

"Good eye. I follow them on an app I have that shows where the ships are. There is a gale warning for Lake Huron, and the ships are heading to port," he said.

The two men got down to the business of Colton's school suspension and Jenny's murder. Colton started by saying, "After talking to kids in school, I'm convinced the killer is someone from outside the school. Luke seems to know who it was, but he wouldn't say. He threatened to kill whoever it was! That's more serious than attacking me."

Doyle took a deep breath. "I hope he doesn't do something stupid. I made calls to my friends in Detroit, and I may have discovered something relevant about Jenny's family. To get the details, though, I have to drive to Detroit. If we get the security video from the school on Monday morning, we can drive there. My friends in the homicide department said they will help with the video and give us the information they have about Jenny's relatives."

"Why can't they tell you over the phone?" Colton asked.

"Because they want me to visit them." Doyle chuckled. He walked over to Copper and said to him. "Do you want to come with us, Copper? I won't let them put you in that nasty jail again. I promise."

"Again?" asked Colton.

"The homicide department gave me Copper as a goodbye gift, and they kept him in a holding cell until my farewell party." Doyle said. "As I understand it, the holding cell worked out great, but Copper didn't like the smells and got quite upset."

Colton considered the offer and agreed to the Detroit trip, but he wondered if Seth would also like to go.

"Call and ask him," suggested Doyle. "While you do, I'll make a quick pit stop."

Getting out of school on a Monday sounded great, so Seth didn't hesitate to accept. "Wow! We'll be at the Detroit Police Headquarters?" He wanted to make sure he wasn't hearing things.

"Yes! Doyle said he can get information about Jenny's family, and he wants to get a copy of the school's surveillance video from last Friday."

"I would love to see that video. Do you think it shows anything?" asked Seth.

"No." Colton knew the camera didn't cover the hallway where the fight broke out. If anything was on the video, it would only be the two guys walking toward the gym. He told Seth to meet him at the office on Monday, and the two of them could drive to Mr. Doyle's house.

Doyle was standing behind Colton, listening. "Sounds like Seth will join us Monday?" he asked.

"Yes. What time should we meet you?"

"Be here at eight. We can stop at the school and get the video. I would love to take the knife, but that might be impossible," Doyle said. He stood silently for a moment. "Call your friend, Ned. You know, the county deputy. Ask him to get the knife for us so we can take it to Detroit for analysis. I bet we can get fingerprints from it."

"Great idea, because I never touched it. I hit Luke's arm, and it fell to the ground. Coach Talbert and Principal Don Zeller touched it. Will we be able to get their fingerprints?"

"All teachers have their prints on file with Michigan. I can get a copy."

Colton reached into his jeans pocket and pulled out his cell phone.

He punched Ned's number and waited. "Ned, this is Colton... No, I'm fine, but I need your help again. Mr. Doyle wants to know if you could get the knife that was used in the fight last Friday."

Doyle could hear Ned objecting. He motioned to Colton to let him talk to Ned.

"Ned, Doyle wants to talk to you," Colton said, passing the phone to Doyle.

"Deputy Ned. We're heading to the Detroit Police Building on Monday. The State Police have a forensic lab there, and I want them to check the knife for fingerprints."

Ned wasn't comfortable letting an outsider handle the evidence. To ease his concerns, Doyle said, "Put the knife in a sealed evidence bag, and the State Police will verify the seal was unbroken."

Ned agreed to the offer and suggested they pick it up in Bad Axe on their way to Detroit. It was getting near dinner time, so Colton thanked Doyle for his help, said goodbye to him and Copper, and headed for home.

Copper went to his outdoor room so he could watch Colton leave. Doyle watched Copper do his business and return to the house. He didn't beg for a treat, but Doyle offered one and the bloodhound accepted.

Considering the events of the last few days, Doyle thought about something Sandy said, and he realized it was true. *I love being involved in a mystery, but I hope Colton can prove he didn't start the fight with Luke, and if someone killed that young girl, Colton needs to find him before he hurts someone else.*

Is He Dead?

Doyle checked his watch and realized he only had an hour to be ready for his Saturday evening date with Sandy.

"Copper, why didn't you remind me to get ready? What's with you, anyway?"

Copper didn't know what Doyle was talking about, but he stayed out of his way, because it was obvious he was on a mission. After a quick shower and shave, Doyle picked out a comfortable pair of tan slacks, a fine gray and brown striped dress shirt, and a gray and tan tweed jacket with leather trim. He checked himself in the mirror.

Copper was watching him, and he seemed to approve of the outfit. His tail wagged, and there was a twinkle in his eyes. "Do you like it?" asked Doyle as he checked himself in the mirror. "Yes, it looks nice... I hope Sandy likes it, too."

The drive to Sandy's home on the south shore of Sand Point took five minutes. He drove onto the long wooded drive and saw an impressive two story home. She had her car parked in the garage and was standing at the door.

"Am I late?" he called out.

"No, perfect timing. Come on in. This is what I call my little castle in the woods." Doyle made sure his shoes were clean and walked into the entryway. The room was bright, but filled with antique furniture and many knickknacks. Cows, chickens, and pigs of all sizes and colors.

"Wow!" he said. "I guess I know what to get you for Christmas."

"You do, and I'll never talk to you again. My family and friends won't stop giving me these things, and I can't throw them away or hide them. I'm trapped in a menagerie of farm animals." Sandy chuckled. "The rest of the house is better. I keep all the animals in this entryway except for Casey, my cat. He goes wherever he wants."

As they walked through the house, Doyle noticed the huge apricot point Siamese cat sneaking looks at them. "Your cat is playing with us."

"He's not sure he wants to meet you yet. He smells Copper on your clothing."

Doyle checked himself for odors, but smelled nothing but his cologne.

"Well, what do you think?" Sandy asked.

"I like the house. It reminds me of my home in Detroit. That was a 1920s three story in Palmer Park... furnished with antiques. My home here is modern. I sold all the antiques with the Detroit house. They made the furniture for that home. Your home is warm and cozy, and here comes your cat. Did I make him angry?"

"No, I think he likes you." Sandy said as she bent down and took the huge cat into her arms. There was an instant purring sound, and when Doyle held his hand out, Casey sniffed it and the purr grew louder.

"There, you are now friends."

Sandy set Casey on the floor and took Doyle's hand. "Let's get going. We can talk about antique furniture on our way to Port Austin." As they walked to Doyle's Buick, she muttered, "You sold all your antiques? Really? All of them?"

Doyle didn't answer. He opened her door, closed it, and got into the vehicle. As he drove out of Sandy's driveway, he said. "Yes. I sold the antiques with the house. You should understand, the house came with the antiques when I purchased it, and the people who bought the house wanted them. When I lived there, I loved the house, but the dark exterior brick, mahogany walls and black walnut floors became a symbol of my past. I needed a change."

"I understand. It just amazed me you sold *all* of your antiques."

"Well, not *all*. I still have my mother's oak desk. It was in her restaurant in Greektown, and I've had it in my office for years. I'll never part with it."

Sandy laughed. "That's more like it. You sold all but the most important antique you owned. So you are sentimental."

As Doyle drove east on M-25 toward Caseville, Sandy's cell phone broke into a raucous rendition from *Annie Get Your Gun*. She answered with, "OK, we'll meet you in Kinde. Bye, see you in ten minutes."

"Al, the gang is having dinner at the Pasta House in Kinde. We'll take the Kinde Road. I'll tell you when to turn."

Doyle remarked on how flat the land was. "Isn't there any place to go that's not a country drive away? I'm so used to being able to walk or take a cab to the theater or club. This will take a while to adjust to."

"We're a long way from Greektown, Al, but you will come to love it here. It's a simpler, slower lifestyle."

Doyle crossed M-53 and drove into Kinde. It took a while to find a parking space. When the couple walked into The Pasta House, Roger and his wife Mindy were holding a table for them. It was a small table set for four. Doyle asked if there would be more coming, and Roger said, "Everyone is at the theater. They had a problem last night at the last rehearsal, so they're trying to iron out the bugs before tonight's production."

"Isn't that a strange thing to say?" added Roger's wife, Mindy. "*Iron out the bugs.* Now that would be messy, wouldn't it? Ironing bugs, I mean."

Roger let out a slow chuckle. "Yes, dear. What I meant is they have to fix the problems with the play."

"Yes, I know, silly. I was just thinking about the image of them ironing bugs."

As they looked at the menu, a tall young man approached the table. Sandy recognized him and said, "Randy, we didn't expect you. Would you like to join us?"

"No, Sandy; I ate. Are you guys going to the play tonight? It should be good. I love Mark Twain, and the play is hilarious."

"Yes, we are all going. Will you be there?"

"Oh, yes. Wouldn't miss it. You know my girlfriend, Mary, is in it. She's been working hard to remember her lines. I helped her... you know? I remember all the lines, so I might try out for a part in the next play. Well I gotta go, bye." Randy turned and walked toward the door.

Doyle smiled. "Is he all there? He seemed to be a little uneasy."

Sandy laughed. "Yes, he's all there. Randy Awold was the valedictorian of his class, but he's awkward around people. They say he's got autism. He hangs around the theater crowd, but he's never tried out for a part. Who knows, he might be an excellent actor."

Mindy laughed, "I bet he would be better than that girlfriend of his... Mary... whatever her name is. She's quite the oddball, isn't she, Roger?"

"Yes dear. It's Mary Ballenger, and she's odd, but Randy likes her, and that's what counts," said Roger. "Now... what are we ordering, Mindy?"

The server was standing next to her, ready to take the order.

"The salmon special sounds good. I'll have that with fries and a salad with blue cheese. And bring me a large glass of house white wine. What will you have, Roger?"

"Everything the same, only without the wine. I'll have black coffee, please."

Both Doyle and Sandy also ordered the salmon, with a glass of wine for her, and coffee for him.

Everyone enjoyed the dinner, and Doyle let Roger and Mindy pick up the tab, provided they come to his party next Tuesday. They agreed and laughed their way out of the restaurant.

They met up in front of the Community Theater in Port Austin. After handing their tickets to the usher, who led them to seats near the stage. Several friends of Sandy, Roger and Mindy, yelled greetings. Everyone noticed Doyle, and the whispering started.

"Any idea who he is?"

"He and Sandy make a good-looking couple, don't they?"

"I bet he's loaded. Just look at that blazer. You can't get that from a catalogue, can you?"

The lights dimmed, and a minute later the play began. Doyle hadn't laughed so hard in years. The players performed well, and there were no technical problems. Sandy told him who was who, and Randy's girlfriend impressed him. She was odd, but it fit the part perfectly.

The play centers on a young painter, Jean-Francois Millet, who is in love with Marie Leroux, but he is in debt to a picture dealer named Andre, and Andre is blackmailing him and wants to marry Marie. The only way the artist could solve the situation was to fake his death, making his paintings precious. He came back dressed like a woman, his sister, the widow Tillou. Now a rich "widow," he must get out of a dress, return to life, and marry Marie.

After the play, Doyle and Sandy went to the Theater Bar and Grill in Port Austin. They sat with Roger and Mindy and later by Sandy's sister-in-law, Kathy Brausch, and her husband, Sam. By the end of the evening, Doyle had met all the cast members and many of Sandy's friends. He had a great time, and they made him feel at home.

At midnight, like Cinderella, Sandy said she had to get home. "I'm the Sunday school teacher this week, and I have to work on my lesson. I hope you don't mind, Al."

"Not a problem."

Together, they said their goodbyes and left the bar. It was chilly, so they hurried to the Buick. Sandy appreciated the heated seats.

As they drove, Sandy reminded Doyle to watch for deer. There were several times he had to slow down to avoid hitting them, but it was still a pleasant drive back to Sand Point.

Sandy said she would love to have him come in for a drink, "but I really have to prepare for the kids at church. We take turns teaching, and it's my turn tomorrow."

Doyle walked her to the door and gave her a tender kiss. She pulled him in closer and added passion. She smiled and said, "Yes, I wish I could invite you in, but we'll have to wait until our next date."

"Soon, I hope," Doyle said. "I'll call tomorrow afternoon. Remember, I'm going to Detroit on Monday with Colton and Seth, so I'll see you Tuesday for the party. Thank you, Sandy. It was a wonderful evening."

"I agree, and please call tomorrow."

Chapter 11

Detroit Police Visit

Doyle prepared a breakfast roll-up and a fruit plate, which he carried across the driveway to Trudy's home. Five inches of snow covered the ground, but the forecast called for warming temperatures and sunny skies. Trudy said she would walk to Doyle's home, but he insisted he do the walking.

She watched him as he trudged through the snow and opened the door for him. "You're going to spoil me, Al; I'm not used to so much attention."

Doyle laughed as he set the dishes on the table. "I hope you made coffee, because I didn't, and I sure could use a cup."

He didn't have to wait since Trudy had poured a cup and placed it on the table before he arrived. The two friends enjoyed their breakfast. Doyle told Trudy about the planned trip to Detroit with Colton and Seth, and Trudy asked if he had heard the news about the young boy who got killed early Sunday morning.

"No. It wasn't Colton, was it?"

"Oh, heavens no, that would be terrible. The radio announcer said it was Luke Hadderton. Isn't he the boy Colton said abused that young girl, Jenny?"

"Yes, but I'm sure Colton wasn't involved." Doyle became concerned and called Colton after breakfast. Colton explained what happened and assured Doyle he was not a suspect.

The snow began melting by the time Colton and Seth drove into the Doyle's driveway. He was ready and waiting in the garage, where he told Seth to park his Charger. Seth called shotgun and jumped into the front seat of Doyle's Buick as Colton climbed into the back. Doyle drove through Bad Axe and pulled into the McDonald's drive-through. "Anything you guys need. I'm up for a large coffee."

"I'll have coffee," said Colton. Seth ordered a big breakfast with apple juice and coffee.

The next stop was the sheriff's office. Doyle and Colton went in, leaving Seth to finish his breakfast. Doyle warned him not to get food on the leather seat. He then laughed as they walked through the office doors.

There was a small sealed package at the front desk with Doyle's name on it. A young blond officer stood by the counter and said, "I need your identification before I can let you have this."

Doyle pulled out his badge, and the girl marked down the name and number. "Please sign this evidence form and remember you're responsible and you must keep it secure."

Doyle had Colton and Seth in stitches all the way to Detroit. He told them humorous stories about his time as a detective.

"You should write a book about your adventures," said Seth.

Doyle grinned with pride and said. "Perhaps. It's fun to remember the happy times, but unfortunately the bad times outweigh them. If I wrote a book, I'd have to talk about those sad events too. I don't think I want to relive them; therefore, I'll just enjoy the adventures of today and tomorrow."

They exited I-75 downtown Detroit and drove to 1310 3rd Ave., where he found a parking space. He gathered the evidence package, and Seth grabbed his laptop. The three walked to the front entrance of Detroit Police Headquarters.

Looking up at the impressive building, Colton asked, "Were you stationed in this building?"

"No, this is a new building. Over the years, the police department went through many changes. The new State Police Crime Lab and some of my old homicide pals have offices here."

They walked into the lobby, and two men in dark suits approached them. The older man with gray hair, a bushy mustache, and a large round belly, opened his arms and said, "You old Irish bum. What did you do, stop eating?"

Doyle laughed. "Maxwell Brown. How the hell have you been? I didn't expect to see you here."

"I wouldn't miss your coming home celebration."

"And no, I'm still eating and cooking; just not as much."

The two men laughed, and Max gave Doyle a hug and introduced him to Lieutenant Detective Howard Smithers. Smithers was a thin man who stood over six feet tall and had a full head of blond hair. He was young enough to be their son.

"Max told me all the tall tales about your adventures with the department. I see you've brought the evidence and your two young friends."

"Yes, Sir. This is Colton Blackwell, football star and a junior detective from Pigeon, and his friend and business partner is Seth Seamoore. These two young men started a security and detective business, and it's because of them I'm turning to you for help." Doyle said.

Lieutenant Smithers shook Colton and Seth's hands and said, "It's great to meet the two of you. We've heard of your adventures and wanted to thank you for your help a few months ago, when you put away more major drug dealers in one sting than four of our men did all fall."

It surprised Colton that the Detroit Police appreciated their effort, so he said, "Thank you, sir, but we stumbled on those dealers by accident."

"It's all about the results." Smithers turned to Doyle and said, "We're glad to help you any way we can, so come on up to the Homicide Squad Room where more officers want to meet you."

Colton and Seth followed the homicide detectives. The group took an elevator up several floors, and when the doors opened, another group of officers threw confetti and sang, "For he's a jolly good fellow."

Turning to Max, Doyle laughed and asked, "What the hell is this?"

"We knew you'd never be able to stay away from being a detective; homicide is in your blood. Besides, it's great having you back with us."

"Thank you, but my return is premature as I'm just helping my young detective friend, Colton. So enough of this celebrating; let's get down to business."

Doyle and Colton gave the knife to the Michigan State Police forensic investigator and followed him into the lab while Seth worked with a video specialist on the school's security video.

After an hour of working on the evidence, they determined Colton did not touch the knife and did not start the fight. The video showed that Luke had the knife in his hand when he passed through the hallway before attacking Colton.

"So, what now?" asked Colton.

Lieutenant Smithers said, "We will send this information to the State Police and the Huron County Sheriff. You must allow them to investigate, and I don't want you involved any further. It's time for the police to take the lead; they will find the killer of those two teenagers."

On the return trip to Sand Point, Doyle stopped at his favorite Eastern Market shop for fresh produce and exotic cheese and wine. Both Seth and Colton enjoyed the adventure. They then stopped at Doyle's former restaurant in Troy for lunch. Both the restaurant and the respect Doyle received from the staff impressed the teens. They could see his former employees missed him.

The trio arrived at Doyle's home mid-afternoon. Colton thanked Doyle for his help in proving he didn't start the fight with Luke and for giving the Sheriff a lead on who the killer might be.

"You shouldn't have any more problems, but please let the sheriff and his men handle this investigation. I don't want you getting into more trouble," Doyle warned. He wasn't sure Colton would follow his advice since the young man had a knack for finding trouble.

"Thank you, Doyle. I'll try to be careful."

Another Death

Copper was waiting at the door with his leash in his mouth, and his tail swishing back and forth. He was glad Doyle came home, but he wanted to go outside, *NOW*.

Doyle laughed. "Wait for a few minutes. I need to make a pit stop, and I want to call Trudy. Did you mind her when she stopped in?"

Doyle noticed Copper had used his outdoor room, so when he returned from the bathroom, he went out with a plastic bag and cleaned the grass. Copper watched every move and kept insisting he go outside. Doyle returned from the bathroom and then called Trudy.

"Hi, did Copper give you any problems?" he asked.

"No, but he wanted to go outside. There's something out there that he smells, but I wasn't about to get dragged around the beach by a bloodhound," Trudy said.

"I don't blame you. I'll take him for a walk now."

Trudy asked about the trip to Detroit, and Doyle explained what the forensics lab found. She replied, "I'm so glad for Colton. He's such a nice boy, and his girlfriend, Lacie, is a wonderful friend. I'd hate if he had more trouble."

"He'll be fine," Doyle said as Copper tugged at his pant leg. "Copper wants out, so I'll talk to you later. Oh, I wanted to remind you. We're having a party in my recreation room, and I hope you'll be there. I believe I mentioned it yesterday."

"You mentioned the party; I'll be there. Thank you for being my friend and neighbor."

When he put his cell phone in his pocket, Copper jumped up and barked. "Copper, what's got into you? You know you don't bark in the house." Doyle put his coat and hat on and connected the leash to Copper's collar. "OK. Let's go find what's so important outside."

Copper pulled Doyle toward the beach. His nose sniffed the air, and his tail wagged. He moved back and forth as if trying to catch the smells. Together, they followed the icy lake as the waves lapped onto the sand. It was November, and there were no boats in the water or on the shore. The homeowners had cleared the beach to avoid damage from the ice that would push ashore during the winter months.

With a violent jerk, Copper broke loose from the leash and ran down the beach. Doyle watched as Copper ran over a quarter mile and then he stopped and howled. It was a howl that sounded like a cry of pain. Doyle could see a black object on the beach next to Copper and he was sure it was an animal that died and washed ashore, so he ran as fast as possible because the last thing he needed was to have Copper covered with the smell of a dead animal.

The closer Doyle got, the less the mound looked like a dead animal. He knew it was the form of a human body, so he sprinted to the body, and there on the cold, wet sand was the old man he had seen in the bar a few days ago. Someone smashed in his head, and blood covered his clothing. Next to the body was an old bloody axe with a long handle. It appeared to be an antique... old, but deadly.

Doyle didn't check for a heartbeat because he could tell the man had been dead for many hours. He grabbed Copper's collar and connected the leach. "You did well, Copper... real good."

He reached into his pocket and pulled out his cell phone and a doggy treat for Copper. There was a strong cell signal, so he dialed 911 and reported that he and Copper had found a body on the north shore of Sand Point, and he gave his name and the location. The operator asked that he stay there until the police arrived; however, Doyle suggested it might be better if he walked to the road so the police could see him. "The body is on the beach, and I don't have an address. I'll stand along the main road, and then I can lead them to the body. I'll be wearing blue jeans and a dark blue coat and a Detroit Tigers cap... Yes, my name is Al Doyle... Thank you."

Doyle avoided stepping on evidence, but he noticed several footprints leading from the road to the beach. It appeared someone had struggled with or perhaps dragged the old man. There were footprints and drag lines coming from the road toward the beach and returning to the road.

Doyle thought, *Perhaps he died somewhere else, and the killer moved the body to the beach, hoping the waves would take him out to deeper water? But why the axe, and why leave the weapon at the scene? That's such a strange weapon to kill someone with. And why kill this old man? What's the motive?*

Doyle's mind was in detective mode. When he reached the road, he checked to see how far he was from home. He estimated it at a little under half a mile. He walked along the edge of the road to see where the foot marks began and noticed tire imprints and a small amount of blood on the road.

Copper watched as Doyle looked for evidence. The Detroit Police trained him as a police bloodhound, so he understood what his owner was doing. Doyle looked down the road and saw an ambulance with its lights flashing, followed by a Huron County Sheriff's patrol car.

Deputy Ned Wooddell stepped out of his car and approached Doyle. "So you found a body? Show me where it is and tell me what happened. Nice dog." Ned approached the ambulance and told the driver to wait until he was ready for them. Doyle and Copper led Ned and his partner Chad to the beach.

When Ned saw the old man, he exclaimed, "Damn, that's Old Man Lancole, I think it's Harold. He lives a mile down the beach. Who in hell's name would want to kill him? I know he was a cantankerous and venomous-tongued old drunk, but I can't think of anyone who would do this."

Chad surveyed the crime scene and took photographs. Doyle instructed him to take photos of the footprints and showed him which footprints belonged to him and Copper. The footprints were here when I found the body. If we don't contaminate the crime scene, we might get good imprints of these prints, plus the tire print next to the road.

Ned turned to his partner and said, "Chad, get some of that plaster in the trunk. We can take imprints now. If we do it after they remove the body, the prints might get destroyed."

It impressed Doyle that Ned was doing a thorough investigation, given the limitations of the Sheriff's office. As they worked on the crime scene, the middle-aged, gray-haired County Sheriff, Carl McNabb, walked up to Ned and said, "What we got here, Ned?"

"Mr. Doyle found Old Man Lancole on the beach."

Sheriff McNabb looked over the body and said, "Well, cause of death is obvious, but who killed him?"

Doyle walked up to Sheriff McNabb and said, "Sir, an autopsy should be completed in this case. I noticed there is blood next to the road and tire tracks. It might be a hit and run. Perhaps the driver tried to make it look like murder to throw us off. It's important to not jump to conclusions about the cause of death, because I've had investigations change directions after the autopsy."

"Your name is Doyle, right?" asked McNabb as he looked over the tall stranger offering him police directions. "And why should I listen to you?"

Ned moved close to the Sheriff and whispered, "Sir, he's the retired Detroit homicide detective we told you about the other day."

"The rich one who just moved here?"

Doyle heard the conversation and said, "Yes, I'm that man, and I have over twenty years of detective work under my belt. I solved more murders in one year than you've had in Huron County during the past twenty."

Sheriff McNabb replied, "I heard all about you, Mr. Doyle, and I'm impressed with your credentials. Are you still interested in detective work? You must be, seeing how you helped that Colton boy solve his mysteries."

"I will admit, it gets in your blood, and you can call me Doyle."

"Doyle, we could use your expertise in Huron County. How about working with us?"

The offer startled Doyle; he didn't answer the question.

"Cat got your tongue?" Sheriff McNabb asked. "We need a seasoned homicide detective on our team. Look, we've had more crime in the past two months than we had in the previous two years. Times are changing, and I can't afford a full-time detective. What I need is someone who will work by the case."

Doyle mulled the idea for a few seconds and then said, "Give me some time to think about it."

"There is no time! I have a dead man here, and I would rather not turn this case over to the Michigan State Police. I know they're good, but we should be able to handle our own cases."

"Could you assign an assistant?" Asked Doyle.

"Who would you like?"

Doyle looked toward Ned, who was pouring plaster into the footprint. "Deputy Ned Wooddell would be a great assistant detective. He's smart and dedicated, and I know I could work well with him."

"If that means you'll take the job, then yes." The sheriff walked over to Ned and said, "Deputy, would you be willing to work with Mr. Doyle if I made him a Deputy Homicide Detective?"

Ned burst out laughing, but Sheriff McNabb wasn't smiling. "This is not a joke. Doyle says he will take this case if you assist him."

"What about the State Police? We hand homicide cases over to them, don't we?" Ned asked.

"How many cases have we had in the past ten years? Accidents, overdoses, and suicides are our most common. I know we could hand this one over to the state, but we have an experienced man here in the community. What do you say, boy?"

Ned knew the sheriff was serious. Turning to Doyle, he asked, "Do you honestly think I would be any help to you?"

Doyle smiled, "Hell yes! I'm the one who suggested you, Ned. I can tell you have the skills and dedication to be a good detective. If I pass on my knowledge, you will soon be able to take the job over. Until then, we'll work as partners."

Ned smiled at the compliment and said, "OK. When do we start?"

"Now," insisted the Sheriff. "I'm heading back to Bad Axe, so, Doyle and Ned, you're in charge. By the way, Doyle, I now designate you as the official Huron County Deputy Homicide Detective. Now it's legal."

The Sheriff walked away laughing to himself. Doyle turned to Ned and said, "I'm calling the State Police CSI Crime Scene Department. I want to get them up here because we need to know if Mr. Lancole died on the street or here on the beach. They can test blood splatter and look for any other evidence we might miss."

Doyle took his cell phone out to make the call. He had the number as a contact, and while he dialed the number, he said, "Can you get us a pop-up canopy to cover the body. We'll need one." There was an answer on his cell phone, and he said, "This is Detective Doyle, Huron County Sheriff's Office, can you hold a minute? Ned, the ambulance might as well go home until we clear the body. Also, does Huron County have a coroner?"

"Yes, but he prefers not to visit the accident or crime scene."

"Call him and tell him he has to be here ASAP. Don't take no for an answer," Doyle insisted.

Doyle turned back to the cell phone. "Is Richard Ketlinger on duty today? Yes, please connect me... Richard, Al Doyle here... Just fine, but this is an official call. I'm working as the Huron County Homicide Detective, and we have an elderly man either run over and dragged to the beach on Sand Point or they bludgeoned him with an ax on the beach. Either way, we need a crime scene investigation ASAP....

great... yes, Huron County. It's on the main street of Sand Point, about two miles west of M-25. We'll be here waiting... Yes, we have a canopy coming, and we will protect the scene... Thank you, Richard."

Chapter 12

Who Would Kill An Old Man?

Doyle walked Copper home so he could get food and water. He stopped in to see Trudy. It shocked her when he told her about the dead man on the beach and he suggested she keep her doors locked until he knows for sure what happened. Doyle then drove back to the crime scene.

Deputies Ned and Chad had a white tent set up over Mr. Lancole's body, and police tape now stretched from the road to the water's edge and back, and both County and State troopers were on the scene. Several Sand Point homeowners were milling around, trying to see who had died. Doyle avoided them and asked a County Deputy to make sure no one crossed the police line.

State Trooper Steve Lithowski and his partner were talking with Deputies Ned and Chad as they returned from the scene on the beach. When the four officers reached Doyle, Steve faced him and said, "Mr. Doyle, this is a case for the Michigan State Police. I don't understand why McNabb asked you to handle it, but I suggest you allow us to head the investigation."

"Don't worry about it, Trooper. I'm in charge, I will stay in charge, and I will not argue the matter with you because I have work to get done!" Doyle's tone was blunt and forceful.

Trooper Steve laughed. "Ned, you're right. He is a testy old man, but... it looks like he's doing everything by the book, so I'm not too worried. Doyle, if you need anything, I'd be proud to help you."

"What you and Ned can do is canvas the area. I hope someone saw something. I'm not sure when the old man died, but I would guess last night or early morning." It pleased Doyle that the trooper accepted him as lead detective because quick action is important on a case like this. *The more time we waste on other matters, the less likely we will solve the case.*

The deputy and state trooper gathered their notebooks and agreed on how they would interview the neighbors. Doyle estimated it would take them two hours, so he went to his vehicle and recorded his notes regarding the case so far.

He worked until he saw the police officer return. Dr. Edward Shotingham, the Huron County Medical Examiner, followed them. Ned and Steve had finished speaking with the neighbors and were comparing notes. When the coroner approached, Ned tried to keep Doyle calm. "Remember, we don't get many murders in Huron County, so don't get upset with the medical examiner; he's just doing his job."

"Fine... I'll play nice, Ned." Doyle greeted Dr. Shotingham and shook his hand. "I'm Homicide Detective Al Doyle, and I understand you're the Medical Examiner?"

In a terse voice, the examiner said, "Yes, but what's so important to me being here. If you need a death certificate, time of death, or autopsy, I don't have to be here for that. The EMT can bring the body. I've got a lot of work you're keeping me from."

As Doyle listened to the Examiner complain, he noticed the white van of the Michigan State Police Crime Scene team parking next to the patrol cars. Doyle excused himself and walked toward the van. A burly man in his early sixties approached Doyle with his hand out.

Doyle laughed and said, "Richard, it's good to see you. How long has it been?"

"Too long, Doyle, and since when are you working for Huron County?"

"The sheriff hired me a few hours ago. Or should I say, he appointed me the official Deputy Homicide Detective. My bloodhound found the body on the beach, and the Sheriff asked if I would head the investigation."

"Didn't you retire?" asked Richard.

"Yes, twice. This gig is just for fun," Doyle laughed. "Follow me and I'll show you what we have." Doyle approached the Coroner and said, "Dr. Shotingham, this is Richard Ketlinger, the State Police CSI leader from the Bridgeport station. Richard, Dr. Shotingham is the county medical examiner. Show him what you need."

The men walked down to the tent, and Richard barked out orders. Doyle knew enough to walk away and let him work, so he went back to the road where the police still discussed their notes.

"Did any of the neighbors hear or see anything?" Doyle asked.

Ned's face turned solemn. "Nothing, but there are residents who may have been around last night, but are at work now. I can check again later."

"Thank you for trying, Ned. I'd like you to find out where Mr. Lancole was last night. Any bets he was at the bar in Caseville? I saw him there a few days ago, and you said he was a known drunk."

"Good idea! Chad and I can drive into town and ask. Chad's brother is tending bar, and if anyone knows, it's him." Ned said. "What do you plan on doing, Doyle?"

"I'll wait for Richard and the medical examiner's results. I know they won't have everything until the autopsy, but I would like the time of death. Also, I've been looking on the internet for information about our victim. He's quite a wealthy, eccentric drunk. We will have to visit his home, but first things first. I will also call Seth and Colton. They set up cameras to catch the robbers last week. And I hope they have a video of the main street from last night."

Ned thought it was an excellent idea. After the two deputies drove off to Caseville, Doyle walked down to see how far the coroner and CSI had gotten.

"Come on over," Richard yelled when he saw Doyle. "We're almost done here."

Doyle walked up to the tent and noticed that there were several evidence bags setting in Richard's case, including the enormous axe. "What did you find?" Doyle asked.

"Identification, credit cards, keys, a lot of money, and blood," Richard pulled the fabric away from the old man's leg and thigh. They cut the pants to inspect an injury. "See this bruise? We found paint chips on the pants and, from the height of the injury, I'd say someone hit him with a pickup truck or large SUV, perhaps an F-150. But that didn't kill him. The blow to the head did him in."

Dr. Shotingham listened to Richard and added, "Doyle, we estimate the time of death around eleven o'clock last night. I'll do an autopsy in the morning along with a forensic toxicology test, and Richard wants me to check his clothing for random fibers. I learned a lot from Richard today. Thank you, Doyle; I'll call you in the morning; however, some results may take a while."

"Dr. Shotingham, thank you for your help. Richard, when can I expect your findings?"

Richard looked at his notebook and said, "I can email you what we have in the morning, but I don't have your address." Doyle reached into his pocket and pulled out a business card. "This will do for now. I need to set up an official address with the county. I'll let you know when it's done." As the two talked, the ambulance EMT crew lifted Mr. Lancole's body onto a stretcher and enclosed him in a black body bag. They carried him up to the road and placed him in the back of the ambulance. Doyle followed them

The sunset was beautiful over the lake, but the white canopy looked out of place. Several homeowners milled around the street and watched from their backyards. A newspaper reporter was standing next to Doyle's Buick, waiting for information. The memory of past investigations rushed back as Doyle considered the task ahead. *Do I really want this job?* He asked himself.

"Mr. Doyle," yelled the young reporter from the Huron County

Gazette. "Can you give me a statement? I'm with the local newspaper."

"What's your name, kid?" Doyle yelled back.

"Rodney Billings, I'm with the Huron County Gazette. Can you tell me who died and how he died?"

"Rodney... not yet. As you know, until they notify the family, we keep the names out of the press. As for how he died, until we have the medical examiner's report, I can't say for sure. I'm sorry, but that's how it is. Besides, it would be better if you talked to Sheriff McNabb in the morning."

Before Doyle could reach his Buick, Barry Cummings ran up and grabbed Doyle's arm. "Doyle, how did Old Man Lancole die? Did someone kill him? That's the word in town."

"Barry, who the hell told you about this?"

"I stopped at the Blue Water Inn when Deputy Ned was interviewing the staff. Oh, there they are now." Barry pointed to Ned and Chad as they pulled up behind Doyle's vehicle. "I left just before they did... so... what's the skinny? Is it another murder? There's been too many of them around here, you know?"

"I can't say, Barry. We won't know anything until the medical examiner completes his autopsy, so please don't spread gossip." Doyle wasn't surprised the news spread so fast, and Barry was right. There have been too many murders on Sand Point in the past two months. *I think I'll enjoy living in this community,* Doyle thought. "Barry, perhaps I'll have more news at my party tomorrow. You will be there, won't you?"

"I wouldn't miss it for the world. You are cooking, aren't you? We always loved eating at your place in Greektown. I'm surprised we never met you there."

"It could be I was working at one of my other places, and yes... I'm cooking."

Barry grinned from ear to ear. "Hot damn, I'll see you tomorrow... Bye now, I have to tell my wife about the murder." Barry hurried down the street and ran into his driveway, just a few houses down the road.

Deputy Ned and Chad approached Doyle. They were both laughing, and Ned stopped and said, "Did Barry tell you about our conversation with Chad's brother, Will?"

Doyle chuckled and said, "Yes, he said he heard you interview Will, so tell me what you learned."

"Will said Old Man Lancole was in the bar all afternoon, drinking and complaining about everything. Around ten thirty yesterday evening, Will took the old man's car keys and had Larry Adderman, the cook, drive him home. Larry said the old man insisted he drop him off at the market on the corner of Main Street and M-25. Jeffery watched him as he staggered his way toward home, and then he continued on to Bay Port. Lancole's 1958 Caddy is behind the bar. We checked it, but there wasn't anything of interest. It's a nice car, but it's full of trash. Mr. Lancole isn't good at being neat."

"Where is the car now?" Doyle asked. He was thinking there may be evidence in it.

"The Sheriff is having it moved to the station in Bad Axe. They'll check it for prints, but we may want to go through the trash to see what the old man has been up to these past months."

Doyle agreed and said, "Great work. For now, I guess we can head home. I have a party tomorrow evening that I need to get ready for. If you and Chad want to stop in, you're always welcome. Cocktails begin at five, and the buffet dinner is at six-thirty tomorrow evening, and it will last until ten, perhaps later if we are having too much fun."

"We'll try to make it," Ned replied. "Chad and I may be on patrol, but we could stop for a snack; because I hear you're some kind of cook. I would like to grab a taste."

Doyle smiled. "Yes, I'm some kind of cook."

Getting Ready To Party

Doyle parked his Buick in the garage and passed Copper's fenced-in room. Copper watched Doyle through the large patio door. The bloodhound was not begging for a walk... instead; he rushed to Doyle and rubbed his leg, as if saying, *Everything will be fine, I understand how tired you are.*

"Yes, I'm tired," replied Doyle, as he walked to the kitchen counter and picked up a bag of Copper's favorite treats. "You deserve this treat, Copper. You found that poor old man on the beach, and now I'm the new Deputy Homicide Detective. If this new adventure turns bad, it's all your fault! Do you understand what I'm saying, Copper?"

Copper didn't care about Doyle's statement; his mind was on the treat and his water dish, which Doyle filled with filtered ice water. Doyle made himself a flavored coffee and studied his notes regarding Mr. Lancole's death. He realized there is nothing more he can do on the case until the State Police CSI and the Bad Axe Medical Examiner give him their reports.

"Copper, I'm going downstairs to get ready for my party tomorrow. You know, this party will be a lot of work, too. Sandy will be here early tomorrow to help, but it's still a big job."

Doyle walked down the steps to the lower level. The room was a replica of one of Doyle's Irish Pubs. When he sat down with the decorator to remodel the house, Doyle insisted that this area be his entertainment room. The kitchen is larger than many restaurants, with the latest stove, grill, deep fryers, several ovens, a walk-in refrigerator and freezer, commercial dishwasher, and his favorite ice cream maker.

One wall with two large patio doors faces the beach and Lake Huron. Outside, the patio features tables and chairs so guests can enjoy the summer breeze, and inside there are a dozen tables with four matching chairs. The style is typical pub and grill. Photographs grace the wood-paneled walls, and there are several huge televisions and a pool table in the back. Doyle walked up to the bar and sat his coffee mug down. He pulled up a bar stool and took out his cell phone. After searching for the number of the Main Street Cafe, he called the restaurant.

"Hello, this is Al Doyle... Could you tell me if Angie Stallmark is working this afternoon? Great... yes, if I could, I would like to talk with her."

Angie came to the phone and said, "Hello Mr. Doyle, how can I help you?"

"Angie, do you work tomorrow evening?"

"No, I have the early shift tomorrow."

Doyle didn't give her time to ask why he wanted to know. He said, "How would you like to make a quick hundred dollars for working about five hours tomorrow evening?"

The offer mystified Angie. She wasn't sure what he was asking her to do. "How... I mean, what...?"

"Oh, I'm sorry. I'm having a party tomorrow night at my home in Sand Point, and I need someone to help me serve about fourteen guests. My entertainment room is an actual restaurant, and I'm serving buffet style."

"Are you serious? If you are, yes! I can use the money. Oh, yes!"

Doyle felt relieved. "Wonderful, Angie. Do you know someone who could help with dishes and tend bar? It pays the same amount."

"Yes! My husband works here in the mornings as a prep cook, and he was a bartender before he got this job. He would love to help you." She was excited but had orders to deliver. "I have to get back to my customers... what is the address?"

Doyle gave her the street number and told her to stop in at four o'clock to help him set up. "Thank you, Angie. I'll see you tomorrow."

Copper made his way downstairs and was watching Doyle. He

couldn't understand why Doyle looked like he had just won the lottery. Excitement filled his face, and he bent down and gave Copper a hug. "Isn't it great? I have people to help me. Copper, I have a staff. Why aren't you excited?"

Copper walked to the patio door and laid down, staring at the beach and the beautiful pale pink and blue sunset. "Yes, it's lovely, but...." Before he could complete the sentence his phone rang. It was Sandy, and he was happy that she had called.

"I'm so glad you called. I must tell you, I hired Angie and her husband to help tomorrow night."

"Angie and Alex from Main Street?" she asked.

"Yes, she's helping with the buffet, and he will be a bartender and dishwasher. That way we can enjoy ourselves and our guests."

"Sounds nice, Al, but I think you know why I called. I heard Copper found a dead body on the beach. Barry called me a while ago. Is it true that Sheriff McNabb made you a deputy so you could work on the case?"

"Yes, that's true. I got back from Detroit, and Copper wanted to go outside. His nose picked up the smell, and he ran to Mr. Lancole's dead body. It was a nasty scene involving an antique axe and lots of blood."

"Sounds awful. Tell me all about it." Sandy insisted. "Every gruesome detail."

"I was just going to put a hamburger on the grill; why don't you drive over and I'll make you one too? Then, I have to cook for tomorrow. I won't have time in the morning because of the investigation."

"Sorry, I ate earlier. Can't we cook the food when I come over tomorrow afternoon?" she asked.

"Some, but I want to do as much as I can tonight. I miss cooking, and I'm looking forward to testing out all this new kitchen equipment. Sandy, wait until you see my entertainment room. I think you'll like it, since it looks like an antique Irish pub."

"Sounds wonderful. Now let's get back to Mr. Lancole."

As Doyle told the story of the day's events, including his trip to Detroit with Colton and Seth, he worked on his dinner. He put the speaker on and sat it on the bar so he could talk, cook, and then eat. The conversation continued as he mixed dough for his famous pitas. While the dough was rising, he made a marinade for chicken breasts and ribeye steaks. He used metal pans and covered the meat with the marinade, then he moved them into the huge refrigerator on a metal cart.

"What are you doing? It sounds like you're pushing a shopping cart," Sandy asked.

"I walked into the refrigerator."

"Oh, I'm sorry. Did it hurt?"

"No, why would it hurt?" he asked

"You said you walked into it. When I bump into the door of my refrigerator, it hurts," Sandy explained.

"I didn't bump into it; I opened the door and walked in. It's a walk-in refrigerator."

"You've got to be kidding. What kind of kitchen do you have?"

"A really nice one. The upstairs kitchen is normal; this kitchen is special; nice enough for a master chef like me."

After the couple spent over two hours talking, Sandy said good night. She was now eager to see Doyle's downstairs kitchen and said she would be there at one o'clock on Tuesday afternoon. "I'll bring my evening clothes and my make-up bag with me. That way I can help you in the kitchen without worrying about messing up my clothes."

"That sounds great. I'm so glad we met, and I'm looking forward to tomorrow."

Chapter 13

How Could He Live Like That?

Doyle got dressed and had his second cup of coffee before sunrise. It fascinated Copper to see him awake so early in the morning. It's not natural, and Copper knew something was up. He kept staring at Doyle, trying to figure out what he was doing.

After Doyle finished his bagel and cream cheese, he said, "You will spend this morning in the Buick, Copper. I have to investigate the death of that man you found on the beach, and I can't let you go everywhere with me. Try to understand and don't get upset and mess up my nice new vehicle."

Copper wagged his tail in agreement, and Doyle reached for the leash so he could take him for a quick walk on the beach. "Promise you won't find another body? One body a week is sufficient." Copper kept looking down the beach to where Old Man Lancole had been laying. He may have thought his lifeless body was still there, because he kept trying to pull Doyle in that direction, but Doyle kept a firm grip and forced the bloodhound to go the opposite direction.

After a fifteen-minute walk, the two were back in Doyle's yard. Copper jumped in the Buick, and Doyle returned to the house to get his thermos of hot coffee and his notebook and laptop. His first stop was Bad Axe, to meet with the sheriff and Deputy Ned Wooddell.

It took fifteen minutes to reach Bad Axe, the largest city in Huron County, and is the county seat, with a courthouse and jail located downtown. It was only yesterday that Doyle was in the building picking up evidence for his trip to Detroit. He never expected to be back so soon, and not as a visitor, but as a homicide detective. *Amazing how things happen*, he thought as he walked through the double doors into the police station.

A police woman behind the desk greeted Doyle and directed him to the sheriff's office. The door was open, and Ned was sitting across from Sheriff McNabb. McNabb stood and bellowed, "Doyle, glad to see you can get up so early. Ned here says you got a lot done yesterday. Any ideas who the killer is?"

"We're just beginning, Sir. Ned, I hope you had a good evening. Did the medical examiner or the Michigan State Police send us anything?"

"The autopsy report is here, but the CSI haven't reported yet," replied Ned as he handed Doyle the official Medical Examiner's report. Doyle sat down and studied the report. "Did you read this, Ned?" he asked.

"Yes, it's interesting. The Sheriff and I were just discussing it."

McNabb piped in with, "Ole Doctor Shotingham outdid himself. He's never been this thorough. I wonder what got into him?"

"Richard Ketlinger and I told him what he had to do in the autopsy, and he got excited about the investigation."

"So what do you think? Is it a hit and run?" asked the sheriff.

"Good question," replied Doyle. "This confirms that a large vehicle ran into Lancole on the side of the street. Was it an accident? I don't know. Lancole had a high blood alcohol level, so he may have been wandering in the street, but why hit him on the head? This report says he was alive when the axe struck him. That makes it murder even if it started as an accident."

"Damn, you're supposed to have answers; all you've given me are more questions," complained the Sheriff. "Get busy and answer your questions. I have work to do, so scram."

Doyle and Ned looked at each other and grinned. They got up

and walked out of the office, trying not to burst out laughing. Doyle asked, "Is he always like that?"

"Oh yes, he's quite the character. But he lets us do our jobs. He doesn't show everyone how smart he is, or isn't. He does his job and expects us to do ours."

"I want to go to Mr. Lancole's house in Sand Point. There has to be a reason someone killed him. I don't buy the hit-and-run angle. You don't kill a man after you accidentally hit him," Doyle said.

Ned thought for a moment. "You said yesterday that Lancole was very wealthy. Could that be an angle we need to investigate?"

"Let's sit in the Buick. I hate discussing a case in front of everyone," Doyle whispered. He could see several officers trying to hear what the two of them were saying. This case is the talk of the county, and Doyle knows how rumors spread like wildfire.

Copper jumped into the back seat when he saw Deputy Ned open the front door. Ned turned and patted Copper on his forehead. "Hi Copper; are you out for a ride today?"

Copper didn't respond. He was watching Doyle enter the Buick, then he gave a low grunt and laid down. Doyle turned to Ned and said, "Lancole sold his manufacturing business in Detroit three years ago. He made a fortune selling to a Chinese company looking to supply the Big Three auto companies with parts. I heard the price was almost a billion dollars."

Ned whistled, "Wow! He looked like he didn't have a dime to spare. I had heard he was wealthy, but I didn't know. Does he have a wife or kids?"

"Neither, he never married and only has one living relative, his brother's son. Everyone else in the family is dead. I sent a request to the Detroit Police to see if they can get information on the nephew. We don't have a phone number or address for him, and we must notify him of his uncle's death ASAP. We also need to find Lancole's lawyer. He should be able to tell us what the old man's will says. That kind of money would be an excellent motive to kill him."

Copper decided that Ned was OK, and he put his head between the front seats and drooled on Ned's thigh. Doyle laughed and said, "Ned, Copper only leaves his mark on people he likes."

"That's nice, but how do I get drool out of my pants?"

"Run water over it. It won't leave a stain unless he's been eating something greasy."

Ned opened his door. "I'll see you in an hour at Lancole's house. We won't have to break the door down because I have the key from his pocket. When the medical examiner stopped by, he gave us his belongings. He said he took fingerprints and DNA samples from them. Like the sheriff said, *'Ole Doctor Shotingham outdid himself'*. So, I'll see you later."

Doyle agreed, and as Ned walked into the office to clean off Copper's drool, he headed back to Caseville. "Copper, we still have to get that drooling under control."

Doyle was enjoying the country roads and took the scenic route. He drove north on M-53 into Port Austin and then followed M-25 around the shoreline. It was beautiful even if it was a chilly November day. It surprised him how few cars were on the road. "Copper, this is the downtime around here. The vacationers went south, and the locals are working somewhere else."

Doyle drove through Caseville, and he stopped at the corner gas station and filled his vehicle. While inside, he picked up the local newspaper, which had a front-page photograph of the crime scene and a full-color photo of him. Above his photo was the headline, "Why is this man investigating Mr. Lancole's death?"

The clerk looked at the paper and then at Doyle. "Look, that's you in the paper."

"No, really?" responded Doyle as he paid and walked out of the party store. Several other people noticed him and whispered to each other. Being recognized was not new to Doyle. As a wealthy restaurant owner, many people in Detroit would ask for his autograph, and when he was a detective, the press hounded him for information on the latest case. But today it came as a surprise.

Doyle drove into Mr. Lancole's driveway. The house was a one story old cottage on the north shore. There were two ultra-modern mansions on each side of his house. The contrast between the three homes was astonishing. Lancole's home looked out of place, hidden in what appeared to be a forest. It needed repairs; the wood siding was falling off, and the crushed stone driveway had weeds cropping up everywhere. Someone mowed the lawn, but there were clumps of grass piled everywhere. Whoever mowed it didn't want to rake up the long grass.

Doyle and Copper walked around the yard and down to the beach. There was clutter everywhere: an old shed that might have once been for storage, and a boathouse next to the water leaned toward the lake like a weathered tree leaning away from the wind. "Wow, Copper, this is a mess. Why didn't he fix this place up?"

Something about this place frightened Copper. He sensed that this was not a normal home, and he smelled Mr. Lancole's scent everywhere. Doyle circled the house and saw Deputy Ned pull into the driveway. Ned got out of the patrol car and walked down the driveway and stopped at Doyle's Buick.

Doyle yelled, "Ned, I'm over here. I'll be there in a minute, provided something doesn't jump out and attack me. Looks like a jungle, doesn't it?"

When Doyle reached the Buick, Ned broke out laughing. "Looks like the thistles attacked you."

Doyle looked down and saw masses of round thistles clinging to his pants. Then he looked at Copper and burst out laughing. "Copper, you've changed color." Thistles covered his fur, and he was trying to bite them off. Instead of coming off, they were getting attached to his face.

Doyle bent down and gently pulled the thistles free from Copper's fur. He then turned his attention to his pants and worked until most of the thistles were all off. Ned assisted him by telling him where the last few were located. Free from thistles, Doyle turned to Ned and asked if he had ever been to Lancole's home.

"To tell you the truth, Doyle, I knew he lived somewhere around here, but from the road all you see is a rustic path into the woods. Did you find anything of interest?"

Doyle threw the last thistle down and said, "Just thistles and the worst lawn I've ever seen. For a rich man, Lancole didn't take care of his house."

"I saw his car this morning, that he took care of on the outside, and left it go to hell on the inside. We sifted through all the trash, and bagged it as evidence; just in case, but I saw nothing useful."

Doyle opened the back door of the Buick and told Copper to jump in, which he did. He grabbed two sets of foot covers and rubber gloves and handed one set to Ned.

"What are these for?" asked Ned.

"They will help in protecting the evidence. If we contaminate the crime scene with our footprints and fingerprints, it can destroy any existing evidence. Just put them on." Doyle took out his cell phone and selected the camera icon. "I'll take photographs as we walk through the house, because we may need them later. Are you ready to see what's inside?" he asked after they had their shoes and hands protected.

"No, but we have to do it anyway," Ned replied. "I hope I don't see mice. I hate mice, and rats, and spiders, and snakes."

"Don't worry, I'll leave the door open so you have an escape route." Doyle laughed and took the keys from Ned. He looked at the door and could see that it was open. Someone broke the lock, and it looked like they had used a crowbar to break in. "Look, Ned. Someone was here already."

Ned studied the damage and agreed. I guess you won't need the keys."

Doyle pushed the door open, and they both stepped back. The odor of rotting trash was overwhelming. "Oh... my... God, what's in there?" Ned asked.

Doyle kicked the door wide open and looked in. "It's the dump. I think the old man was a hoarder. Look, there's a single path into the dump, and piles of junk on both sides." He looked at Ned, who was turning a deep shade of green, and said, "Come on, Ned, man-up; we're going in." He took several steps and gathered his senses. "It looks like Lancole's living area is to the left. Don't step on the rats."

"RATS? Where?" screamed Ned.

"Just kidding, Ned. I didn't see any rats; settle down. Haven't you been in a hoarder's home before?"

"Yes, of course. But this beats them all."

Doyle stopped at an open area. There were a daybed and a chair next to a desk piled with papers. Doyle looked at the desk and noticed mail from the day before. "Yep, this is his personal area. The old man must live here, in the middle of all that trash. How sick is that, Ned?" Doyle turned and saw Ned's back. He was sprinting out of the room.

"There are rats in there; I saw one, and it's the size of a cat!" Ned screamed.

Doyle looked down at a dark brown and white cat. "Oh... Ned... it's a cat. Come on back; if the cat lives here, there won't be rats or mice around."

Ned poked his face into the doorway. "Are you sure?"

"Yes, I'm sure. Come here and help me go through this junk. Perhaps we can discover what the old man was up to other than collecting junk. God, the least he could have done was pay for trash pickup. Look over there — bagged garbage piled to the ceiling. Someone will have fun going through that mess."

Doyle checked the desk and noticed that the intruders had emptied all the drawers. The contents were on the floor, perhaps just the contents the person who broke in didn't want.

"I wonder what they were looking for?" asked Ned.

"I don't know, maybe his last will or a letter; who knows? Let's put this all in a bag and bring it outside where there's fresh air. My eyes are burning." Ned looked around and found a box of large black garbage bags. He pulled out two bags and gave one to Doyle. While he scooped up the files on the floor, Doyle worked on the items on top of the desk. They walked around the room as much as they could and found a bag of cat food. Doyle dumped it on the floor and put water in the cat's bowl.

"We should call someone to come and pick up this cat," suggested Doyle.

"Not in this county. There are no kennels that accept stray cats. Only a few crazy women who take in all they can get, and I won't give any cats to them," Ned said.

"You know, Ned, we should have someone dust the door and desk for fingerprints. We need to know who and why they broke into this place."

"Any suggestions? We could call your friend Richard from the State Police."

Doyle thought for a moment. "I have a better idea. It's too far to have Richard's team drive down just to look for fingerprints. Why don't we assign Trooper Steve to the task? I'm sure he would appreciate having to muck around in this trash bin of a home."

Ned broke out laughing. "You have a very warped sense of humor, and I love it! I'll radio the sheriff and have him call in Steve. They should be able to sweep for prints this afternoon."

After leaving the house, Doyle tried to close the door. The cat rushed out and ran into the wooded area. Ned laughed, "I guess the cat heard us talk about him."

"I guess, but how do we keep this door shut?" Doyle asked.

"We don't. I'll let the sheriff know. Perhaps he can get it condemned, and someone will tear it down."

"Not until we solve the old man's death," Doyle insisted. "You never know what we'll need from this house and the junk it holds."

"Yes... later," agreed Ned. "Where should we examine these

papers?"

"My place. I have an office I can use for the rest of this investigation if you don't mind driving to Sand Point to work."

Ned smiled. "Makes no difference. In fact, it will be nice if we're out of McNabb's sight. He makes me nervous."

"Me too," Doyle said as he threw the two bags into the back of the Buick. Copper had to smell them, and he acted like they were poison. He sniffed and then went back to his seat. Doyle got behind the wheel and yelled out the window. "You can park in the driveway. I'll park the Buick in the garage."

Ned And Sandy Know Each Other

Ned Wooddell parked the patrol car and walked into the garage to help Doyle carry the evidence they bagged at Mr. Lancole's home. Doyle put Copper in his fenced-in yard and led Ned onto the second floor kitchen.

"I'm impressed," Ned said as he looked around the beautiful home. "When did you move in?" he asked.

"Almost three weeks ago, I think. With all the craziness going on, I have trouble keeping track of time," Doyle said as he set the two black garbage bags on the floor.

Ned walked around the room, stopping at the enormous windows overlooking Lake Huron and the beach. "Nice view. Do you own a fishing boat?"

"Everyone asks that question when they look out that window. No, I never considered getting a fishing boat, but perhaps I should rethink the idea. Do you fish?"

"Yes, I own a small powerboat... more like an oversized rowboat with a motor. I love going out early in the morning or late in the afternoon. I go alone so that I can think. It's sort of like therapy for me. I know we don't get the crime like you dealt with in Detroit, but we have drug and alcohol problems and poverty; I hate dealing with kids with addictions or overdosed on drugs. My heart breaks, you know?"

"Yes, I understand. I would cook up a storm when I got stressed over the job. In my early years as a detective, before my wife left me, I drank myself numb. It ruined my marriage, and my addiction led me to a depression that almost killed me." Doyle confided.

Ned pulled up a stool and sat at the kitchen counter. He enjoyed being able to talk with Doyle, and he enjoyed his company. "So how should we attack this pile of trash?"

"One at a time." Doyle pulled an empty wastebasket from under the counter. "Trash goes here. Trash will include anything that isn't relevant to the case. Everything else can go on the counter."

"OK, let's dig in," said Ned. "I suggest we first do a quick sort. Then we can study the relevant items later. Otherwise, it will take forever to go through it all."

"Agreed," said Doyle. "We need to use gloves and hold the paper by the edges. We have to preserve this evidence." He then grabbed a few papers and sorted. There were more items going into the trash than on the counter, and it took over an hour to get it all sorted. When they finished, they had about fifty items that could be important to the case. The wastebasket was overflowing, so Doyle dumped it into one garbage bag, marked it as trash from Lancole's home, and took it to the garage to keep until they solve the case.

As he walked back, Sandra drove into the yard. Doyle looked at his watch and gasped, *One o'clock!* He walked to her car and helped her with her things. "It has been busy here. Deputy Ned Wooddell and I went through Mr. Lancole's house. He was a hoarder who kept everything, including his trash. What a mess! I'll tell you all about it later. So, welcome to my little cottage on the lake."

Sandy looked at the three-story mansion. "Little?" she asked. "Why such a large home?"

"It was the location. My friend Trudy lives next door, and she suggested the place when it came up for sale. I spent a fortune remodeling it, and now it's becoming a home. There are still a few things I want to change, but I'm growing fond of the place," Doyle said. "Come on, let's go inside. I'll show you around."

Ned shuffled through the letters, reading the details to determine if it was important to the case. Sandy walked through the door with Doyle and said, "I knew it was your patrol car in the driveway. How have you been?"

"Fantastic! I'm assisting Doyle in the investigation. So far, it's been interesting. How are Ron and Ray doing? I haven't seen them in over a month."

"They're fine, still battling each other but no bloodshed yet," chuckled Sandy. "Doyle, Ned, attended school with my oldest son, Ronald. They spent a lot of time at our house; he's been like a third son."

Ned smiled, "Thank you, Sandy. That means a lot. Well, Doyle, I'm going back to Bad Axe to pick up Chad; we have to patrol this afternoon. When do you want to continue our investigation?"

"Tomorrow morning. Stop in for breakfast around eight a.m. I'll be cooking."

"OK, I'll try to stop by your party tonight. If I can't, I'll see you in the morning."

"That sounds good. Thanks again for the help." Doyle said as Ned walked out the side door.

Chapter 14

Party Preperations

Doyle asked Sandy if she wanted a drink, and she requested coffee, so he set up the coffeemaker. While it was brewing, he showed her around the family kitchen, dining area, living room and office.

"This level is the master living quarters. It's nice because everything I need is on one level. Upstairs there are four bedrooms with a bath in each, and downstairs there was one bedroom, which I removed to enlarge my entertainment room." He explained.

"You were correct when you said it was modern, but I find it comfortable. I've seen many large homes that feel like the interior of a bank, you know, industrial. This is nice. Did you pick out the wall decor?"

"No, and I would like to replace the artwork. I want to personalize the space and make it more about this area. I mean, that picture of the beach has palm trees, for heaven's sakes; this is Michigan!"

Sandy nodded in agreement. "Your decorator was more interested in color than subject; most decorators are. If you like, I would love to help you pick out art; not right away, but over time we could replace the ones that don't fit in. There are several local artists who do beautiful work. I'll introduce you to them, and we can go to the art fairs this coming spring and summer. There are also several wonderful gift shops in town. It'll be fun."

"That would be nice, Sandy. I'm sure we'll have a good time, and this place could use a woman's touch."

Sandy smiled. "Are you ready for the party, or do we have a lot of preparations to do?"

"Oh, yes... the party. I did a lot of prep work last night. I made pitas, prepared the chicken, steak, and shrimp, and I made the pumpkin pecan roll-ups. What we have to do now is make two or three salads, but I'm not sure what I want to do for a carb. I have a lot of yellow potatoes, but I don't know... that might be too much."

"I take it the guests will make pita roll-ups with salad on the side. What about a pasta salad?" Sandy suggested.

"Perhaps. Do you think they would like spicy sweet potato wedges or yellow potato wedges?"

"I would, and I think they would be better than another salad, but you're the chef, so it's your choice."

"Potato wedges. Like I said, I have a lot of yellow potatoes, so we'll use them."

Having made his menu decisions, Doyle asked Sandy if she wanted to put her things in the master bedroom. Together, they put the garment and make-up bags away. The layout of the master quarters impressed her, but she was eager to see the downstairs kitchen with its walk-in refrigerator.

Doyle led the way. "The home is a modified try-level. The entertainment room is four steps lower than the second floor."

As the couple entered the room, Sandra gasped, "Oh... my... God. This looks like the Doyle's Irish Pub in Ann Arbor. What possessed you to put one in your home?"

"Because it was easy to do. When we built the Doyle's Pubs, we used a contractor who could set one up in a week. I decided I wanted an entertainment room in this space. I loved my Irish pubs, and now I have one in my house. See... I can play pool, watch sports, cook meals, drink at the bar, or play darts. What more could I ask for?"

Sandy walked between the tables, mesmerized by all the wall decorations and large screen monitors. When she saw the kitchen, she gasped. "Doyle, I'm impressed! This makes my little kitchen look like a dollhouse. My God, an actual restaurant in your house. This takes the cake. I can't wait for our friends to see this. They'll die. I mean, it's fantastic... breathtaking."

"Thank you. I appreciate your enthusiasm. Now we should get busy. We only have four hours before the party starts, so come into the kitchen and I'll show you what we need to do."

Doyle assigned Sandy to preparing the salads. He planned a Greek style salad, a watermelon salad, and a yogurt and cucumber salad. While she was chopping ingredients, he cleaned and chopped potatoes into wedges. Until ready to cook, he placed them in a bucket with lemon water. Angie will spread them onto large baking trays and place them into the oven.

"How do you cook everything so it's ready for the party, and not cold?" asked Sandy.

"That's the restaurant chef's secret, but I can spill the beans. I'm precooking the steaks and chicken breasts in the oven so the inside is rare. Just before I want to serve, I throw them onto a blazing hot grill, and out comes a nice steak, sizzling on the outside and just the right temperature on the inside. Same with the chicken. While I'm cooking the meat, the potatoes will finish in a hot oven. Everything will be ready to eat."

As the couple did their tasks, they discussed the murder of Mr. Lancole. Sandy mentioned that she had read something in the Pigeon Museum years ago about the Lancole family, but she couldn't remember what it was. "I'll be working there tomorrow, so if you like I can look for the article," she suggested.

"Anything you can find will help. It's a tough case, but I'm sure Ned and I will solve it. Did you know what kind of house he was living in?"

"I heard rumors he was an eccentric drunk. Other than that, I never heard much. He wasn't in my circle of friends. I don't think he had any friends in the area. Like I said... eccentric."

"And he was a hoarder... big time!"

"Really?"

"Yes, his house has trash piled to the ceiling, and someone broke into it either before or after his death. They were looking for something; I hope they didn't find it, but it's hard to tell."

After a few hours of work, they were ready for the party. "Angie and her husband Alex will be here in an hour, so we can relax. I have to take a shower, but I can use the one upstairs."

"Don't be silly, use your bedroom and bath. If you shower and change first, I'll have lots of time to do my magic."

"Good.... let's go upstairs. I'm sure Copper would like food and water. I'm surprised he hasn't been down here begging," Doyle said.

When they entered the upstairs kitchen, Copper came running. He had been at the large patio door watching deer walking on the beach. "Are you hungry, Copper?" Doyle asked, and Copper rushed to his dish.

Sandy laughed, "He listens well, doesn't he?"

"It's amazing. This is the smartest dog I've ever seen."

"I can't wait to have him meet my cat, Casey. I think they'll get along. Casey can be possessive and bossy."

"So can Copper. I've found that you can't take his food when he's eating. That's not a smart idea." Doyle said. "He doesn't bite, but you know he's not happy."

"Well, it's getting late, so why don't you get ready?" Sandy suggested. "I'll stay and visit with Copper."

Doyle agreed and left to get dressed. He took less than half an hour to shower, shave and change clothes. Then he returned wearing khaki dress slacks, a light blue button-down shirt, and a deep burgundy cardigan.

"Wow, don't you look nice," remarked Sandy. "Are you done in the bathroom? I promise I'll be ready before the party is over," she quipped.

"It's all yours. I'm going downstairs to get ready."

"Aren't you afraid of getting your clothes soiled from cooking?"

Doyle grinned, "I'll use a chef's coat and a long apron while I'm at the grill."

Sandy smiled. "I know; you're a professional chef. I'll get ready now."

Party Goes Well

Doyle removed his cardigan and put on a black chef's top, a cap and a long black apron. He mixed the watermelon salad, cucumber salad, and Greek salad and put the bowls into the refrigerator. The buffet has a hot side and a cold side. He arranged serving pans for the meats, and large bowls for the salads. The desert would be at the far end, near the ice cream machine. He already had the butter pecan mixed, and it only took a few minutes to run the mix through the automatic ice cream machine, filling a large bowl with soft ice cream. He then packed the frozen delight into a bowl and placed it in the freezer, so it would firm up.

As he walked out of the freezer, he saw Angie and Alex standing in the doorway, staring into the room with a look of wonder on their faces.

Alex spoke first. "Hi, Mr. Doyle, I'm Alex, and this place is... amazing."

"It sure is." Angie said, turning toward Doyle. "When you said you were having a party downstairs, I never dreamed it was an actual restaurant. Why did you... what were you...?"

"I owned twenty-six Irish pubs that looked exactly like this. There is one in Ann Arbor, Grand Rapids, and at locations in ten other states. I sold them all, but when I moved, I wanted one of my own because I'm Irish and I'm a chef."

Alex walked to the bar and looked around. "Good story, sir, but we're here to help, so let's help, Angie."

Doyle showed Angie what he wanted done while Alex set up

the bar. Once he was sure the bar was ready, he helped Doyle in the kitchen. The two men talked about cooking and business. Alex's skills were impressive, and Doyle was happy to have two professionals helping him.

Sandy walked down the steps as Angie was putting the finishing touches on the tables. Sandy wore a beautiful beaded cream sweater with brown silky slacks and matching flats. Angie looked up, saw Sandy and said, "You look very nice tonight. Isn't this quite the room?" she asked.

"It sure is, and Doyle is quite the man," Sandy whispered.

"I heard what you said, Sandy, and you're looking beautiful too," replied Doyle. He approached her and gave her a big hug and a light kiss. "We're ready for our guests. All we need is background music. Do you have any requests?"

"Yes, something light... perhaps instrumental. Why don't you let me pick?" she suggested.

Doyle showed her the entertainment system, and she searched until she found a channel with soft, romantic music featuring classic songs from the 1980s.

Alex and Angie put food on the buffet while Doyle prepared the chicken, steak and shrimp for the grill. He had already grilled tomatoes, green peppers, red onions and zucchini slices, and placed them on a platter... topped with feta cheese and olive oil. The buffet would hold them at the perfect temperature.

The first guest to arrive was Sandy's sister, Kathy Brausch, and her husband, Sam. Sandy took their coats, showed them around, introduced them to Doyle and answered their many questions.

Barry and Barbara Cummings arrived with Roger and Mindy Harding. Sandy went through the routine again, but Roger was intent on talking to Doyle. He stood in the kitchen chatting until Doyle advised he had to move so he could finish dinner.

"Roger, we can talk after dinner. Why don't you grab a drink and talk with Alex at the bar? I bet he'd love to visit you."

Mindy and Roger sat at the bar. Mindy told Sandy how much she loved her outfit and wanted to know what Doyle was like, how much money he had, and why he made his house into a restaurant. "Is he a little eccentric?" she asked.

Sandy laughed, "Not any more than you are, Mindy."

Roger burst out laughing. "So he is a little over the top?"

Mindy gave her husband a stern look, then she also broke into a laugh. "I guess we all are eccentric, in our own way."

Roger wanted to know about Mr. Lancole's death, but Sandy wouldn't talk. She told him it's Doyle and Deputy Ned's case and she couldn't discuss it. Roger then walked over to Barry to find out what he knew.

Edna and Harvey Sykes arrived with Clyde Leaming. Clyde wore a tight tee shirt and stretch jeans. His physical condition was that of a younger man, but his face looked every bit his age of 65. Sandra welcomed them and repeated her introductions and explanations.

Clyde reached his hand around her waist and gave her a hug. "So... you got something going on with this Doyle guy?" he asked.

"Clyde, you and I are not *a thing*, and the sooner you realize it the better we both will be." She walked away while he said, "Can't help it, Honey... you drive me wild with your good looks and sexy ways."

Before starting the steaks, Doyle walked across the driveway to escort Trudy Hoffstarter to the party. Sandy met them at the door and hugged Trudy.

After they found a table for Trudy, Doyle took Sandy aside. "Is Clyde going to be a problem? I heard what he said to you."

"No... I have to keep him in his place. He has a crush on me and thinks he's God's gift to women. He has a big ego."

"Well, just remember. He may be bigger and stronger than I am, but I can use a fry pan better than he can. One whack and he'll be on the floor."

Sandra laughed, "Hilarious, Doyle. I think we should get the party going. Do you want to welcome everyone?"

"Yes." Doyle stood in front of the buffet and said, "Friends... if I can have your attention, I want to welcome all of you to my home. I know it looks like a restaurant, but that's just the way I like my entertainment center — or should I call it my man-cave?"

There was light laughter, and Doyle continued. "I'm new to this area, but my family settled in Caseville in the 1860s as commercial fishermen, so I feel I have roots here. I was lucky to have met Sandy, a beautiful and caring woman. We wanted to have this party so I can meet you, some of Sandy's best friends."

Barry made a toast to Sandy, and everyone applauded. "Thank you, Barry. Now I'm going back to the kitchen to cook our main course. We're having a Greek buffet with pita bread, grilled chicken breast, rib-eye steak, and shrimp. There are salads and dressings set on the buffet. You can make your dish any way you like. I hope you enjoy the meal. Everything will be ready in six minutes, so find you seat and prepare yourselves for a Greek treat."

Alex had the four foot indoor grill on, and he had just turned the steaks. "This grill gets super hot... super fast. I almost think it's easier to use than an outdoor grill, too," he said. Doyle agreed and placed the shrimp on the grill. The two cooks took turns with the chicken breasts.

As Doyle placed the meat on the trays, Angie sliced it and arranged the slices for serving. It was six minutes when the buffet was ready, and Barry and Barbara were first in line, eager to get started.

Doyle turned the grill off, took his black chef's top and apron off, and joined Sandy and Trudy at the table. Sandy reached over and took his hand. "You're fantastic. I was watching you in the kitchen, and I can see how much you love cooking. You put yourself into it more than anyone I know."

Trudy agreed, "He's been cooking like that since he was ten years old... working at his mom's Greek restaurant."

"I enjoy cooking, especially when I can cook for my friends."

Doyle looked around and smiled. "Sandy, isn't it nice that everyone is eating and not talking? That's a good sign."

"You didn't think they would like your cooking?"

"It's always a fear, and that fear keeps me on my culinary toes. All it takes is one bad dish to trash your reputation," Doyle said.

Trudy smiled and said, "Sandy, he's full of crap. If they don't like his food, it's their fault, and he knows it. You'll discover that our friend here has an oversized ego, even if he projects the appearance of a humble man."

As the guests finished eating, they milled around the room. Barry asked if he could put a few tables together so it would be easier to visit, and Doyle thought it was a good idea. He asked Alex to help.

As the tables were being moved, the door swung open and Deputy Ned walked in. All the guests looked at him and, in unison, they yelled, "Ned!"

Doyle welcomed Ned and showed him the buffet. While they were talking, Chad walked through the doors. In unison, the other guests yelled, "Chad!" Chad walked over to Doyle and Ned. Together, they filled a plate with food. Unexpectedly, the door opened again, and Sheriff McNabb walked into the room dressed in full uniform. He stopped as the guests all yelled, "Sheriff!"

Barry stood and yelled, "Doyle, does the Sheriff know you're running a speakeasy in your house? Could be a problem, you know?"

Doyle didn't know what to say. He approached the Sheriff who was laughing. "Doyle, I heard you were cooking tonight. Nice man-cave you got here. Care if I sample your food? As you can tell, I'm an expert on food." The sheriff patted his huge belly and laughed. "You aren't charging anyone for this party, are you?"

"No, but donations to my favorite charities are always welcome," Doyle said, as Sheriff McNabb piled food on a plate. "Are you on duty?" Doyle asked.

"No, and yes, I'd love a brewski... Bud Lite, if you have one," the sheriff barked at Alex. "Doyle, I haven't seen food like this since I was down in Greektown. Your place, if I recall. Loved it."

"Thank you, Sir. We can talk after you're finished."

"Man, don't call me Sir. The name is Carl or Sheriff, and it may take a while to fill this empty tank."

Doyle returned to Sandy and Trudy's table. Sandy's brother-in-law moved a table. Sandy's sister, Sam, was sitting next to her. Sam said to Doyle, "We enjoyed dinner, and thank you for the invitation, but could you tell me about the man who died on the beach yesterday? Sandy says you're investigating, but she won't give us any details. Can you?"

"Yes, I'm heading up the investigation, but I can't talk about it. We have only begun, and it isn't proper for me to discuss the details."

McNabb yelled, "Ned says the old man's house was a pigsty. You'd think Old Man Lancole could have afforded a housekeeper, don't you, Doyle?"

Doyle could tell the sheriff wouldn't be following proper police procedure. "I guess, Carl, but we can talk about it later."

"Later, gator." The sheriff laughed and turned to Ned. "I love to talk crime over dinner. Makes the food go down easier. Son, tell me about that house again. Was it as nasty as you said?" Ned accommodated the sheriff. It was an easy way to deal with him.

Clyde, along with Harvey and Edna Sykes, was the first to leave. Harvey and Edna thanked Doyle and Sandy for the lovely party, and Clyde told Sandy he was going to the Blue Water Inn. "If you want to have fun, stop in later, Honey."

Doyle interrupted him and said, "It must take a while for facts to sink into that head of yours. Did you have an accident when you played football or are you just dense?"

"Are you calling me dense?"

"Yes, Sandy said she didn't appreciate you hitting on her, so please don't."

Clyde's face turned red, and he said, "Come on, Harvey and Edna, let's get out of here."

Edna smiled and patted Sandy on her shoulder. "He means well;

like your friend said, Clyde's a little dense."

The Party Is Over

Once one couple left, the party wound down. Sandy offered to walk Trudy home, and Doyle announced that anyone who wanted a to-go box should help themselves. There was a scramble to fill the box with meat, and in no time the leftover food disappeared.

Roger took Doyle aside and said, "I need to talk to you about Mr. Lancole's death."

"Roger, I told you everything I can. I..."

Roger interrupted him. "I have something to share that is very important."

Doyle leaned in and said, "Tell me what you have."

The two men sat at the bar and Roger began, "You've seen Lancole's house. Can you imagine how that hellhole made his neighbors feel? His two next-door neighbors, Arthur Wilcone and Jerry Stratman, made threats on Lancole's life. They took him to court, and lost. After the court case, Arthur said, *'One of these days you will walk down the road, and I'll squash you flatter than a squirrel.'* Then Jerry added, *'When Arthur's done, I'll throw your dead body in the lake so the fish can eat your rotting flesh.'* Doyle, I never heard such angry men. Like I said, they lost the case in court because Mr. Lancole sold them the property, and he set up their association so he could make all the rules. They were at his mercy."

"And where did this conversation take place?" asked Doyle.

"Outside the Huron County District Courtroom. I was there because Arthur and Jerry's lawyer called me as a witness. I live a few houses down the street."

"Thank you, Roger. I'll talk to them, and don't worry, I won't let on who told me about their threats."

"I better get going; my wife looks like she's ready to hit the road, or me if I don't take her home soon. She doesn't like to be away the house for too long," Roger said as he got up. "Good luck with the case, Doyle. I had a wonderful time, and remember, we need you down at the Chamber."

Sandy had been talking with Mindy while Doyle and Roger visited. She approached Doyle and said, "If you don't mind, I should get my things and go home. It's been a long day, and I want to do some research at the Pigeon Museum tomorrow morning."

"Let me walk with you. I want to make sure Copper hasn't been tearing up the living room. Sometimes he gets frustrated and takes it out on the pillows." The couple walked up the steps, where Copper greeted them. There was no destruction, and Copper looked rested.

Sandy grabbed her bag and work clothes. Doyle escorted her to her parked car, and he opened her door and said, "Thank you for all the help you gave me. You are a special woman, and I had a wonderful time."

"So did I," she replied. "I'll call tomorrow. Are you still working at the Community Center for Thanksgiving?"

"Yes, and you're going to your son's home?" he asked.

"Yes, but I wish I were helping you." She gave him a hug and a passionate and long kiss. "Bye, now."

Doyle beamed as he headed back into the house. Copper came out of his room and greeted him. "Perhaps I'm in love, Copper." Doyle swore the bloodhound smiled... sort of. *It could be gas,* Doyle thought.

"Come with me downstairs, Copper. Ned is there, and so are Chad and the Sheriff. I believe you'll like them." Doyle stepped into the room just as the sheriff belched. "Sorry, Doyle... that was the best damn food I have eaten in a long time. You can come cook for me anytime you want. My wife's idea of dinner is Chinese takeout."

"That is a treat sometimes," Doyle said.

At first, Copper was reluctant to enter the room. When he saw the crowd had left, he relaxed and walked up to Ned. Ned pet Copper's head, and the bloodhound moaned with pleasure.

"What have we here? A bloodhound? This must be the dog that smelled Old Man Lancole's rotting body. Good doggy."

Copper looked up at the gigantic man and then turned to Doyle. Both were grinning. Doyle smiled at the sheriff and said, "Yes, he's a good doggy."

As Angie and Alex finished cleaning the kitchen and dining room, Doyle told the Sheriff and Deputies what Roger reported.

"I know all about it. They made quite a scene at the courthouse. That was a year ago. You going to talk with them?" asked the sheriff.

"Yes. I need to see Richard's report, and we must finish going through Lancole's letters. Did Trooper Steve check for fingerprints at the Lancoles's house?"

Ned said he did, but they still need to check the database for a match. "Should we have Richard and his team go over the house to check for anything? It's such a mess, it could take him quite a long time, and I'm not sure what he would find."

Doyle thought over the question and said, "Not now, Ned. Let's do the interviews and see what happens. Perhaps our killer or killers will be easy to find."

Chapter 15

They Hated The Old Man

Doyle's phone rang at six-thirty, waking both him and Copper. He reached for the cell phone, checked the number and answered, "Ned, why are you calling so early?"

Last night Chad's brother, Will, told him Arthur Wilcone and Jerry Stratman are going to Florida after Thanksgiving. They plan to leave on Saturday, so I called them and set up an appointment for nine this morning. I hope you don't mind."

"Not at all; I appreciate your taking the initiative. Why don't you come over for breakfast and we can drive down together?"

Ned agreed and asked if he should pick up anything? Doyle laughed and said no. "I'll make French toast, so I can use up some of my eggs and bread. You could stop at the Farm Store and buy two bags of Bacon Strips for Copper. Buy the bacon and cheese and the original bacon flavor. They're his favorite. I'll pay you back when you get here."

"OK, I'll be there in an hour," Ned said.

Doyle used the bathroom and took a long hot shower while Copper stood next to the shower doors. An empty Bacon Strips bag was lying on the floor in front of him. When Doyle saw him, he laughed. Copper pulled the bag out of the trash and wanted to make sure Doyle knew he needed more.

"Don't worry, I'm getting more. You know, if you keep eating like you've been, you will be a very obese dog. Too fat to help me find the killer, perhaps too fat to get through your doggy door."

Copper paid no attention to the warning. He returned to the kitchen and ate from his dog bowl, not his favorite treat, but still food.

Ned arrived just as Doyle turned the French toast and bacon. He placed maple syrup, butter, and sliced oranges on the counter, and let Ned in and asked if he wanted coffee, juice, or something else. Ned selected coffee, and they ate breakfast.

"I wanted to thank you again for inviting me to the party last night. We had a great time. Sometime I would like to bring my girlfriend if she ever gets a day off. She works at the hospital in Pigeon. She's been pulling a double shift. I think she's trying to save up for a home here on the Point."

Doyle laughed, "I know a house that might be real cheap."

"If you're thinking of Old Man Lancole's, no way! Besides, the property would be worth more than I make in a year."

"Perhaps." Doyle gave Copper one of the bacon treats, and Copper's tail went into overdrive.

"What's in those treats? He acts like he's addicted," Ned asked.

"I don't know, but now I'm sorry I got them. I might need to sign Copper up for doggy rehabilitation."

After breakfast, Ned and Doyle resumed working on the papers they found in Mr. Lancole's house. They sorted out the evidence, but now they needed to check each letter. A task that would be slow.

Wearing gloves, they opened and read letters, shuffled through file folders and scanned the contents for any leads.

"I've got a letter from a lawyer. It's regarding the lawsuit his neighbors filed against him." Ned advised.

"Anything important other than the name of the lawyer?"

"Yes, at the end of the letter he reminded Lancole about a meeting set up to change his last will and testament. That was last summer, July 20th, in Troy, Michigan."

"Good lead, put it in this pile and mark the information in your notes," instructed Doyle. Doyle also found letters from Lancole's lawyer. There were statements from investment companies, banks, insurance and utility bills, and an important letter from his nephew, Andrew Lancole, Jr. Doyle didn't take the time to read the entire letter. He showed it to Ned and added it to the pile of evidence.

Fifteen minutes before nine, the two left for the ride down to Arthur Wilcone's home. Both Arthur and his neighbor, Jerry Stratman, would be there for the interview. Doyle said he would lead the interview, and he asked Ned if there were questions he wanted asked.

"Yes! Ask them if they killed the old man. I want to watch their reactions."

"Are you an expert in body language?"

"No, but sometimes you can tell when a person is lying."

Doyle smiled. He agreed with Ned, but he would not admit it. As the two walked up to the door of the enormous home, Mr. Wilcone greeted them and welcomed them into the front room. The four men sat at a small table.

Wilcone offered coffee, but they declined. Doyle began with, "I am aware the two of you didn't like Mr. Lancole and you made threats against his life. Did you run him over and throw his body into the lake like you said you would?"

Mr. Wilcone exploded and yelled, "What the hell? I don't have to answer these kinds of questions."

"Yes, you do, but if you like we can all go to Bad Axe. As of now, you two are our prime suspects. You had a motive, means, and the opportunity to kill him. Now, answer the question or prepare to see the Sheriff!" Doyle insisted.

Jerry Stratman gave his friend Arthur a stern look. "Arthur, we have no reason to get upset. When we blew up in the courtroom last summer, we both realized it would come back to bite us in the ass. Let's answer all of Mr. Doyle's questions. We have nothing to hide."

Jerry settled down, and after a few moments he said, "We didn't kill the old man. I'm not sad that he's dead, but I had nothing to do with his death."

Doyle stood and walked around the table. "Tell me where you were between eleven p.m. last Sunday and two a.m. Monday."

In unison, the men said, "Sleeping!"

Ned interrupted, "Doyle, that almost sounded rehearsed, didn't it?"

"Sure did, Ned." Doyle sat down again. "Now, why should we believe you? Is there anyone who can support your statement other than your wives?"

Jerry said, "My wife was with me, and I had my son and his wife here. We were playing cards until twelve and then we all retired to bed. The kids got up early and left for home. I can give you my son's phone number. He's also a doctor, and he took over my practice in Troy."

Doyle looked at Arthur. "Was there someone other than your wife who can back up your alibi?" he asked.

"Nope. We went to bed, and that's the truth. I have too much to lose. I would never do something stupid, like kill that bastard of an old man. He would die soon enough... the way he drank and let himself go to hell. Trust me, I could wait!"

Doyle and Ned continued asking the two men about their relationship with the old man. It was very obvious they hated him. The problem was the old man's home was not visible from the road, so when the authorities drove by they didn't see how rundown it was, and being an association, the property owners could set their own standards of upkeep.

Arthur lamented, "It was my fault. I should have studied the paperwork better, but it was such a good deal. When I learned that the old man was in total control of the association, I was furious. We couldn't sue him, and the authorities wouldn't enforce the county blight laws, so we ended up with a junkyard as a neighbor. I even had to hire people to kill rats coming from his house, and the smell in the summer got so bad we wanted to go back to Florida, even though it was too hot there."

Doyle's phone rang. He checked the number and told Ned he had to take the call and walked outside. Doyle replied, "Richard, how is my favorite CSI man?"

"Fine, thanks. I have some interesting news, but I don't want to tell you over the phone," he said.

"Come on, tell me something. We are at a standstill here, and with the holidays coming, I don't want to wait on the mail."

"I'll be there this afternoon. Is that soon enough?"

"Hot damn, yes it is. But it's such a long drive, so would you rather have me drive down and pick the report too?"

"No. My wife and I are going to our daughter's for Thanksgiving. She lives in Port Austin. I'll drive over, drop my wife off in Port Austin, and then circle back and meet you at your place, if that's ok."

"Perfect. What time will you be here?" asked Doyle.

"I should be at your house around three o'clock. You can have coffee ready and perhaps some of your best homemade cookies."

"I will. Thank you, and I'll see you at three."

Doyle put his cell phone in his pocket and started into Mr. Wilcone's home. Before he could open the door, his phone rang again. It was Sandy.

"Doyle, I found some interesting facts about the Lancole family. I get out of work at one o'clock, so can I stop over?"

"Yes, and I'll have coffee and some homemade cookies ready, just for you."

Doyle returned to Mr. Wilcone's home and spoke with Ned. Ned said he covered all the questions and advised the two men not to leave Michigan until the investigation was over.

"I bet they didn't like that suggestion," Doyle said.

"No, but they said they would comply with the request," Ned said. "We might as well go unless you have more questions."

"Only one." Doyle approached the two men and asked, "What do you know of the broken door on Mr. Lancole's house?"

Arthur looked at Jerry as if asking him to speak. Jerry didn't say a word, so Arthur said, "Well... we didn't break into the house. The old man came over three weeks ago and accused us. He thought we broke in, but I assure you, there's nothing I want inside that house. I told him I had seen a pickup truck parked in his driveway the day before, but I didn't see the driver. When I told him that, he got angry. Not at us, just angry.."

"Ok, gentlemen, don't leave town, and if you remember anything else, here's my number."

Doyle handed them each a business card.

Ned and Doyle walked out of the house. On their way to Ned's patrol car, Doyle said, "Let's head back to my place. Sandy is stopping in at one o'clock with some info. She found in the museum. Something to do with the history of the Lancole family. And then Richard will stop in at three o'clock with his CSI report."

When the two men reached Doyle's place, Ned stayed in the car. "I have things to do," he told Doyle, "but if you don't mind, I'll come back at three to learn what Richard has to say."

"Good. You should be here since you're my partner in this investigation."

Sandra Finds Something Interesting

Doyle greeted Copper and put fresh water and food in his dishes. He then went into the walk-in freezer and found the container of chocolate chip cookie dough he had brought with him from Detroit. Already made into small balls, they are ready to drop on a pan to bake. He didn't make them, but he will bake them, so his conscience will be clear.

Sandy rang the doorbell just as Doyle emptied the last batch of cookies into the large cookie jar. He baked three dozen and had a pot of coffee ready for his guests.

"Come on in," he told her. "I'm eager to hear what you found, but first you have to try my cookies. I' baked them, but I'll confess... the team in Detroit mixed and froze them, but it's my original recipe. Now, how do you want your coffee today?"

"A little light cream if you have some," she replied.

"That was my guess, but I wanted to make sure," Doyle said as he poured her coffee. "Tell me what you found that's so important."

"I mentioned I remembered reading something at the Pigeon Museum about the Lancole family. I couldn't recall what I had read, but I remembered it was unusual, so I did a search and I found a newspaper article. They published it in the April 21, 1919, Pigeon Progress. Once I read the article, I remembered the story." Sandy grabbed another cookie. "I want this recipe. They're good! Now where was I?"

"The newspaper articles. Did you bring a copy of it?"

"Yes," Sandy said as he dug into her purse. "I made a copy and then I typed it up. I considered sending you the file, but I wanted to see your reaction."

Sandy handed the paper to Doyle. "Here, you can read it aloud. It's a fascinating article. I'm not sure how it fits into your case, but I bet it does."

Doyle took the paper and read.

From Pigeon Progress, April 21, 1919
Four Murdered Near Bay Port
Alexander Lancole Kills Mother and Three Children at His Home Saturday Evening

One of the most horrible crimes ever committed in Huron County occurred near Bay Port last Saturday evening when Alexander Lancole aged 43, killed his mother and three of his children.

"They were ready to die, and it seemed the proper time for them to be taken."

That was the only explanation obtainable Saturday from Alexander Lancole, aged 43, for killing with an axe his 69-year-old mother and three children, from 18 months to four years of age, at their farm home near Bay Port, Saturday night. Lancole, who gave himself up to Samuel Cochran immediately after the crime, told Mr. Cochran he had killed his dear ones as a religious sacrifice and also intimated that others among his immediate associates were ready to die and he would like an opportunity to kill them.

The farm colt which he could not catch after he had killed practically all other livestock on the farm also as a sacrifice, "had too much electricity and was unfit to die," he declared, and the family cat was possessed of "too much deviltry."

Three of the bodies — those of two of his children and his mother — were found in the living room of the Lancole home, huddled close together. The crime apparently had occurred just after they had finished their suppers and when Lancole had come in from doing the farm chores. In each instance, a blow from the blunt end of the ax had dashed out the brains of the victim.

His little son John, aged 3, evidently had some realization of his father's purpose - and tried to get away from him.

He was half-way up the stairway when struck down by the frenzied man. Like the other three, a blow on the head also killed him.

After killing the three members of his family, Lancole killed most of the farm livestock with the same ax.

Mrs. Lancole was absent from home and on her return was ordered from the house by her husband and her life threatened.

On one or two previous occasions, Lancole had shown signs of mental weakness, it is stated, but none of these expressed themselves violently and little attention was paid to them.

The Lancole family came to Bay Port about two years ago and made their home on a 120-acre farm about a mile south of town.

That Mrs. Mary Lancole, the aged mother of Alexander Lancole, fought desperately Saturday night to save the lives of his three children and herself before he killed her and them with an ax in a religious mania, is the belief of Huron County officers.

The Lancole home was literally strewn with broken furniture, particularly the blood stained room where the bodies of the woman and two of the children were found. No less than 6 broken chairs, which must have been used by the woman to defend the children against their crazed father, were found, some of them smashed almost to bits. Her fight is even more remarkable when it is considered she was 69 years old and the man was 43, of sturdy build.

The bodies of all the victims were mutilated, almost beyond recognition. After they were killed with the blunt end of a single bit ax, they also were chopped with the blade. Some bodies showed the victims had been choked before they were struck with the ax.

Lancole was the father of seven children. Besides the three victims, Edith, aged 1, John aged 3 and Sally, 18 months old. There are 4 older children, three of whom were with their mother on a shopping expedition at the time of the murder. When Mrs. Lancole and the children drove up to the house, Lancole met them at the door holding the axe and told them he had killed the children and his mother and threatened to kill his wife if she did not leave immediately. Then he went to town and gave himself up.

Lancole was taken to Bad Axe on Saturday night and lodged in the county jail. Yesterday he was judged insane by Probate Judge Cornell and will be taken to an asylum. The funeral of the victims of the tragedy was held on Tuesday, and the remains were laid to rest in the Old Bay Port Cemetery.

═══

Doyle laid the paper down. "Wow. That was a nasty situation, but are we sure this is the same family?"

Sandy smiled. "I wondered that too, so I did a genealogy search, and the father who killed his family was Mr. Lancole's grandfather. His dad was one of the older sons who were with their mother. I thought it was interesting because of the antique axe used to kill the old man. Don't you agree?"

Doyle laughed, "Sandy, are you getting the detective bug?"

Sandy looked surprised. She thought about it for a moment and had to admit that this mystery had piqued her curiosity. "Yes! I think I am getting the bug. Being a detective is like being a history buff. I love to learn about the past."

"Same here. I'm not sure how it all fits. Richard Ketlinger, my CSI friend from Bridgeport, will be here in about an hour. He also has news to share about Mr. Lancole's death. Would you like to stay and hear his report?"

"Yes, I would, but I have a doctor's appointment in Pigeon." She looked at the clock on Doyle's kitchen wall and added, "In fact, I should get going now. Call me this evening so you can tell me what Richard said." Sandy picked up her purse and grabbed a few cookies. "These are fantastic."

Doyle put Copper on the leash, and they walked with Sandy outside. He gave her a big hug and promised to let her know all the details. "Bye Sandy. Say bye, Copper."

Copper watched her drive away and pulled Doyle toward the beach. They walked along the edge of the frigid water. Copper's nose was twitching, and Doyle told him, "Don't even think of finding another body. Let me get this mystery solved before you drag me into another one. Is that understood?"

Copper pulled the leash, and the two started back toward home. Copper understood.

Chapter 16

Richard Has A Surprise

Doyle was inside Copper's fenced-in room when Richard Ketlinger drove into the driveway. As Richard walked toward the door, Doyle yelled, "The door is open. I'll be there in a few minutes; I'm cleaning up after Copper."

Richard looked around, but he couldn't find Doyle. "Where are you?"

"I'm in here."

"In where?"

Richard looked behind the fence and saw Doyle. "There you are. Did you get this cage from the Detroit Zoo?"

Doyle grabbed the plastic bag and opened the door. "It's Copper's room. He has a doggy door in the house and can go outside whenever he wants to."

The two men entered the house. Richard carried a large bag with the Axe and a briefcase with a laptop and folder. He set the evidence on the counter, and Doyle arranged a cup of coffee and some cookies as Richard walked around the room and admired the fantastic view. "How's the fishing?" he asked.

"I don't know; I never go fishing."

"You own a boat, don't you?"

Doyle laughed at the question. "No, but I might buy one this summer," he relented.

"I would," Richard said. "There's nothing like sitting on the deck of a boat, drinking a beer and soaking up the sunrays. Best way to spend an afternoon; if you like... you could even fish a little."

"Sounds enchanting, Richard. So what's the word on Old Man Lancole?"

"You read the report from the medical examiner, didn't you?"

"Yes."

"A pickup truck or large SUV hit Mr. Lancole, with just enough force to knock him to the ground. More of a bump than a hit. There wouldn't be any damage to the vehicle. He hit his head on the pavement, resulting in a minor scrape. At first we thought there was black paint from the incident, but it came from the old man's '58 Cadillac. I gather Lancole never dry cleaned his black suit, or took a bath. The paint peeled off the door next to the driver's seat."

Doyle remarked, "You should look at his house. We thought about having you come and do a sweep for evidence, but he was a hoarder, and finding evidence would be impossible... like wading in water while trying to find one special drop of water."

Doyle opened his laptop and turned it on. "I took photographs so you can see for yourself." He opened Lancole's folder and turned the computer so Richard could scroll through the images. While Richard studied the pictures, the doorbell rang; it was Ned.

"Sorry I'm late. The sheriff got talking, and you understand how that goes. I see Richard is here, so what did he say?"

"Come on in. Richard just got here, and he's looking at the pictures of Lancole's house," Doyle explained.

Richard looked up and greeted Ned. "Welcome to the funhouse, Ned. So what do you think of Lancole's home? Quite a junkyard, isn't it?"

"Fun like hell. It was so bad I almost lost my lunch." Ned looked at the table and saw the axe in the sealed clear plastic evidence bag.

"I'm sure the two of you are eager to hear what we found. Ned, I told Doyle earlier that a truck or SUV had hit the old man, causing only a scrape on his forehead. The impact knocked the old man off his feet. We found a little blood from a head injury on the road, and footprints led to the beach where the killer hit him with the axe. That blow killed him. We found older tire tracks, footprints and some trash on the beach that did not relate to the case. The tire tracks on the road are standard issue, and the shoe prints are common Nike tennis shoes. It appears the old man ran from the road to the beach before being killed. The evidence does not identify who the killer is. However, the axe tells another story; a strange and perplexing tale. We took the axe head off and found old blood in the grooves. We estimate the axe and blood are about one-hundred years old."

"Amazing," Doyle said as he picked up the newspaper article Sandy gave him. His mind was racing with questions.

Richard continued. "I did an analysis of the blood on the axe. We found animal blood and fur plus human blood and hair in the wood under the axe head. We did DNA tests on the blood and the human hair, and I have those results here." He lifted the folder and waved it around as if taunting them. "Are you interested in seeing the findings?"

Ned jumped out of his seat and said, "Hell yes! Finish... this is like a late-night movie you can't stop watching, even though you're scared silly."

"OK," Richard continued. "The blood is a hundred years old, and it is from someone related to Mr. Lancole. Not a father or son, but probably an uncle, aunt or cousin. Doyle, tell me how that happens in a case like this?"

Doyle smiled and handed the newspaper article to Richard. "Read this article from Pigeon's local newspaper. It's dated April 21, 1919. Read it aloud so Ned can hear it too. I haven't shared it with him yet."

Richard read the article while Doyle and Ned listened. Ned looked like he was about to explode. When Richard put the paper down, Ned said, "What's going on here? Is this investigation turning into a paranormal event with ghosts and goblins?"

Doyle laughed and took a cookie. He bit it in half and followed with a sip of coffee. Ned kept watching and wondered why Doyle remained calm. "Well?" Ned asked. "Aren't you going to say something?"

Richard laughed. "Is this newspaper article a joke?"

"No," said Doyle. "Sandy found it this morning, and it's real. Now we know Mr. Lancole's family history. Ned, I'm sure it wasn't a ghost, but someone had the weapon that his grandfather used to kill his uncles and aunts. We have a lot of investigating to do before we'll know who killed Lancole."

The three men continued their discussion. Ned left first; he had to get ready for a date. Richard said he should get going, but he wanted to see the rest of Doyle's home. He seemed impressed with the Irish Pub, but he said if it were his house, it would be a bowling alley instead.

Doyle put Copper on the leash and walked with Richard outside.

"If you have more questions or another mystery, you know where I am," Richard said as he walked down the driveway.

Doyle shook his hand and thanked him again for the report. "We'll solve this mystery, and I'm sure there will be many opportunities to work together."

Richard sat behind the wheel and opened his window. "Have a good Thanksgiving, Doyle."

Copper jumped and put his paws on the door and poked his nose into Richard's car. He licked his face before Doyle could stop him. "Sorry, Richard. That's a first for him, so I guess he likes you."

"Great, I'm glad somebody does."

More News About The Old Man

Copper and Doyle walked down the road. When they reached the Cumming's house, Barry was standing by the road watching them approach. Doyle considered turning around, but Barry gave him useful information about Lancole's neighbors.

"Barry, I wanted to thank you for the information you gave me last night."

"Andrew told me you visited them. He asked if I had told you about their fight; I lied. Sure hope you didn't tell them it was me who ratted them out."

"I said nothing about you, Barry. You'll learn I'm a man of my word."

"So what did they say? Are they the killers? Andrew has a bad temper, and his buddy would lie for him. He was a doctor, but he's been Andrew's friend since they were teenagers." Barry was almost out of breath.

"Barry, that's too many questions. The case is young yet, and we only have a few suspects. When I learn something important, I'll clue you in. Until then... relax... take a deep breath... I'm on the job."

Barry smiled. "The word is you're helping at the Community Center tomorrow. I'd be there too, but my wife won't let me because I have to help her cook our Thanksgiving dinner. The whole family will be here; it's a riot, if you know what I mean."

"Well... enjoy tomorrow, and I'll talk to you later. Now I should get Copper home so he can eat more doggy treats."

Doyle made his way home without running into any other neighbors. When he entered the house, Copper insisted on more Bacon Treats. Copper took one and laid down on his rug to savor it. Doyle checked the time and decided he could call Sandy now.

"Hi, how was your doctor appointment?" he asked.

"It went well, the doctor said I'm in excellent health. I guess it pays to eat well. I've always taken care to eat and drink healthy food. Do you realize wine is great for the heart?"

"I sure do, and if you were here, I'd open a bottle so we could drink to our good health."

Sandy laughed, but she wondered about the investigation and asked, "What did Richard say about the newspaper article? And did he find any interesting evidence?"

"Oh, yes... something very interesting. The axe that killed Mr. Lancole was the same axe that killed his great great-grandmother and his aunts and uncle. The blood and hair DNA matched."

"Oh God! That's beyond strange, Al. Who would want to keep that weapon all these years?"

"I keep asking that question. We discovered someone had broken into Lancole's house several weeks before he died. If the axe was in the house, that might be what the killer stole."

Sandy took a deep breath. "This is exciting, Al. I've always enjoyed reading mysteries, but we're actually involved in a mystery of our own."

"Yes, it's exciting, Sandy. As a police detective, I got overwhelmed at the viciousness of humans. Violence became a part of my life, and each death hurt a little more than the last."

"Doyle, I am sorry. Perhaps I should I stay out of this?"

"No, I didn't tell you that for sympathy. Today, I approach the mystery in a different light. This is a mystery, and we have to find the killer. Sandy, this time around I'm having fun because I enjoy sharing with you. I am thankful that we met."

"I'm thankful too, Al."

The two talked for a few more minutes. Doyle told her he was going down to the Community Center to see what they wanted him to do.

"First, I'm going to The Blue Water Inn for a cheeseburger and fries. If Chad's brother, Will, is working, I might ask him a few questions about the old man," he explained.

"Do you ever just relax, Al?"

"When I'm with you," he replied.

Cooking All Night Long

Doyle left Copper alone in the house while he drove into Caseville for dinner. He walked into the Blue Water Inn, and it took several seconds for his eyes to adjust to the darkness.

"Doyle," a friendly voice called out. "Over here."

Doyle looked around. Chad, Ned, and a woman who Doyle assumed was Ned's girlfriend were sitting in the far corner. Ned asked Doyle to join them, and after Ned insisted, Doyle pulled a chair up to the table.

Will, the bartender, approached the table and asked what Doyle wanted to drink. Doyle said, "I want a cheeseburger with fries, and a diet cola, and get my friends another round of drinks."

When Will left to get the drinks, Ned introduced his girlfriend, Alice Webb; a plain-looking girl in her late twenties. Alice smiled and held her hand out to shake Doyle's hand.

"It's good to meet you, Alice. Ned told me how hard you are working these days. It must be nice to get the holiday off."

"It sure is, Mr. Doyle. Ned told me all about you and the case he's helping you with."

Ned grimaced. "Not everything. I only told her about Mr. Lancole's death."

"That's OK, Ned. I confided in Sandy, too. So, Chad, did your brother say anything else about Mr. Lancole? He was a regular drunk around here; I wonder if he had any run-ins with other patrons."

"I'm not sure, but we can ask him. He goes on a break in a few minutes."

Chad asked his brother to stop at the table during his break. Will said he would after he had a smoke. Chad admonished him. "Stop smoking, damn it. You saw how Dad was in the last days of his life, and you still want to smoke?"

"Drop it Chad, It's my life, not yours," Will replied with resentment in his voice.

When Will returned, he joined their table. "So what information do you need, Mr. Doyle?"

"Did you ever notice Old Man Lancole arguing with another

patron?"

Will mulled the question for a moment. "To be honest, a lot of my customers argued with him. He was the most obnoxious man I knew, and he smelled like pee and garbage. There were several times I got upset and threw him out."

Doyle smiled. "That's understandable, but think back. Did anyone sit and argue with him? We're looking for the person who broke into his house three weeks ago. I realize it's a longshot, but try to remember."

"Yes, about a month ago the old man showed up, and a younger man came in and joined him. They talked, and then the old man yelled at him, and the younger guy got angry and left."

"Did you hear the conversation?"

"Hell no! I stayed as far from that old man as possible. I heard him yelling at someone." Will sat while he reminisced about the event.

Doyle thanked him and asked if the man had come into the bar before or after that run-in.

"Not that I can remember. I would have recognized him if he had been a regular. He had a medium build, height, and so on... you know... an average guy."

"Would you recognize him if you saw him again?" Doyle asked.

Will smiled. "If he were a girl, I'd say yes. I wouldn't recognize him; I don't pay attention to guys."

Doyle felt good about the information he gathered from Will, even if he didn't recognize the man who Lancole argued with. *At least there is another suspect to look into*, he thought.

He left the bar and drove to the Caseville High School. Several cars had parked in the lot. He parked next to one with a bumper sticker reading, *God loves you!*

At the door, Marge Dutwiller, the manager of the Community Center, greeted Doyle.

"Mr. Doyle, I'm so glad you're here. Let me introduce you to our chef, Galen Zeller. She led him to the school cafeteria. "Galen, this is

Mr. Doyle, the man I told you about."

Galen was a thin man in his seventies. Doyle could tell he was a retired chef from the kitchen he managed. "Galen, it's a pleasure to meet you. I see everything is under control, so if there is anything I can help you with, I'm at your service."

"How good of you, Mr. Doyle. Your reputation proceeded your arrival, and it is you who should be the Master Chef here."

Marge laughed, "You two can cut out the niceties. There is work to do, and I quickly tire of small talk."

Doyle and Galen laughed. "She is a tiger under that soft exterior, Galen said."

"So what do you need?" Doyle asked.

Galen began, "Well... the money you donated has helped us this year. Last year we were begging for food, but this year we bought the best. We are short on desserts, though. Our order got lost," he looked at Marge, "and we ended up with only a few pies that the Village Market had left. There isn't another pie for sale in this village. Do you have any ideas, Mr. Doyle?"

"Yes, I can do pies for dessert. How many would you suggest?

"We're expecting over a hundred for this dinner. We serve at noon and end at seven in the evening. Perhaps you can come up with a dozen pies? We can cut them smaller so they go around."

"I can do that. I have a lot of the ingredients at home, but I'll stop for a few things at the market. They're open until eight, if I recall."

"Yes, but how can you bake them? There isn't enough oven space in this kitchen. I thought you could just go to the Walmart in Bad Axe and buy them for us."

"Trust me, Galen, I can bake them in my home. My kitchen is equal to the one here. It won't be a problem, and I'll bring them in the morning."

"Wow! I don't know what to say." Galen said. "Thank you, Mr. Doyle."

"It's just Doyle, Galen."

Doyle asked Marge what time the school doors would be open, and she said they would open at seven a.m. "There will be cooks working on this dinner until midnight and then early in the morning."

Doyle thanked her and said, "I'll have the pies here by nine, if that's OK?"

"Wonderful, I'll see you then," she said.

Doyle ran into the grocery store. The store was busy with last-minute holiday shoppers. Walking down the aisles, he considered what he had in his kitchen and what else he needed to make sixteen pies. Like a madman, he grabbed bags of apples, large cans of pumpkin, several bags of pecans, a few dozen eggs, fresh peaches, several cans of prepared pie filling, and aluminum pie tins. He was sure he had pie pans in the storeroom of his downstairs kitchen, but he couldn't remember how many. If I don't have pie pans, I don't have pies; he thought. Doyle purchased every aluminum pie pan in the store. He even had the manager check the storage room, where they found five extra pans.

He parked the car in the driveway and walked around the house to the Irish Pub door and returned to his car with a metal cart. It took one trip to carry the ingredients back into the kitchen. Copper soon became tired of watching him work behind the stove, so he returned to the upstairs living room where he fell asleep on his rug.

Chapter 17

Ready To Serve

The alarm on Doyle's phone rang, and Copper tried his best to wake him. Doyle turned over when Copper licked the back of his neck and barked.

"What?" Doyle jumped and looked Copper in the eyes. "What do you want?" he repeated.

He realized where he was and what day it was, and with the speed of Superman, he flew into the shower. Copper observed as Doyle shaved and brushed his teeth. "You know you're staying here, don't you?" he asked the bloodhound.

Copper sulked and walked through the doggy door. He remained outside while Doyle dressed and loaded the pies in the Buick.

Before leaving the driveway, Doyle called Sandra and wished her a happy Thanksgiving. Her oldest son invited her to be with his family. "It should be a nice dinner. My daughter-in-law is an excellent cook, and she'll keep my sons busy so they won't have time to argue."

Next, Doyle called his neighbor, Trudy. "Hi," he said. "I'm sitting in the Buick, ready to head to the Community Center Dinner at the high school, but first I want to wish you a happy Thanksgiving," he said.

Trudy looked out her window and saw him parked in the driveway. "Yes, I see you now. Colton and Lacie are picking me up before noon. It will be nice to be with them and their families. I wish you could have come too, but I'm sure you'll have a pleasant time working with the Center. Did you help cook last night?"

Doyle laughed, "Yes, sort of.... I made sixteen pies for the community center; they're in the Buick now. Wish me a safe drive."

"OK. Be careful, and I'll talk to you this evening," Trudy said.

The drive to Caseville proceeded slowly. Doyle's pies sat precariously on all five seats and in the back of the Buick. One sudden stop and he would tragically be covered in delectable desserts. Every corner and stop sign was a landmine. He was lucky because only a few cars were on the roads. He pulled into the high school parking lot and backed up to the door. Every pie reached its destination.

Chef Galen saw him approach and pushed out a metal cart to carry the pies into the kitchen. "Wow, these look wonderful," Galen remarked. "How late were you up cooking?"

"The last pie came out of the oven at one o'clock. I cut corners by doing streusel tops on the fruit pies, and I found a case of nine-inch glass pie pans in my storage room. I used them and then the throwaway aluminum pans I purchased last night. Everything worked out well."

Inside, Doyle helped cut pies and placed slices on small paper dessert plates. Chef Galen then had him help carve the turkeys. Dinner was ready at eleven-thirty, so the volunteers gathered in the kitchen to visit. The variety of people who gave up their family gathering so they could serve those in need impressed Doyle. They included business people, teachers, doctors, lawyers, and laborers.

Several of the workers asked Doyle about the death of Mr. Lancole, but Doyle resisted saying anything. He acknowledged he had worked on the case, but it ended there. At noon, the doors opened and a mass of guests walked through the line. The workers served them a plate, asking each guest which items and how much they wanted. It pleased Doyle that almost everyone chose his pies over the store-bought varieties.

At three o'clock, only a few guests still passed through the line.

Galen said there wouldn't be many more until dinnertime, around five p.m. Doyle thought about Copper and announced that he had to go out for a short while.

"I'll be back before the rush at five," he said.

At home, Copper was still in his doggy room, sulking. When he saw Doyle, his tail sped into overdrive, and he joined him in the kitchen. Doyle shook his paw and hugged him. "I'm sorry you had to stay home, but you wouldn't have liked all the people."

Doyle reached into his pocket and pulled out a plastic bag filled with dark turkey meat. Copper went mad and chomped the meat down like it was Bacon Treats. "Tastes good, doesn't it?" Doyle asked. While Copper finished his treat, Doyle made a cup of coffee and checked his messages. He had over an hour before he needed to return to the Community Center, so he sifted through the rest of Mr. Lancole's mail.

One letter that intrigued him was from a detective agency in Westland, Michigan. The letter read: *'This is to inform you, Mr. Lancole, that we have found the person you were looking for. Please call my office, and I will give you her address, but I will not give you the information until you pay the bill in full. P.S. I only accept cash.'* The letter was dated seven months earlier, and Doyle could tell Lancole read it many times, because there were finger marks, a variety of stains, and the paper was limp from being folded and unfolded. There was an invoice enclosed with a balance due of $3,250.00, for time and expenses.

As he sat at the counter, he considered the options for the future of the investigation and concluded that he and Ned must go to Detroit. There are three people needing to be spoken to: the lawyer, the nephew, and now the detective agency all require looking into. A web of clues is forming, and he hopes to catch the killer soon.

Copper watched his every move and put his paws up on the counter. He smelled the letter and barked. "Yes, Copper, it's the old man's, and this letter might lead us to a killer. I sure wish you could talk because it seems like you might know who the killer is." Copper barked again and walked to his water dish, which was dry. "Or perhaps you just want more water."

Doyle returned to the high school. There were almost as many guests attending the evening Thanksgiving meal as did the noon meal. Doyle kept seeing the pies disappear, and he wondered if he had made too few.

Galen watched as the servers placed Doyle's last pie onto dessert plates. "That's the last one, but I don't see anymore guests lining up, so we may be OK. I still have the two pies I saved for the crew. After we serve our last meal, we get to eat.

"I was wondering why none of the volunteers were eating. What would we do if the food was all gone?" Doyle asked.

"Be thankful that we can go home and cook a meal for ourselves. Many of the people here either don't have a home, or enough money to pay for food. Our food pantry distributes food every day. And the lines keep getting longer. The rich are getting richer, but too many people are being left behind."

"Amen, Galen. I was wondering where you worked as a chef?" Doyle asked.

"I was a culinary teacher in Detroit for twenty-five years. My son is the principal at Lake Community School in Pigeon. I'm retired now, but I still love to cook and serve my community."

"That's an admirable goal. I hope I can do the same. My family was from this area, but as you know I grew up in Detroit's Greektown community."

"Yes, I ate there when your mother owned the restaurant and then a few years ago when you were there. Why did you quit after becoming so successful?"

"My doctor insisted I slow down and enjoy life, but I can assure you, I may enjoy life, but I have no intention of slowing down."

Galen laughed. "Wonderful attitude. Let's grab a plate and join the rest of the volunteers for Thanksgiving dinner. We have much to be thankful for today. I saved two wonderful pecan pies you made.

It is a custard, correct?"

"Yes, it's my favorite. Sweet, but not sticky sweet."

After dinner, a group of teens helped clean the kitchen. They were doing this as a community project. Doyle and the other adult volunteers headed home at eight o'clock. Doyle put his pie pans in the back of the Buick and sat for a moment.

Sitting in the Buick, Doyle watched an elderly couple walking to their vehicle. *They must be in their eighties. I hope they enjoyed the meal;* he thought. She was holding onto his left arm for support, and he had a cane in his right hand. He opened the car door and helped her into the seat. With care, he bent down and kissed her. The love that Doyle shared today touched his heart in ways he never imagined. His thoughts went to Sandy, Trudy, and Copper, and he was thankful. He wiped the tears away and drove home.

Planning for the weekend

Copper met Doyle at the door with his leash laying on the floor in front of him. Doyle frowned and said, "Really? No... it's too late for a walk, and I'm too tired. Let's sit and spend an evening in front of the television."

Copper wasn't happy when Doyle put the leash on the counter, hung up his coat and hat, and made his way to the leather chair. The bloodhound joined him and put his paws on his lap. Doyle spent a few minutes scratching Copper's ears while he also checked messages on his cell phone.

"Copper, I got a message from Sandy. Please get down; I need to call her back." The message was cryptic and suggested she had something important to tell him. His mind was racing, and he wondered if she wanted to break off their relationship.

Long-term relationships have always been difficult for Doyle. Trudy once told him he shouldn't allow insecurity to rule his life. "You can't insulate yourself from people and expect to find someone to share your life with," she would say. "Open your heart and accept that you might get hurt. Don't dwell on your pain; brush it off and keep an open heart."

He gathered his courage and called Sandy back. When she answered he said, "I got your message, and it sounded ominous... what's the problem?"

"Problem? What are you talking about?" she asked.

"Nothing... I guess. How was your Thanksgiving?"

"Very nice, but I ate too much. Did the dinner at the high school go well?" she asked.

"Wonderful. Have you met Galen Zeller? He was the head cook and ran the kitchen."

"Yes, I met him a few times, but I've never talked to him. He always seemed like a giving person, a religious man."

"That was also my opinion. He liked my pies, so he has good taste. Now what was your message about? You piqued my curiosity."

"My sister and her husband's sister asked me to join them for a girls' weekend out. They want to attend two craft shows tomorrow and then spend the rest of the weekend at Soaring Eagle Casino in Mount Pleasant."

Doyle immediately felt relieved. "Are you going?"

"Yes, they convinced me to go. I don't like to gamble, but a weekend with the girls will be fun. The two of them are crazy when they get away from their husbands, and I always enjoy their company. I would prefer to be with you, but I'm sure you'll understand."

Copper put his paws on Doyle's lap to comfort him and begged to have his ears scratched more. Doyle obliged as he continued his conversation with Sandy. "It sounds like fun. When will you be returning?"

"That's the other thing I wanted to talk about. I will be back early Sunday afternoon, and I want you to come over at five p.m. for dinner. This time I'll cook for you."

"I would love to. Is there anything you want me to bring?" he asked.

"Yes... bring a bottle of the wine you had at your party," she suggested. "Also, please bring more cookies. I love your cookies, Doyle."

"Wine and cookies... it will be my pleasure."

"Be sure to bring Copper, too. It's about time he met my cat, Casey."

Doyle laughed, "That should be an adventure. Do you suggest bringing a first aid kit?"

Sandy said she had one, so he didn't have to bring his. "I don't expect trouble... just warn Copper to watch his manners and bring some Bacon Treats as a bribe."

Sandy asked if there was anything new in the investigation and Doyle discussed his plans to call and visit the Westland detective, Lancole's lawyer, and his nephew in Detroit. "We need to get to the root of this case, so Ned and I will drive down next week, Wednesday or Thursday."

"I'll keep looking for information at the museum, but I doubt there is anything else. It looked like Mrs. Lancole took her kids and left the county. I understand her family was from out of state, but I'm not sure."

Doyle and Sandy continued talking until Sandy suggested she had to get her suitcase packed. "We're leaving early in the morning. You know how Black Friday can be, and my sister is eager to get out as early as possible."

Doyle laughed, "OK, Sandy. Have fun and say hello to the girls."

"Bye, and have a good weekend, Al."

After his talk with Sandy, Doyle called Trudy to see how her Thanksgiving with Colton and his family went.

"I had so much fun, Doyle. I enjoyed being with people who appreciate me, and Colton's family made me feel at home. We laughed through dinner, and Colton's mom even let me help in the kitchen," she explained. "Did the dinner at the school go well?" she asked.

"Yes, we served a lot of guests, and everyone enjoyed the meal. I found it amazing how many people took advantage of the dinner, especially senior citizens. I expected a younger crowd, but the seniors outnumbered the youngsters by two to one."

"That's because this area has more retired people than youngsters. Most young families leave the area to find work, and the seniors come back to Huron County to retire, just like you and I did."

Trudy asked about Mr. Lancole, and Doyle explained how the investigation was going. The news about the murder weapon surprised Trudy. She said, "By using that weapon, the killer showed the crime was personal. It's as if he were trying to complete what the grandfather had started in 1919. Doyle, find out where that axe has been all these years. Perhaps the old man had it, but if he did, he had a fixation on his family's secret, and perhaps that's what drove him to drink and never marry."

Doyle considered what Trudy said. As a psychiatrist, he trusted her observations, and her insight ran through his mind all evening. *Where has the axe been all these years*? He asked himself.

Doyle and Copper spent the balance of the evening watching television. He caught up on the Detroit Lions football game and then he switched the television to The Animal Channel and watched a dog show, which Copper enjoyed.

Chapter 18

Summonsed By The Sheriff

Doyle's Black Friday was to be a quiet day at home with Copper. Shopping is not his favorite activity, and shopping while hundreds of people are in pursuit of the latest deals sounds horrid to him.

After eating breakfast, he received an urgent call from Ned. "Doyle, the sheriff has summoned us to his office. The newspapers are all over him about Lancole's death, and he said he needs an answer today... *Not tomorrow! TODAY.*"

"What time is the meeting?"

"I am standing outside his office now. Can you be here in fifteen minutes?"

"No! I need to shower and shave. Tell him I'll be there in half an hour, but he shouldn't expect too much. It's been less than four days since Copper found the old man's body. What does he expect? A miracle?"

"Yes, he wants a miracle," Ned said. "I'll see you when you get here, but please hurry. You realize the sheriff gets on my nerves, don't you?"

"I'll hurry."

Before leaving for Bad Axe, Doyle went into his Irish pub and filled a takeout box with a dozen cookies. He made a mental note to bake more cookies before Sunday's dinner with Sandy. He told Copper he would be back soon and handed him a Bacon Treat.

Copper didn't eat the treat; instead, he watched Doyle drive out of the garage and down the street. Then he returned to the kitchen, where he savored the treat.

Doyle passed the Walmart and shuddered at the number of cars in the parking lot. He couldn't imagine any sale being worth the time and effort it would take to make his way through that crowd.

Ned was standing outside the courthouse waiting for Doyle. He looked stressed and was pacing back and forth. Doyle walked up to him and put his arm over his shoulder. "Ned, learn to relax. The sheriff is just a man... a loud and oversized man, but he's still a man. I am sure his bark is worse than his bite."

"It is, but he barks too loudly and too often."

Doyle laughed and said, "Come on, let's bark back at the sheriff. Perhaps we can make him nervous. I brought him cookies to soften his tone."

When Sheriff McNabb saw Doyle at his door, he yelled, "About time, Doyle. Why are you taking so long to find that old man's killer? Why, I could have solved this murder days ago."

"Yes, you could have. But then, you would have made the wrong decision. Rushing a case often results in reaching the wrong conclusion. You rushed to your conclusion that Jenny Stillmore committed suicide in the hot tub a few weeks ago, and now you're looking for her killer. How did that decision make you look?"

"Yes, perhaps you're correct. My problem today it but that pesky reporter, Rodney Billings. He keeps badgering me to tell him what's going on. Reporters make me nervous, and he always has his tape recorder on, and he pushes it into my face. One of these days I will snap and break his skinny neck."

Ned laughed at the thought of the sheriff being nervous, and McNabb didn't appreciate it. "Don't laugh, Ned. Someday you might have to answer to the newspapers. If I say the wrong thing, then the headlines will tear me apart. I have to get elected to this office, so I can't screw up too many times."

Doyle winked at Ned, who appreciated how he handled the Sheriff. "Now let me tell you where we are in this investigation and offer you homemade chocolate chip cookies." Doyle handed the white takeout box of cookies to the sheriff. He opened the lid, and a huge smile ran across his face. "Thank you! These cookies look good. Perhaps you can also tell me what to say to the reporter?"

Doyle told the sheriff what they had uncovered so far, including the axe from the 1919 murders that the killer used to kill Mr. Lancole.

The sheriff yelled for someone to bring him another cup of coffee, and he told Doyle to keep talking. "This is becoming a strange case. Who do you suspect besides the next-door neighbors?"

"I don't think they killed him. Their alibis are flimsy, but why would they kill the old man? He was an old and unhealthy drunk living in a germ infested rat hole. I'm looking at the Nephew in Detroit. I don't know what the old man's will says, but he could be the type who would leave all his money to his cat. The Nephew is Lancole's only relative, but then there's the girl the detective in Westland found. We are also looking for the man who argued with the old man in the Blue Water Inn about a month before he died. I want to find him if I can."

The sheriff sighed. "So there's nothing to tell the reporter?"

Doyle leaned in toward McNabb. "You tell we are digging deep into this case and when we find the killer, he will be the first to know."

"Ok. So I have bullcrap to tell him. That works fine for me. I was a farm boy before I became the sheriff; I can spread manure. Now... what's your next move?"

"We're going to Detroit to speak with the nephew, the lawyer, and the detective. If we find the girl, we can talk to her too."

Ned looked surprised since Doyle had never told him the plan. "Detroit? When do we go there?" he asked.

"I'll make calls this afternoon to schedule meetings for next Wednesday or Thursday. So try to keep your schedule open. I'll drive down in my Buick."

"Sounds good," replied Ned. The prospect of the trip excited him.

"I'll stay on my regular schedule for the next few days." Ned said. "There was a threat to Colton's life, so we've been looking out for him."

"Is he in danger?" asked Doyle.

"I don't think so, but we're still looking for Jenny and Luke's killers. It's been a busy month in Huron County, so I would imagine that's why McNabb is in such a foul mood."

Doyle watched Ned get into his patrol car. He considered the danger Colton could be in and thought about how fast life changes. He said a brief prayer for his young friend and headed back to Sand Point.

Copper Is Angry

When Doyle pulled into the driveway, he noticed the garage door was open; he remembered closing it. He parked in the driveway and walked past Copper's room. Since he didn't see Copper, he assumed he was on his rug sleeping.

Doyle walked up to the door and froze. Someone broke the lock, and the door was ajar. Doyle went back to the Buick and grabbed a pair of rubber gloves from the glove box. He heard Copper barking, so he knew the bloodhound was alive. Before entering the house, he called 911 to report the incident.

"This is Albert Doyle, from Sand Point. Someone broke into my home this morning. I was with Deputy Ned Wooddell earlier this morning; is he still in Bad Axe?"

"I understand... we all are busy today. Can someone come out now? I didn't enter the house yet; however, I need to go in because my dog is still inside."

"Yes, the state police would be fine... Yes, fifteen minutes is OK." Doyle ended the call and decided Copper's rescue couldn't wait so he stood behind the open door and called; "Copper, come here... come here boy... it's me, not a burglar."

Copper came running to the door and pushed it open with his nose. "Are you OK? I bet you scared them away, didn't you?" Copper's tail was wagging at full force, and he kept as close to Doyle's leg as he could get. Doyle walked back to the garage and found a spare leash, which he connected to Copper's collar.

It took the state police ten minutes to respond to Doyle's call. The blue patrol car drove into the driveway, and Trooper Steve Lithowski got out and meandered to where Doyle and Copper were sitting on the porch steps.

"Isn't this interesting? The great Mr. Doyle had to call 911?" Steve chided.

In a mocking falsetto voice, Doyle said, "Kind officer... someone broke into my house and scared my little doggy."

"OK. I'm sorry for the comment, Doyle. I was just surprised when I got the call."

"Thank you. When I got home, the garage door was open, and someone had broken the door lock. I don't think they got into the house, but I haven't gone in yet because I felt it would be better to have the police check the door for prints first."

"Good choice. Most people just rush in and rummage through their things trying to see what the robbers took," Steve said as he walked back to his car for a fingerprint kit. "I'll check for prints first."

Steve reported that there were no prints on the door handle or door. "He must have worn cotton gloves, or they wiped the prints clean."

Doyle was standing behind Steve when he pushed the door open. There was no sign of an intruder inside, except for the trashed rug in front of the door. Doyle laughed, and Steve asked, "What's so funny?"

"Look at Copper." The bloodhound was hiding behind Doyle's legs, peeking into the doorway.

"Bloodhounds are not the best guard dogs," Doyle said. "He must have terrified the intruder because it looks like someone walked in, saw Copper and tried to run. He might have fallen, and I wouldn't put it past Copper to jump on his backside. Doesn't look like he bit him... no visible blood."

"I'll make a report so you can get the insurance to fix your door. Perhaps you should call Colton and Seth's new company for a security system," said Trooper Steve. "There have been a lot of positive reports or *reviews* for their business."

"It was my understanding you didn't like Colton?" Doyle questioned.

"Who said that?"

"Colton and Seth. They say you project a poor attitude regarding teenagers."

"I do. At least I make them think I do. I like to give them a hard time... it's just my way of dealing with teens."

"There are better ways to deal with them. Are you involved in Colton's investigation? I heard the police are handling the search for Jenny and her boyfriend's killer."

"I helped with the case. We're looking at two suspects and should have one guy behind bars soon. This weekend I'm shadowing Colton while he does his paper route. You know, keep him safe." Steve handed Doyle a copy of his report and said, "Take pictures of the damage and send a copy of this with them to your insurance agent. They can get an official copy from the Caro State Police office."

"Great. Thank you, Steve; it was a pleasure working with you."

Steve walked to his patrol car. He yelled back to Doyle, "Call me if you ever need help again, Doyle."

After making sure the intruder didn't steal something, Doyle called Richard Waters, the contractor. Richard agreed to fix his door later that day. "I have an identical door in stock, so it won't take long to swap them," he told Doyle.

Doyle's second call was to Seth Seamoore, Colton's partner in the security company. When Doyle told Seth about the break-in, it surprised him. "It's strange that someone would do that in the middle of the day. I wonder if it has anything to do with Colton. Someone painted graffiti on his Jeep while he and Lacie were shopping at Walmart today. They believe he's the guy who killed Jenny. Maybe he knows you were helping Colton."

Doyle thought for a moment. "That never crossed my mind. I should let Ned know about the connection. Anyway, can you put a system in yet today or tomorrow?"

Seth said he would talk to Jim Owens, the man who does his installations. I'm sure he can fit you in. Will you be around all afternoon?" Seth asked.

"Yes, I have calls to make, but I should be here," Doyle said. "Seth, I want you to know Trooper Steve gave you and Colton a high recommendation. I don't think he's as bad as he wants you to think he is."

"I know; he just likes to appear tough."

"That's what he told me, too. He's one odd Polish trooper, isn't he?" Doyle said with a chuckle. "Are you convinced Colton will be OK?"

Seth sighed, "I hope so. I'm going with him on his route as often as I can, and I take my baseball bat for protection. The police are shadowing him too."

"That's what Ned and Trooper Steve told me. Anyway, if you can install a security system with all the bells and whistles, you will make me happy."

Copper watched Doyle put the phone down. He seemed to understand what the conversations had been about because he relaxed.

"There won't be another intruder, Copper." Doyle reached down and petted his friend. Copper begged for a treat, and when he got two treats, images of the almighty Bacon Treat god replaced his memory of the break-in.

Security At Last.

Doyle made a quick salad with sliced chicken breast for lunch. He wanted a beer or a glass of wine, but decided on coffee instead. *I don't want to become a drunk like Old Man Lancole... do I?*

"Copper, do you want a piece of chicken breast?"

Before Copper could answer, Mr. Waters was at the broken door, removing it from its hinges. Copper barked at him and then ran to greet him with his tail wagging.

Doyle laughed, "Richard, my bloodhound loves you."

"That's nice, just don't let him get out or he'll be chasing deer all afternoon."

Doyle realized Richard was correct, so he grabbed Copper to put his leash on his collar. "Stay Copper."

When Richard had the new door hung, he opened a box with a new lockset. "We were lucky. I had the same door and locks we used before. This won't take long," Richard said as he worked.

"Thanks for the quick service. Did anyone else order a doggy room?"

"It's on my website, and I got a ton of comments. I would say next spring people will call to order one. How does Copper like his room?"

"It took a lot of coaxing to get him to use it, but now he loves it," Doyle said.

Just as the contractor drove out of the driveway, a van with a large security logo drove up. The driver of the van approached Doyle, who was sitting with Copper on the steps.

"Good afternoon, Seth called me and asked if I could do a rush job. This is the correct address, isn't it?"

"It sure is, and your name is Jim Owens?"

"Yes, Sir." Jim pulled a business card with his photo from his shirt pocket and handed it to Doyle. "I understand you had a break-in this morning?"

"Yes, while I was in Bad Axe, at the police station of all places."

Jim smiled. "That's a bummer. We've been getting a lot of work these days. Seth said you wanted all the bells and whistles. Let me walk through the house, and I'll give you a plan of action. I can get started today, and if I don't get done, I'll finish in the morning."

Doyle showed Jim the entire house and garage. Jim liked the Irish pub and suggested a better door and lock for that entrance. "You want to foil the teenagers looking to steal alcohol. I have a catalogue of commercial style security doors, and we have two styles in stock."

While Jim was installing the security system, Doyle finished his lunch. Copper enjoyed the chicken breast, and Doyle thought about the Bacon Treats. He grabbed the bag and studied the ingredients. *Damn*, he thought. *I'd never eat this, so why am I letting my dog get addicted to it?*

He studied dog nutrition requirements on the internet and resolved to make his own. *I know he likes smoked fish and chicken breast, so perhaps I can make all natural treats. It would be nice if they stopped his drooling, too.* Doyle laughed out loud, and Copper wanted to know what was funny. He looked around but couldn't see anything, so he concluded Doyle needed fresh air. The bloodhound brought him the leash and suggested a long walk.

Doyle told Jim to lock the front door when he left, in case he and Copper were still out.

"No problem, Mr. Doyle. Have an enjoyable walk."

Chapter 19

Return To The Scene Of The Crime

Copper and Doyle walked to the beach. It was a beautiful November day; the sky was clear, and even though it was almost freezing, the warm sun was comforting. Copper wanted to return to where he had found Old Man Lancole. At first Doyle resisted, then he decided it was time.

"OK, Copper, we can go there." The two walked along the beach, staying just inches from the lapping waters of Lake Huron. Copper kept watching the seagulls, and several times he pulled the leash, showing Doyle he wanted to chase them. Doyle resisted, and soon they were at the spot. The waves from yesterday's storm had removed all traces of the murder, but Copper could still smell something.

After covering the beach, he wanted to go to the road. His nose followed the exact path the killer used to reach the beach. At the road, Copper smelled the remaining blood and released a mournful howl.

"Yes, it's sad, Copper. I'll catch the killer, and this will all be over soon."

Doyle returned to the beach. He hadn't walked the length of Sand Point's famous beach yet and figured this was an excellent opportunity. When they reached Mr. Lancole's home, he didn't recognize it. It looked different from the waterside as all cottages do.

"Look, Copper. The stinky house you wouldn't go into. Want to see it?"

Copper pulled the leash toward the house, giving Doyle his answer. When they reached the home, it surprised Doyle to see that the grass had been mowed again and someone had trimmed the shrubs. There was a pile of grass and branches at the edge of the property. As he approached the house, he saw Arthur Wilcone, the next-door neighbor, with pruning shears.

"What the hell are you doing, Arthur? Didn't you see the police tape telling everyone not to cross it?"

"Yes, but I took it down. It made the place look awful, and since Lancole is dead, he can't complain if I clean this mess up, can he?"

"Arthur, do you want me to arrest you for trespassing?"

"You can't do that, can you?" Arthur got nervous and looked like he wanted to run.

"Yes, I can. Did you go into the house?" Doyle asked.

"No, I didn't go in. I just cleaned the yard."

"Go home and don't leave the area until I'm finished with my investigation," Doyle told him.

"So, who do you think killed him?"

"I can't and I won't say, but we will find the killer soon."

"I hope so. See if you can arrange the sale of this property. I want to buy it before Jerry Stratman does. Perhaps we could split the land between us... that would be nice. Find out what the new owner intends to do, OK?"

Doyle didn't answer the question. He hurried Arthur off the property and walked around the house. The state police had posted the front door with a notice and added a chain and lock.

Looks like Trooper Steve is on the ball, Doyle thought.

Doyle and Copper followed the street back home. As they walked past Barry's house, he noticed Barry outside and tried to hurry past. No luck... Barry rushed to the street and asked questions, faster than Doyle could answer.

"Did you catch the killers? It wasn't Arthur or Jerry, was it? I didn't think so. They get a little crazy with the old man, but they aren't kill-ers. So who did it?"

Barry, I can't say yet. We're still checking all the suspects. Where were you the night of the killing?"

"ME? You don't suspect me, do you? I couldn't kill a mouse, let alone a man."

Doyle was laughing, and Barry smiled. "Too many questions?"

"Barry, we're looking into all the leads. Did you ever see the old man argue with anyone at the Blue Water Inn?"

"No, but I'll ask Barbara. She keeps tabs on everything and every-one. You want me to stop down at your place when I find out?"

"That won't be necessary," Doyle said as he handed Barry a busi-ness card. "Just call me."

Doyle hurried away, pulling Copper behind him. Soon the two were in unison, with Copper finding a scent to follow and then becom-ing disappointed when Doyle refused to follow him. They reached home as Jim Owens was finishing up the new security system.

"All ready to stop the robbers in their tracks?" asked Doyle.

"Yes, it is. I put cameras on all the doors with lights that come on if someone approaches the home. I also put a camera and light in your dog's fenced-in room." Jim said. "You have a cell phone, don't you?" Jim asked.

"Yes." Doyle reached into his pocket and pulled out his phone.

Jim took the phone and said, "Let me set this up so you can monitor people coming onto your property. I can add the app to your computer and laptop if you like."

"Do you have time to do all three?"

"Sure do. Let's do it now," suggested Jim.

In a few minutes, Doyle was watching all the cameras on his smart television, phone, computer, and laptop. Jim smiled as he watched the expression on his customer's face.

"Jim, I'm impressed with you and your service. Tell Seth and Colton they have another satisfied customer," Doyle said.

"Great to hear. We're trying to build this business on customer satisfaction, and so far it's growing by leaps and bounds."

"Good to hear. How do I pay you?"

"I'll have Colton's mom, Cyndi, email the invoice. You can set up the monthly charges for automatic payment, or we can bill them. Just follow the info on the invoice."

The two men shook hands, and Doyle walked out with Jim. As Jim left, Doyle noticed Copper watching them in his fenced in area. Doyle took a plastic bag from the garage and went into the room. In a few minutes he had cleaned up the area and was inside the kitchen again, with Copper begging for another treat.

"Later, Copper. You will get fat and sick from eating those treats."

Copper sulked and went down the steps and into the Irish Pub. Doyle wondered if the bloodhound planned on cooking his own treats, or perhaps he wanted to watch the seagulls on the beach. *Must be the seagulls,* he concluded.

Doyle checked the time and realized he needed to make his planned calls to Detroit now, or wait until Monday. He found the letter from the Westland Detective Agency and rang the number.

The soft voice of a woman answered, "Westland Investigations, how can I help you?"

"Hello, this is Homicide Detective Albert Doyle, from Bad Axe calling. Could I speak to Robert?"

"Hey, Bob, it's for you," the woman yelled. "He'll be right with you," she said in a soft voice again.

"Bob here, what do you need?"

Doyle explained who he was and why he was calling. When he asked for the name and address of the woman Mr. Lancole hired him to find, Bob said, "Hell no! The old man owes me over three grand for that investigation."

"Bob, like I told you, Mr. Lancole is dead. Contact his lawyer for payment, but I need the name for my investigation into his murder,"

Doyle argued.

"NO! If you want the name, you come down here with cash or a court order. Cash will be easier for both of us." Bob slammed the phone down, and Doyle sat listening to silence.

Well, that went well, didn't it? Doyle thought.

Next, Doyle called Lancole's lawyer, Stratford and Son's. There wasn't a first name for either the father or son, so he would ask for the father. *He probably knows more about Old Man Lancole*, he decided.

The phone rang, and an elderly male voice said, "Steven Straford here, how can I help you?"

"Mr. Stratford, I'm Homicide Detective Albert Doyle, and I am investigating the death of your client, Mr. Harold Lancole, here in Sand Point."

"Oh yes, I've been expecting a call from someone on this. Let me get a cup of coffee, and we can talk." The phone went silent for a few minutes. Enough time for both Doyle and Mr. Stratford to get coffee.

"I'm back. I found out about Harold's death two days ago, so I expected someone from Huron County to call. Aren't you the cook who used to be a Detroit police officer?"

"Yes, should I know you?" Doyle asked.

"My former partner was your lawyer. What a coincidence... small world, isn't it? What are you doing investigating my client's death?"

"Long story," Doyle said. "I retired from this job, and yes, it's a fascinating coincidence. How is Jackson? I haven't heard from him in years."

"Oh, my... he died four years ago in a car accident. I got his wife a million dollar settlement. A wonderful lawsuit, lots of money. Now why did I call you?" Mr. Stratford asked.

"I called you, Steven... about Mr. Lancole."

"Oh, yes. Did you know Harold is dead? He died a few days ago."

"Mr. Stratford, do you have his most recent will? We need to find out who killed him."

"Yes, I have Harold's will. When would you like to come down and see it? I'm always here. I live in the back room now." Steven cleared his throat and continued, "I will also have the people named in Lancole's will attend the reading. You can be like that Hercule Poirot character on PBS. I think it was an Agatha Christie mystery. He's funny. Do you look like him, Mr. Doyle? I think he's French... no... Belgian, and he walks funny, but he always solves the crime."

"What day should I come to your office?" asked Doyle. He tried not to laugh, but it was getting difficult.

"Thursday at one o'clock, but you didn't answer my question, Mr. Doyle. Do you look like Hercule Poirot?"

"No, Steven. I have gray hair, I don't have a mustache, and I don't walk funny, but I too always solve the crime."

"Oh... that's wonderful. I'm eager to meet you."

"Be sure to write the appointment down, Steven."

"Why? I have a wonderful memory; I won't forget," Steven said with a chuckle in his voice.

Can't Wait Until Sunday

Doyle spent part of the evening talking to his sister, Sam. She had left a message, and he returned the call after dinner. The two caught up on family and health issues.

Sam wasn't surprised that her brother was a homicide detective again. "It's what you wanted to be since you were in grade school. I remember how you would read those true crime magazines and pretend you were a police officer like Dad, walking his beat."

"Yes, I remember every mystery I uncovered in Greektown. I'd watch the customers in Mom's restaurant and pick out the crime bosses. Little did I know who was who; I would just make it up as I went along. When I was fourteen, I told Mom the mayor was a drug dealer because he looked like a mobster. Like I knew what a mobster looked like. He got word of what I said, and Mom spanked me hard. Dad just laughed and said the mayor was a crook, but not a crime boss."

Doyle suggested Sam and her daughter drive up for a visit, and Sam said she would talk to Laurie to set a time. "Your niece has a role in a production at the Detroit Repertory Theater this winter, so we have to work around her schedule. Perhaps you and your new girlfriend can come down for the show. I'll ask Laurie to get tickets, if you like."

"That would be nice. In fact, I might ask some of Sandy's friends, who are in a local theater group, to come with us. We could rent a bus and make it a theater party."

"Oh, wouldn't that be fun? We can talk about it after Christmas. The production dates are in late January, so we have time to make plans."

Saturday morning, Copper was up early and Doyle slept in late, which didn't go well with Copper, who was eager for his walk on the beach. He watched several deer meandering in the yard during the sunrise and wanted to follow them. When Doyle awoke, he had an urge to call Sandy, but knew he shouldn't. She left for the weekend, and if she wanted to talk, she would call him.

With no plans for the day, Doyle called Ned to see how Colton was doing. Ned had nothing new to report, but he wondered about the meeting in Detroit.

"We have to be at the lawyer's office at one o'clock, Thursday. The lawyer is a little senile, but he has Lancole's will and plans on reading it at the meeting. He wouldn't tell me what is in it, so we have to wait. I need you to do something for me."

"Sure, what do you need?" said Ned.

"We have to get a court order for the name of the woman the detective agency found for Mr. Lancole. He won't give it to us without a court order, or cash, and I will not pay for information."

Doyle emailed the address and name of the detective agency so

Ned could request the court order. "I should have this before the day is over. The judge usually approves these," Ned said.

"Good. We can drive down early Thursday morning and get the girl's name, and then we'll go to the lawyer to learn about Lancole's will. Perhaps the lawyer will know something about this mystery girl."

"Sounds good, but I have to get going. I only have a half day, so I better go see the judge, and then I'm off to see my girlfriend. We're shopping for Christmas today."

"Have fun. I'll call you Monday."

After lunch, Doyle's phone rang. It was an unknown number, but he answered.

"Mr. Doyle?" The man asked in a firm voice.

"Yes, how can I help you?"

"My name is Kenneth Lancole Jr., Harold Lancole's nephew. The police in Bad Axe told me you would let me into my uncle's home in Sand Point."

The call didn't surprise Doyle, because he figured the nephew would show up, but he expected a warning.

"Where are you now?" Doyle asked.

"I'm parked in the driveway of my uncle's home."

"I'll be down in fifteen minutes," Doyle advised. He called Copper and put the leash on his collar. "We're going to the stinky house again. I want you to smell the old man's nephew. If he's the killer, bark two times," Doyle half joked.

Copper listened as if understanding the request. Doyle drove to the Lancole home and parked along the street. When he walked back to the house, he saw a huge white Cadillac Escalade and a slim man in his late 40s standing next to it.

Doyle and Copper approached the man. Copper's tail was wagging, and he didn't bark. In fact, he acted like he had found his long lost best friend.

"Mr. Lancole, I'm Albert Doyle, homicide detective for Huron

County. I want to extend my condolences on the death of your uncle."

"We expected it. My uncle was a drunk and never took care of himself. The total opposite of my dad, who was younger and did everything he could to stay healthy. Dad died ten years ago, while my crazy uncle never got sick a day in his life. It's not fair, but that's the way it goes."

"I have to tell you something, Kenneth. I don't have the key to the lock. The state police put the lock on, and I don't know who has a key. It might be at the Caro station, or the sheriff may have it."

"Just tell me, does the house still have a mountain of garbage in it?" asked Kenneth.

"Yes, it's bad. I can show you the photographs we took if you like. But it was so bad my assistant almost lost his cookies from the smell, and my dog won't go in."

Copper betrayed what Doyle said by putting his nose to the door, begging to get into the house.

"I have a few questions regarding your uncle's death. I hope you don't mind, but we are still looking for his killer. Did you know about the 1919 killings south of Bay Port? Your great grandfather killed three of his children and his mother."

"Yes, Dad told me all about the tragic event. I believe my uncle avoided getting married because of those killings. He told Dad that his grandfather's sickness was in his genes. Dad wasn't like that; he talked about it, understanding that his grandpa had schizophrenia and couldn't help himself."

Kenneth Jr. was forthcoming, and Doyle didn't believe he had a killer instinct, but he couldn't be sure, so he asked; "Where were you on the night of the killing?"

"I was wondering when you would get around to that question. My wife and I were in Paris with our two daughters. We flew to Paris two weeks prior and returned two days ago. We like to visit Paris twice a year. My wife and daughters enjoy buying clothing there. Fall and spring... it's hell having money and three women in the family," Kenneth said with a smirk.

"And they will vouch for you?"

"Yes, but I bought the airline ticket stub and the hotel receipt. Here is a list of numbers you can call in Paris. They will vouch for us."

"You've come well prepared. The other question I have is regarding your uncle's last will. Do you know to whom he left his estate?"

Kenneth pulled another piece of paper out of his suit pocket. "Yes, here is a copy of the will. It's dated two years ago, and I'm named as the only beneficiary. I don't need the money, but I can always find something to do with it. Perhaps another trip to Paris for the wife, or another home on some exotic island."

"You could move here and fix up your uncle's house," Doyle suggested.

"Never! This area was unkind to my family in the past, and I have no intention of letting this house stand. I plan on having it taken to the nearest dump and buried, like the rest of my father's family."

"I understand. Come on, Copper, we can go home now. Mr. Lancole, I'll be seeing you Thursday at the lawyer's office," Doyle said.

"Yes, he called yesterday evening. I guess he wants to make the will official."

Doyle and Copper walked to the street and returned home. "Did you like him, Copper?" Doyle asked. Copper didn't say, but in Doyle's mind, he wasn't the killer; however, he concluded the man was a pompous ass. He didn't know him well enough to be sure, but if first impressions matter, he was!

Chapter 20

Copper and Casey Meet

Doyle spent Sunday reading the newspaper and baking cookies for his date with Sandy. He also baked two batches of natural dog treats with peanut butter and bacon. When Copper finishes the store bought Bacon Treats, he can eat the new homemade treats.

Copper watched him put the new treats in a bag and looked sad when Doyle put them away without letting him sample one. "You'll eat these next week, Copper," he told the bloodhound. It was no consolation to Copper, who wanted them *NOW*.

Sandy called at one o'clock to let him know they were on their way home. She didn't have time to talk about the weekend; however, Doyle sensed she enjoyed herself. At four thirty he put a bottle of wine, a takeout box with two dozen of his chocolate chip cookies, and several of the new dog treats in a cloth bag, and then he called Copper.

Copper came running to him, looking for the new treats he baked. Instead, Doyle put on the leash and led him to the Buick for a quick ride to meet Sandy's cat. Doyle wasn't sure this would be a friendly visit, but Sandy insisted on letting the two pets meet each other.

Sandy met him at the door and took the bag of goodies into the kitchen. Copper stood still. He kept smelling the air, trying to figure out what the strange odor was. Sandy bent down and scratched him behind the ears, which he enjoyed.

"Copper, can you find Casey? I think he's hiding from you because he doesn't like guests. Go find him, Copper."

Copper did just that. He smelled out the Siamese cat, going from room to room. Sandy and Doyle stood back and watched him search with his nose, eyes, and ears.

"It's amazing, isn't it?" Doyle exclaimed. "He acts the same way when he's searching for the police. Once he gets a scent in his nose, he doesn't let go, and he positions his ears to scoop up the scent and push it toward his nose."

"I know," said Sandy. "Look, Copper knows Casey is behind that door."

Copper stopped at the half-open door. He knew there was another animal behind it, but he didn't want to startle it, so he laid down and put his front feet out and laid his head down on the ground. Casey peeked out to see who it was. When the cat saw Copper, he jumped and scared the bloodhound. Copper ran back to Doyle with a look of terror.

"It's OK, Copper," Doyle said as he walked to the door. Casey stepped out and looked at the bloodhound. The two animals walked toward each other. Casey circled Copper and used his front paw to tap him on the face."

Doyle feared Copper would get scratched, but Sandy said Casey didn't have claws on his front paws. Eventually, Casey and Copper sniffed each other and realized they didn't need to fear each other.

"I think everything will be fine now," Sandy suggested. "Let's get dinner started."

"You haven't started dinner?" Doyle asked.

Sandy picked up her phone and made a call. "What do you want on your pizza, dear?" she asked.

"I like it all. Pepperoni, mushrooms, green peppers, olives, onions, anchovies, and anything else they offer," Doyle said.

"I'd like to order a large supreme pizza delivered to Sand Point," Sandy instructed. She gave the address, and they advised they would deliver it in forty-five minutes.

Doyle was grinning from ear to ear. "So that's how you make dinner?" he asked.

"Yes, when I don't have the time or energy to cook, I order take-out."

As they set the table and opened the wine, Sandy nibbled on a cookie. The two sat and talked about her weekend with the girls.

"I kept thinking about how I would have rather been with you, but it was nice spending time with my sister. I ended up losing money at the casino, and I ate too much junk food... it was fun.

"Did everyone lose money?" Doyle asked.

"No, my sister is always lucky at the slot machines. She won a jackpot worth five hundred dollars and then put it all in another machine. She ended up with a few hundred dollars more than she took. But, like I said, we all had fun."

Sandy asked, "Did you find any additional evidence in Lancole's investigation? I kept thinking about the mystery all weekend."

"Yes, and no. I think I told you it appears his neighbors didn't kill him, but they sure hated him, and now Arthur Wilcone, the neighbor to the west, is busy cleaning Lancole's yard and planning to buy the property."

"Did you find out who broke into Lancole's house?"

"No, but Trudy got me thinking about the axe. If the old man had it in the house, perhaps the killer broke in and stole it. The break in happened before someone killed him, according to his neighbors."

"Interesting... when are you going to Detroit?"

"Early Thursday morning. Ned's getting a court order for the name and address of the girl Lancole had the detective find. After we get that from Westland, we're driving to Troy to meet with the lawyer and Lancole's nephew." Doyle remembered the nephew and said, "I didn't tell you the nephew showed up Saturday afternoon. He wanted to see the house, and he had a copy of the will. He gets everything, and he said he will bulldoze the house and bury it in the dump."

"No! He can't do that. There might be valuable antiques in that house," Sandy insisted.

"Yes, but it's covered with trash."

"We need to go through that trash and make sure they preserve the historical items. That house is one of Sand Point's oldest cottages, and it's important that we save as much as we can."

"You certainty are dedicated to preservation, aren't you?" Doyle asked. It surprised him how deep Sandy's feeling were.

"Yes, I am. If you spent as much time working at the museum as I do, you would also want to preserve more."

"I understand, and perhaps I'll spend more time there, now that I have a friend to share my time with." He took her hand in his and smiled.

The doorbell rang, and Sandy jumped up to let the deliveryman in. The pizza was on time, and both Copper and Casey wanted to know what was in the large box. Doyle asked Sandy if she had treats for Casey, and she did. Together, they gave their pets treats to take their minds off the pizza. Sandy had a bag of commercial treats, and Doyle gave Copper one of the new treats he had baked earlier.

"Now you're making your own doggy treats?" Sandy asked.

"I tried. Let's see if he likes them." There was no question Copper had a new favorite treat. He ate one and begged for another. Doyle broke one into smaller pieces and offered it to Casey, who also enjoyed the bacon delight.

Sandy laughed and told Doyle she would need a large bag ASAP. "You should go into business selling these."

"No, they're just for our pets," said Doyle.

After dinner, Doyle and Sandy sat on the couch watching their pets play. The animals soon cuddled, as did Doyle and Sandy.

Getting Ready For Detroit

Doyle and Copper got home after midnight. Copper did his business in the outdoor room and became fascinated with a deer looking through the fence. Doyle watched as Copper tried to coax the deer closer, but the deer grew concerned and ran away when Copper barked.

Copper returned to the kitchen, and Doyle said, "Don't make friends with the deer. They eat our shrubs and flowers, and I don't want them walking through my garden next spring. Do you understand, Copper? They are not our friends. Besides you made one friend tonight, you don't need another."

Copper drank water, begged for a treat, and then laid down. They were both tired and slept soundly.

Doyle was wide awake before dawn. Instead of fixing breakfast, he fed and watered Copper and told him, "I'm going out for breakfast, and you can't go."

Copper looked devastated, so Doyle relented and let him ride with him. Several people had suggested he visit the local restaurant located downtown and open only for breakfast and lunch. Barry said, "Walt's is where I get and share the latest news."

At first, Doyle didn't understand what Barry meant, but as he grew to understand Barry and the residents, he knew he was talking about gossip, or as Trudy would call it, *sharing*. Doyle parked on Main Street, and even though the sun hadn't risen, there were cars parked on both sides of the street.

When he entered the establishment, Roger yell, "Doyle.... come on in and sit with us." Doyle looked to where the voice came from and there was Barry, Roger, Deputy Ned, and Chad, sitting at a large table with plates overflowing with breakfast food.

Doyle sat between Ned and Chad, feeling it was the safest place to be.

"So, does everyone eat breakfast here?"

Ned laughed, "Just those who have to eat early."

"I come here to learn what's happening in the community," reported Barry.

"Same here," remarked Roger. "So, Doyle, are you going to come to the Chamber meeting tomorrow evening? We sure could use your professional input."

"I thought you said the meetings were on the second Tuesday of the month. Tomorrow is the last Tuesday."

Roger laughed. "We changed it because we have to make plans for our Christmas party. Last year we had it the first week of December, so we thought we should plan early."

"That makes sense. You can plan on my being there, just to keep you from hounding me. There isn't a good reason I would want to be a member... I mean... I'm not a business owner anymore," Doyle said.

"Not all our members are. We have a lot of retired men and women interested in keeping our community vital."

Barry piped in, "Barb and I are members. We represent the Caseville Museum, and I agree with Roger; you would be a wonderful asset to our group."

"Only if you don't expect me to volunteer for a big job. Last time I joined a Chamber of Commerce, they made me the president, and I hated it."

Roger and Barry smiled... an evil smile. "We would never do that, Doyle... never."

The server was waiting for Doyle's order, but he hadn't had time to look at the menu. "I'll have coffee with cream, and two eggs over easy, with bacon, hash browns, and rye toast."

"Yes, sir, a number three with rye," she yelled to the kitchen. "You guys need more coffee?"

They all said yes at the same time. Chad chimed in with, "Remember, I'm decaf."

"You sure are, Chad," teased Ned.

The service was quick, and the coffee was hot and strong. "So, Ned, how is Colton doing?"

"Well, we have a good idea of who is trying to mess with him; now we need to catch the guy. So far, he hasn't been in the area."

"Who is it?" Doyle asked.

"I'll tell you later. The sheriff doesn't want the name released since we have no evidence he killed either Jenny or Luke, but he fits the bill," Ned confided.

Barry chimed in, "Have you noticed how many deaths there have been lately? Ever since Colton became our newspaper boy. Is that a coincidence, or what?"

Doyle defended Colton with, "Coincidence! This community has been lucky in the past, but times are changing, and crime is moving out of the cities and into rural areas. Look at the drug busts. The sheriff says there have been so many overdose deaths he's lost count. Is that the sheriff's fault or just a coincidence?"

"Coincidence... but I was just saying... lots of murders. When will we know who did in Old Man Lancole, anyhow?" Barry asked.

"Soon, we're going through the suspects now. I mean, right now!"

The room grew silent as Doyle scanned the looks on everyone's faces. "The killer could be here now, you know... someone in this room."

Ned laughed so hard, he knocked over his coffee mug. "Damn," he yelled, "Carol, clean up on table three."

Carol came racing out of the kitchen with a towel and cleaned the table. "You boys make such a mess," she said.

An elderly man, bent over with pain, walked over to Doyle and said, "Bob over there told me you think I killed Harold Lancole. I didn't do that, you know... why would you say such a thing?"

"I didn't say that... did I, Ned?"

Ned looked at the old man. "Henry, Bob is being an ass again. Doyle knows you wouldn't kill anyone."

"Bob, you're a son-of-a-bitch.... I'll kill you," the old man yelled back to his table. "Sorry, Ned, I didn't mean that, honest."

Doyle shook his head. "I guess I need to be careful about what I say in here. Word travels faster than the speed of light."

"Sure does," said Barry. "That's what I like about this place."

On the way back home, Doyle picked up the Monday Metro Times, since there is no delivery on Monday. While at the counter, he looked at the video monitor behind the counter and noticed that a young man was watching him. He wasn't sure where he had seen him before, but it was obvious the man didn't want Doyle to see him, because when Doyle looked in his direction, he turned around and walked behind a display rack. Doyle made a mental note of what he looked like and thought, *It may be someone who recognized me from Detroit, or perhaps I'm getting paranoid.*

The sun rose as Doyle drove into the driveway. He put the leash on Copper and together they took a long walk, enjoying the freezing November air. Copper enjoyed being outside, and even though there were many smells to follow, he stayed next to Doyle.

Chapter 21

Boring Times In Caseville

As soon as Doyle entered his home, the phone rang. He checked the number and answered, "Ned, what can I do for you?"

Ned told Doyle he was at the County Courthouse and had the court order for the name of the girl Lancole was looking for. "At first the judge didn't want to sign the order, because the detective is out of town, but since the murder took place here, he signed it. You might owe the Judge a homemade dinner because I told him how good your meal was at your party."

Doyle laughed, "I'm not into bribes, Ned. But perhaps we can work something out. So what do you have going today and tomorrow?" he asked.

"Were still on Colton's case. Is there something you need me to do?"

"No, I was just looking for something to do. It looks like I can rest until the trip to Detroit. I hope we find something new when we're there. Every time we think we have a motive or suspect, we come up short."

"Yes... sorry, but I have to get going. Chad is driving with me again, and he's getting eager to go. I'll see you on Thursday. What time should I be there?"

"I want to get on the road by eight, so get here at seven-thirty."

"OK. I'll see you then," advised Ned.

What does a retired homicide detective and master chef do when he has nothing else planned? Doyle asked himself that question. *Television is boring... Sandy is busy today volunteering at the hospital... the investigation is at a standstill, but Copper is fine.* Then it came to him: *Copper needs a bath, and since he loves my homemade bacon treats, I should bake more.*

"Oh... Copper... guess what you're getting?"

Copper came running into Doyle's waiting arms. "Do you want a bath?" He smelled the bloodhound's fur and knew it was time. "Yes, you do... don't you?"

Doyle thought giving Copper a bath would be a simple task. It wasn't. As soon as Copper saw water running in Doyle's large tub, he ran for the kitchen. *I think he's had a bath before*, Doyle conjectured. He walked into the kitchen and grabbed one of Copper's Bacon Treats. Copper followed Doyle back to the tub, and while he was eating the treat, Doyle grabbed him. *Copper, don't fight this because I don't want to get too wet*, Doyle instructed.

When he finished, Doyle was soaking wet, but Copper was clean and also soaking wet. He looked like a mangy mutt with his fur clinging close to his body. Doyle took a huge bath towel and covered his friend with it.

"Come on, Copper, let's go into the living room so we can dry off." He picked him up, carried him into the front room and set him on his rug. Doyle was on his knees, drying him off with the towel, and Copper loved it. When Doyle finished, Copper turned and licked his face. *Wow, no drool. Perhaps it's getting better*, thought Doyle.

Doyle and Copper spent the balance of the day being lazy. After dinner, he talked to Sandy for an hour, and then he watched a murder mystery on television. Doyle enjoyed detective stories, but he had a tendency to second guess the writers.

Tuesday morning, Doyle rushed outside to get his newspaper. There was snow on the ground, and the wind chilled him to the bone since he wore nothing but a robe. Copper also ventured out into the snow. His outdoor room now featured a snowdrift running from one end to the other, and he wasn't sure what to do. He found a dry corner to use and rushed back to get warm.

The two settled in the kitchen, where Doyle offered Copper food, and he accepted. Doyle read the newspaper, laughed at the funnies and wished he had something else to do. Then he called Sandy.

"Doyle, it seven in the morning, what are you doing up?"

"Getting bored. I'm sorry if I woke you, but I need a hobby or something. Did you see the lovely snow?"

"Don't tell me it snowed?"

"About four inches last night, unfortunately they think it will stay around. They're forecasting an arctic winter." Doyle sipped his coffee and tossed Copper his last old treat. His next treat will be homemade.

"What do you have planned for today?" Sandy asked.

"That's why I called, to see what you had planned."

"Today I volunteer at the elementary library for its reading program. They have grandparents coming in and reading to the kids. I love reading to them; I'll be there for about four hours."

"Oh, that sounds like fun," Doyle lied, and Sandy knew it.

"I enjoy it even if it sounds boring to you. Perhaps you should call the schools and see if they need someone to teach kids how to cook, or catch robbers with a fry pan."

"That's low, Sandy. I only used the fry pan trick once, and it worked well." They both were laughing, and Doyle felt better. "Perhaps I'll just work on my family tree. I'm finding relatives I never knew I had. I wonder if it would upset them if I called."

"How close are they?"

"You mean in miles or on the family tree?"

"Both," Sandy said.

"There is one local. He's my relative because his great-great grandmother's sister married my great-great-grandfather," Doyle explained.

"That's too distant. Are there any blood relatives? I wouldn't even count him as an actual relative."

Doyle sighed, "Nope... He's the closest. The rest are members of his family line who moved away. I guess it's just me, my sister and her daughter, and a son who hates me. That's my family."

"Don't get all depressed, Al. Sometimes friends are more important than family, and you are making friends here."

"Thank you, Sandy. I'll let you get ready for your school kids."

Sandy said she would talk to him after she got home. "You could stop over this evening. I'm sure the pets would like to visit again."

"Sorry, I'm going to the Caseville Chamber meeting. Roger and Barry's smart idea."

"Have fun and tell them I said hello. Bye, Al."

Copper was watching Doyle's conversation, and he sensed his friend felt better. Doyle got down on his knees and hugged the bloodhound. "You're a good friend, Copper. Can I consider you part of my family?"

Doyle knew the answer was yes because Copper wagged his tail and licked his face. "Thank you."

Welcome To The Chamber

Doyle dreaded having to attend the Caseville Chamber of Commerce meeting. He made a quick dinner for himself and Copper. Copper loved salmon, so Doyle baked two pieces. One for each of them. He cooked a package of baby carrots and added brown sugar, butter, and dill as a glaze. With a small salad on the side, and he was ready to eat.

So far his weight is stable, but he has a fear of becoming fat, like his sister and his mom. The doctor suggested the Mediterranean diet, which is what he's been eating all his life. The only change he's made is to cut down on sweets and white bread, and it's been working.

Copper enjoyed the salmon and begged for more, but Doyle was not giving him any of his. "This is mine. I can't help if you ate yours so fast you couldn't taste it. Next time, slow down."

Doyle dressed casually and instructed Copper to be a good dog while he was away. "I'll see you in two hours, I hope."

The meeting was taking place at the Caseville Bank, just south of the small chamber office. There were several cars parked along the road, and more in the bank's parking lot. Doyle entered the front door, and Roger greeted him.

"I'm so glad you came. I half expected you would skip the meeting."

Doyle shook Roger's hand. "Roger, you'll find I am a man of my word. Now where is the meeting?"

"It's in the boardroom; just take a left and then a right. You'll hear lots of talking... just follow the voices."

Roger was right; the room overflowed with men and women talking, some arguing, and a few whispering. It was a typical meeting, which Dole had attended many. Roger entered the room followed by his wife, Mindy. At the head of the board table was a heavy-set younger man, who Doyle didn't recognize. The name card said, Elwood Fritzenburg, Chamber President.

Elwood stood and announced, "I call this meeting to order. Let's say our pledge." Everyone put their hand over their heart and looked toward the flag. Afterward, they sat down, and Elwood began the meeting. Doyle found it to be as boring as the past two days, then the conversation turned to the Christmas party.

"I don't think we should hold the party so early," one woman yelled.

"Me either. Christmas parties should be at Christmas, not Thanksgiving," a man replied.

Elwood yelled, "Let's have order here. Is there a motion for a date?"

Roger stood and said, "I move we hold the party the second week of December on Friday at six-thirty pm."

"I second the motion," yelled a girl in the back."

"Who seconded it?" questioned Barbara, the secretary.

"That was Mindy," yelled Roger. "You know... my wife."

"Yes, Roger, I know your wife, but that didn't sound like Mindy."

Mindy stood up and said, "You're right, Barb. That was Elizabeth, but she made the second for me."

"Why didn't you speak for yourself, Mindy?"

"I don't know; I asked her to say it for me. If I'd known it would cause a problem, I would have seconded it myself."

Elwood hammered his gavel and said. "Enough of this crap. All in favor say yes." Everyone yelled yes. "Opposed say no." There was one no.

"Now," Elwood asked, "where will we be holding this party on the second Friday of December at six-thirty?"

"Doyle's house!" yelled Barry. "He has a nice man-cave with a bar, enormous kitchen and enough tables and chairs for all of us."

"I object," said Doyle. "Barry, you didn't even ask me about this. My entertainment room is not a hall to be rented out."

Roger laughed. "Did you hear what he said, guys? Doyle said We don't even have to pay rent. I second the motion."

"So, there is a motion on the floor, which has been seconded."

"Objection, Elwood," Doyle stood and yelled, "I will not allow you to turn my private home into your party place, and if you think I'll stand for this, you are all mistaken!"

Barry stood and spoke in an apologetic voice, "I'm sorry, Doyle. I rescind my motion. Everyone, it wasn't proper to assume that Mr. Doyle, a good friend of ours, would want to help us with our little party."

Several people apologized to Doyle. "Sorry, Barry can be a little crass," one woman said. Barry's wife said, "I suggested the idea to Barry, Mr. Doyle. It's just that we had such a good time at your place last week, and we thought you might share your home with us."

Doyle felt guilty. "Well, I understand, but I'm not in business, and if I catered a party in my house, I could get in trouble with the health department. My home is residential, not commercial."

A young woman said, "Two years ago we had the party in Elwood's heated garage. That's residential and not commercial. We didn't need a permit to do that, did we?"

Doyle thought for a moment. "Here is an idea. I won't cook or supply any food or drink, but I will get my kitchen certified by the Department of Health. If you buy the food, drinks, and pay my friends, Angie and her husband Alex, for their catering service, you can borrow my pub."

The room broke into applause, with whistles and many thank you's.

Barry walked up to Doyle and asked, "Do Alex and Angie own a catering company?"

"They do now, Barry. I just have to tell them about the new business they started tonight."

The meeting proceeded with talk about the Village Holiday celebration, the School Christmas Concert, and plans for Shanty Days in February.

"Shanty Days? Are you kidding me?" Mindy yelled.

Elwood asked, "Why not Mindy?"

"It rained last year. Every year we plan this event, and every year we have either too much snow and ice, or no snow and ice. I remember one year it was ten below zero all weekend."

Doyle wasn't sure what shanty days was all about, so he asked. Everyone laughed. Elwood told him, "Shanty Days in an annual event to break up the long winter. We have an ice fishing contest, a polar dipping event, broom hockey and a concert in the school auditorium. It's fun as long as the weather cooperates."

Doyle commented, "Sounds like fun. I might suggest a dog and cat show, then I can show off my bloodhound."

"What a clever idea!" Mindy said. "My cat would like that. I think we should add that event to the schedule."

Elwood laughed, "Mindy, a minute ago you said it was a waste of time to hold Shanty Days. Now you want to add a cat show."

"Yes, why not?"

"No reason. I need a volunteer to be this year's chairperson of the Shanty Days event." Elwood looked around the room as everyone avoided eye contact.

"Barry, will you take the job again? You did such a wonderful job last year; we need you, pal. Please say yes."

Barry was beaming with pride. "Yes. Thank you."

Everyone clapped their hands, and Barry bowed with joy. "Doyle, could you help with the fishing contest?"

"What does it entail?" Doyle asked.

"Oh, it's a simple job; you'll like it. Lots of fun, and I'll help."

"I suppose I can help," Doyle said, and again everyone clapped their hands. Barry named a few more members and soon he presented his committee. "We'll meet in December. I'll call and tell you where and when," Barry announced.

The meeting ended before eight thirty, and Doyle was home by nine. Since he had an early day, he and Copper went to bed before ten. Throughout the night, Doyle dreamed of snow, ice, and freezing weather. It somehow involved fish, but he wasn't sure how.

Chapter 22

Doyle Returns To Detroit

Ned rang the doorbell, and Copper ran to the door, barking, with his tail wagging and his nose twitching. "Get down, Copper, I know it's Ned; you don't have to tell me." Doyle yelled, "Come in, Ned, the door is open."

Copper stood back as Ned walked in and bent down to give the bloodhound a few pats on the head and some important scratching behind the ears. "I heard you calling my name, Copper," he said. "It's nice to see you again. Doyle, are you ready to rock and roll?"

"No, but I am ready to drive. I hope you remembered to bring the court order. You have it, don't you?"

"Of course I do. On my way, I wondered, what we do if the detective isn't home?"

"He will be there. I led him to believe I would pay him his three grand, so now he has a big incentive to be in his office when we get there."

"Smart move. Are we taking Copper with us?"

"No, I talked to Anne, my cleaner, and she's coming in later this morning to clean house. After she's done, she will help Trudy come over. Trudy will stay until we get back. It shouldn't be too late, provided you don't talk too much."

"Me? You're the one who is always jabbering." Ned liked to tease his new friend and fellow deputy.

Doyle laughed. "Is that an actual word?"

"Hell if I know. Let's get going, Mr. Jabber." Ned laughed as they walked into the garage. The two men never stopped talking. They did, however, agree to get a hamburger on the way to Detroit, but Ned wanted McDonald's and Doyle wanted Burger King. They agreed on Wendy's. When they reached Westland, Ned watched for the street names and yelled when they got near the address. It was a residential home, with a front room office. The sign on the door read, *Detective Agency ... Ring Bell*.

Doyle rang the bell, and a man who looked like he stepped out of a 1930s detective novel opened the door. "You Doyle?" he asked with a gruff voice.

"Yes, and here is what you wanted me to bring you." Doyle handed an envelope to the detective. He opened the envelope and pulled a lone piece of paper out. "Oh crap. This is a court order. What about the money you promised me?"

"I lied... sorry about that. Officer Ned would like the paperwork you have on the girl that Mr. Lancole asked you to find. If not, we will escort you to the Troy police station and place you under arrest for contempt of this court order."

"You're a bastard, but here it is." He picked up a large envelope labeled Lancole and handed it to Doyle. "I hope that old man rots in hell. You know he promised to pay me three months ago. I don't see why he asked me to get this name if he didn't need it. The old buzzard was a crazy drunk; I could tell he was a drinker the first time I met him. Was it the booze that killed him?"

Doyle took the paper and looked at it. The name of the woman is Linda Cotter, born in 1958 to Mary Cotter, a single woman. The father is unknown. She is now living in Livonia, Michigan, under the name of Linda Shepherd. Doyle looked up at the detective and said, "No, it was an axe that killed him. I need to ask where you were last Monday night between ten o'clock and...?"

"No, you don't. I haven't been out of Westland for over a year. You can ask anyone. I don't leave this town... ever." The detective sounded nervous and defensive.

"We'll ask around. In the meantime, don't leave town," Doyle advised.

Ned chuckled as they walked back to the Buick. "That was fun. You don't think he could be the killer, do you?"

"Hard to say, Ned. Anything is possible in this case." They got into the Buick and were off to Troy. Ned watched the streets and house numbers again. The lawyer's office was in an old residential area established in the 1950s. Ned counted down the house numbers, and when they found the driveway, Doyle drove up to an old ranch style home in ill repair. There was no sign showing a lawyer's office.

"Is this it?" asked Ned.

"I hope so; otherwise, we're lost," Doyle said as he turned the engine off. Let go knock on the door and see who's home. As they approached the house, Lancole's nephew parked next to Doyle's Buick. Doyle tapped Ned on the shoulder. "That's the nephew. We're at the correct address."

The three men knocked on the door, and an elderly man in his seventies greeted them. "Can I help you?" he asked.

"We're here for the meeting," Doyle said.

"Meeting... what meeting is that?"

"My uncle's reading of the will — I'm Kenneth Lancole Jr., don't you remember me?"

"Oh yes, and you must be Mr. Doyle, the man who called me the other day," the lawyer said.

"Yes, Steven, I called about Mr. Lancole's death. May we come in?"

"I guess. Where is the young woman?" Steven asked.

"What young woman?" asked Kenneth.

"Never mind. She'll be here soon," Steven said in a soft voice.

The men walked through a foyer and into a small office. There were papers stacked everywhere, and Steven walked behind his ancient wooden desk and sat down. He left Doyle, Ned, and Lancole with only one other chair in the office. Doyle told Ned to find three more chairs, and he brought them in.

"Here you go, Doyle," Ned said. The men sat down just as someone knocked on the front door. Ned walked to the front door and met a woman. She was in her early sixties, slim, with dark brown hair. Ned felt she looked familiar, but he didn't know where he might have met her. They walked back into the room.

Steven Straford looked up at the woman and asked, "Are you Linda Shepherd?" he asked.

"Yes, but please tell me what this is all about?" she asked.

"In due time, Linda. We are now all here, so let's get started. Now where was I?"

Steve appeared to have forgotten what he was doing, so Doyle interjected, "You were about to read the will, Steven."

"Ned gave Doyle a *what the hell look*, and Doyle whispered, He's old, in the mind... he's very old."

Steven started, "Mr. Harold Lancole wrote this will three weeks ago. It's a simple will, and I can attest to its authenticity, as I witnessed it along with a notary public. The will states, *Being of sound mind and body, I execute this last will and testament. In the event of my death, I bequeath my entire estate to my daughter, Linda Shepherd. To my nephew, I bequeath one dollar, and to my lawyers, five percent of my estate as administrative payment. Signed this fourth day of September."*

Linda looked very perplexed and asked, "How did he know I was his daughter?"

"I investigated until I found you a few months ago. I had a DNA sample taken without your consent, and it matched Mr. Lancole's DNA. You are his daughter, and he wants you to have all of his estate."

Doyle pulled the Westland Detective's paper from his notebook and held it up, saying, "Why did Mr. Lancole hire a detective if you had the name of his daughter?"

"I told him not to, but Harold was a stubborn man. When I gave him Linda's name, he said he wouldn't pay the detective."

Kenneth was in deep thought. The lawyer asked, "Kenneth, do you have questions?"

Doyle wondered what his reaction would be since he said he was to get everything. But Kenneth stayed calm and asked, "Is there any question regarding Linda being my uncle's daughter?"

"No, there is no question. I'm sorry Harold dropped you as his beneficiary, but I think you can understand why your uncle wanted to find his only child."

"I understand, and it's great that you found my cousin."

Linda seemed to be in a daze. "I still don't understand. Years ago my mother said she worked for a man named Lancole, and my aunt suggested he might be my father. Mother said she never told my father about me because she didn't love him. I thought my aunt was lying, and I even thought perhaps Mom was a rape victim. She lived in a dangerous neighborhood. If it's true that this man is my father, could you please tell me about him? What did he have that I might want?"

"Mrs. Shepherd, your father has left you a home in Sand Point, that's near Caseville, a 120 acre parcel of land in Bay Port, and five hundred million dollars in bank certificates, bonds, and cash."

Linda passed out and slid off her chair. Doyle reached over and prevented her from hitting her head on the floor. The lawyer pulled his desk drawer open and handed Doyle a vial of smelling salts. "Here, open this and let her smell it. She'll come around. I keep these for clients like her."

Linda coughed several times and regained consciousness. "What happened?" she asked.

Doyle held her hand and said, "You fainted. I guess it surprised you how much money you now have."

"Then I'm not dreaming?" she asked.

"No, you're not dreaming, Linda. You are a wealthy woman now."

"Oh God, this will take time to sink in... lots of time," she added in a soft voice.

Doyle asked questions regarding Mr. Lancole's murder. "Linda, you said you never met or knew your father. Is there anyone in your family, perhaps your husband or children, who might have contacted him?"

"No. My husband, Larry, has been dead since 1998. I was born Linda Cotter, and I married Larry in 1978. We never had children. Everyone knew my father was unknown."

Doyle turned to the lawyer for his next question. Steven, as Mr. Lancole's lawyer, do you know anyone who might have wanted him dead?"

"His brother, and half the people who worked for him. Harold was a bastard when he was drunk. For the past five years, he had been drunk all the time. Kenneth and his dad kept the business going while Harold drank his life away."

"Mr. Doyle, my dad didn't hate Uncle Harold. He felt sorry for him because he lived with demons. I think my uncle had a mental problem, but he would never seek help. We put up with him because he was family and we loved him."

"Well, someone hated him enough to kill him with the axe that his grandfather used to kill his aunts and uncles."

Linda sighed, "He wasn't happy, even with all that money?"

"No, he wasn't happy." Steven, the lawyer, mumbled. "I knew him for years, and I don't remember him ever smiling."

Steven instructed Linda and Kenneth to sign the paperwork to complete Lancole's will. He gave Linda the names of the banks and the account numbers where the money was being held. "This paper transfers the house, and this one the property in Bay Port. Just take these papers to Bad Axe and give them to the clerk. That should be all you need. Now, what was I doing?"

The group explained to Steven what was happening, and he said, "Thank you... I think we're done."

Doyle helped Linda to her car, and she asked him where he lived.

"I live about a mile from your father's home in Sand Point. My dog found his body on the beach."

"If I drive there, would you show me his home? I might want to move there; it would be nice to get away from Livonia."

"Yes, but the house is a mess because your father was a hoarder, and he threw nothing away, including the trash," Doyle said.

"Thank you, but I still want to come up," Linda said in a soft voice. "I can decide about the house after I see it."

Doyle handed her his card and asked if the phone number he had for her was correct. It was, and they agreed to call in a day or two to make the arrangements.

On the way home, Doyle drove past his former restaurant in Troy. The two men were in a solemn mood and talked about how the case was hitting another brick wall. "This is getting to be the murder from hell, Ned," Doyle lamented. "Any ideas about what we should do next?"

Ned chuckled and said, "I'll tell you when I get inspired. Until then, I guess we keep looking under the rocks for a clue."

A Visit To He House Of Death

Copper heard Doyle's car in the driveway, and he ran to the door. Trudy wasn't as fast. She reached the door just as Doyle pushed it open and greeted them. "Hello Trudy. I hope Copper wasn't a bother to you."

"Heavens no, we had a lot of fun. I taught him how to jump for a treat, and he taught me how to find more treats. You are all out of his Bacon Treats, and his other treats are almost gone." Trudy said. She eased herself back onto the stool and reached for her glass of water.

Doyle feigned disgust and reprimanded Copper."How could you bribe my best friend into giving you all those treats?"

Trudy laughed. "There weren't that many left. He sure enjoys the ones in the plain brown bag. I found them next to the empty bag of Bacon Treats. Did you make them?"

"Yes, and Sandy's cat even likes them. Now she wants me to sell them, but I'm too wealthy to be setting up a booth at craft shows to sell dog and cat treats."

"No, Doyle, you're too lazy to do that. Perhaps you could get someone else to bake and sell them, using your name and recipe. I can see it now, *Doyle's Little Bacon Treats*." She moved her arms as if performing in a television commercial.

"I'll think about it." Doyle sighed and walked around the room to see how clean it was. "Anne did a marvelous job of cleaning today. Did she clean out Copper's room, like I requested on the note I left?"

"No, she refused to go in there. She said, it stinks and she... well... you know."

"Yes, I know. I'll hose it down with the chemical that makes the pee smell go away. Speaking of pee, I have to go." Doyle rushed out of the room, and Copper followed him.

Trudy heard Doyle say, "Copper, you don't have to watch me pee. Go away."

When he returned, his face was red. "I imagine you heard me. I'm sorry. If I don't shut the door, he walks in and stares at me. He can be such a chore, can't he?"

"Yes, but he is so friendly. I love him, and so do you."

Doyle nodded his head in agreement and asked if she would like to go to Lefty's for an early dinner.

"That would be nice," Trudy responded. "I surmise you didn't find the killer today."

Doyle shook his head and said, "This case is going nowhere. I met Mr. Lancole's long-lost daughter today. He found her a few months ago and gave her his entire estate. She seems to be a pleasant woman, and she might become our neighbor. She's from Livonia, and her name is Linda Shepherd."

"That's nice, but who killed Mr. Lancole?"

"I wish I knew. The only suspect we have left is the man who argued with him at The Blue Water Inn before his death. The problem we have is nobody knows who he is or what he looks like."

Trudy burst out laughing. "That is quite a big problem. I'm hungry for a footlong and a big hot fudge sundae, so let's go to Lefty's."

"Sounds fattening, Trudy." Doyle knows Trudy never gains weight, no matter how much she eats. *I should be so lucky*, he thought.

After dinner, Doyle walked Trudy to her door and excused himself. "I'd come in for coffee and more visiting, but I told Sandy I would call her after dinner. She worked today at the Pigeon Museum and promised to find what she could about Lancole's family history. I'll see you tomorrow, Trudy." He bent down and kissed her cheek. She smiled and closed the heavy wood door.

Sandy was glad Doyle had called. "I just got home, and I have so much to tell you. Can I come over? It would be easier to talk face to face. Besides, I've missed you all day."

"That would be nice, and I've missed you too. Do you want coffee?" He asked.

"No, I think I need something stronger. Let's talk at your pub so I can have a mixed drink. I'll mix it. See you there, bye." Sandy piqued Doyle's curiosity. After finding nothing out in Detroit, he was eager to hear good news. Even if it's just that Sandy missed him.

Doyle filled a mug with extra strong coffee and cream and walked down to the pub. He turned the lights on and thought about soft music. *No, too romantic*, he thought. *She wants to talk about the murder, not dance.*

Sandy burst through the door, out of breath. Doyle looked at her and asked, "Did you run all the way here?"

"Don't be silly, I'm just excited to share what I found. First tell me what you learned today."

"No, first I want a big hug and kiss." She smiled and opened her arms. It was a warm hug and a passionate kiss.

"That was nice, very nice," Sandy said. "You know I'm falling for you, don't you?"

"Yes, and I, you."

"Now what happened in Detroit? She asked."

The girl Mr. Lancole was looking for is Linda Shepherd. She is a plain-looking woman, thin with dark hair... a nice soft spoken woman. Linda is his illegitimate daughter, and Lancole's lawyer asked her to attend the reading of the last will and testament. Linda didn't know what was going on. She never knew her father, and he left her his house up here and a piece of property south of Bay Port plus five hundred million dollars in cash, she fainted.

Sandy had a look of disbelief. "He had a daughter? Amazing. He must have been better looking when he was young, and perhaps he smelled better."

"I should hope so. I kept my eyes on the nephew to see what his reaction was, and he didn't get upset about being written out of the will. At the end of the meeting, I asked if anyone knew who might have wanted him dead, and they provided a long list, including Lancole's dead brother. No one is an actual suspect, so I'm at a standstill unless you found something new."

"I don't know how important this is, but I found the house where the family died in 1919. We have several old Huron County plat maps at the museum. They show who owned the land during that year; I can guide you to the property tomorrow if you like."

"Sounds like fun. Should I pack a picnic basket?" Doyle teased.

"No, but bring a camera. I called the Bay Port Historical Society, and the woman there said she knows the old house is still on that property. It's fenced off, but you could get police permission, or whatever they call it, to go into the house." Sandy said. She was enjoying the prospect of doing detective work.

"They call it a search warrant, and yes, I can have Ned get one.

Why don't you make your drink and I'll call Ned?"

Doyle told Ned about the house, and Ned said he would get the warrant in the morning. Ned said, "We can plan on meeting at your place for lunch, and perhaps you could have lunch made for us? Hot and homemade?"

"It's the least I can do; Sandy will be here too." Doyle put his phone away, and when he saw the drink Sandy made for herself, he asked if she would make one for him too.

"Yes, but there is no alcohol in it. I love mixed drinks, but only low or no alcohol." She found another glass and mixed his drink. When she finished, they took their drinks and sat in the lounge area on the leather sofa.

"Where is Copper?" she asked. Doyle smiled and went up the stairs. Sandy heard him call for Copper, and soon the two of them were sitting next to her, smiling and happy.

Chapter 23

The House Of The Dead

Doyle rolled out of bed feeling Copper's eyes staring at him. Copper stood in the doorway with the leash hanging from his mouth. Doyle checked the time and said, "Yes, we both could use a walk this morning."

The sun was just rising above the horizon when the two reached the beach. The icy waves splashed onto the frozen beach, leaving piles of ice behind. It was a cold morning, and Doyle was glad he had worn a heavy coat and knit cap. "We won't be able to walk here much longer, Copper. Every morning is becoming more of a challenge. Aren't you getting cold?"

Copper's nose was low to the ground, his ears spread out to trap stray odors. He searched for a clue to some new adventure and didn't hear Doyle's comments. After a bone chilling fifteen minutes of walking, Doyle insisted the two return home. Copper was not happy, but he obliged his friend.

Doyle filled Copper's water and food dishes and prepared himself an egg and ham scramble. While eating, he read through the paperwork he had received from Lancole's lawyer. When he read the property description, he realized that this was the same property Sandy had found on the old plat maps. He reached for his cell phone and called Ned.

"Ned, are you in Bad Axe yet?" Doyle asked.

"No, but I'm getting ready to go there. Is there something you need?"

"Yes. Do you have a pen and paper handy?"

"Yes, why?"

"I'll give you the official property description from Lancole's place south of Bay Port. Write it down and then stop into the County Clerk and get a copy of the deed for that property? We need to learn all I can about that property. This entire case revolves around the old family home." Doyle took a quick sip of coffee. After talking with Sandy, he understood how history can tell us a lot about the present.

Ned agreed and wrote the property description down. "I hope this helps because we're running out of clues, aren't we?"

"That reminds me, I asked Barry to see if his grapevine could find the man who argued with Lancole at The Blue Water Inn. I'll call him when we're done. That man and this property are our only active clues."

"Good luck with Barry. He's a nice guy, and he helps the community, but I find him too... nosey. He asks too many questions, and he's pushy."

"Well... perhaps he'll have some answers this time. I'll see you when you get here for lunch." Doyle said.

"So you're making lunch?"

"Yes. Why are you surprised? I said I would cook lunch, so I'll see you in the pub at noon."

Doyle was ready to dial Barry when his phone rang. It was Barry's number; he said, "Hello, Barry."

"I've been trying to call you all morning. I have info. on that guy you were looking for. His name is Jeffery Edanback. I talked to Barbara, and she asked Barry and Mindy, and Mindy asked the girls on the Bay Port Pool team, and Beth Fortman, the team captain, said she is dating him. Barb said Mindy said Beth told her Jeffery hated Old Man Lancole. It had something to do with Jeffery's father's death. He died six months ago, either of a heart attack or a stroke. I'm not sure because I don't know the man. Does this help?"

"Yes, Barry. Now, catch your breath while I dig into this information. Again, Barry... you did a good job. Thank you."

"My pleasure, Doyle. I enjoy being a detective; perhaps I can help you again sometime. Not that I want another murder around here; we've had too many already, if you know what I mean?"

"Yes. I hope I don't need your help again either," Doyle replied. For several minutes, Doyle sat and reflected on Barry's news. He didn't have a phone book and wasn't sure where this Jeffery guy lived, but he was sure Ned would know. He's always amazed at how much Ned knows about the people of Huron County.

Sandy was the first to arrive for lunch. She walked into Doyle's Pub just before eleven a.m. and asked if he needed an assistant cook. Doyle put her to work making a watermelon salad.

"I remember this from your party. It's so good, but what if I screw it up?" she asked.

"You won't; here is the recipe; follow it and you'll do great."

"I thought chefs did everything without a recipe. Isn't that the way it is?"

"No. If I'm creating something new, I may alter a recipe or create a new dish without one. If I like what I created, I want it to be like the original every time I make it. Following a recipe is the only way to ensure that. An excellent chef's recipe collection is his lifeline."

"Interesting," said Sandy as she cut the watermelon into small chunks. "Do you think we'll learn anything by visiting Lancole's property?"

"I sure hope so," Doyle said while attending the indoor grill. "Today I'm making something new. I flattened chicken breasts, seasoned with Greek spices and lemon, and grilled them until they were just done. When Ned arrives, I'm turning them into a grilled cheese sandwich, using provolone, smoked mozzarella and topped with bacon and avocado slices."

"Sounds good. Are you making French fries?" Sandy asked.

"No. I thought I'd do some baked sweet potato wedges. I'm trying to lose weight by cutting down on carbs."

"That's good; I can afford to lose weight too," Sandy said. She placed the bowl of watermelon salad on a cart and pushed it into the refrigerator.

Walking out she said, "I still can't believe you have a walk-in refrigerator and freezer... it's just amazing."

"But you must admit, it's a great feature," added Doyle.

Ned arrived at noon, and the group enjoyed their lunch while discussing the information they had to share. Ned got the property deed and a search warrant. "Now you owe the judge two dinners," said Ned.

Sandy laughed, "I bet you're talking about Judge Edgar Strandel, aren't you?"

"Yes, he signed our warrants, and he wants Doyle to make him a homemade dinner. Not a bribe, just as a personal favor."

Sandy looked at Doyle and said, "If you saw Judge Strandel, you would understand. He loves to eat and eat and eat. I see him at restaurants all the time."

Ned added, "Have you seen his wife? If she weighs a hundred pounds, I'll eat my shoe. I think he eats her food before she has a chance to."

"It's getting late, so let's get on the road. I'll drive Sandy, and you can follow in the Patrol car. It looks better if we have a police car, in case someone sees us going onto the property."

"Good plan," Ned said.

The group drove out of Sand Point and followed the main highway to Bay Port, a small fishing community on Saginaw Bay. The property was a few miles south on a dirt road. Sandy had the map she made and pointed out the woods where the home was. They drove down an old lane and stopped at a dilapidated gate. They could see the abandoned house through the thicket of brush and trees.

Sandy studied the map. According to this map, there are one

hundred twenty acres of land. "Did you notice the large house by the woods next to the main road? I wonder who owns that?" she asked.

Ned looked at the house. "I'm not sure, but I think Mr. Edanback owned land around here. He died a while back; his son is the guy Barry told us about."

Doyle laughed, "Ned, Sandy, now we're getting somewhere. I think the ghosts here will give up the killer, so let's look at the house of horrors."

Sandy shivered. "You make it sound so grim."

Ned pushed the gate, and it fell to the ground. "There, I did my job."

The three walked toward the old home. To the left, Sandy pointed out the remains of a barn and a small shed. "That would have been where he killed all the animals," she added. The house was a two story home, but the roof now has several open areas, allowing water to penetrate.

Sandy pointed out the clapboard siding, which still had whitewash paint. "This house was pleasant in its time. They must have abandoned it after the killings."

"Wouldn't you?" asked Ned. "Are we going in?"

"Yes," Sandy said. She was excited and fearless.

Ned was less fearless, but he pushed the wooden door further open and Sandy gasped. "Oh God, look at that," she said, pointing to the broken furniture on the floor. "It looks just as I imagined it. Harold's great-grandmother broke the chairs while fighting with her son. He was killing her grandchildren, and she fought with all her might to stop him."

Doyle walked further into the room and studied the wallpaper along the staircase. "Doesn't that look like blood stains?" he asked.

Without speaking, the group stood in the center of the living room, studying the spot where Harold Lancole's grandfather had killed half of his family. There was a deep sadness hanging in the air, and Sandy was the first to ask if they could go. "I can't take more of this," she said.

"Yes, I've had enough too; Ned; lead us out, please."

They walked back to their vehicles. Sandy had tears in her eyes, and Doyle held her. "It's OK. It happened a long time ago."

"I know, but the ghosts of the past may have caused Mr. Lancole's murder. It's sad," she said.

Sandy wiped the tears away and looked at the map again. She gazed at the land, with a look of wonder filling her face. "There's something wrong here," she said. "Look, the property line runs straight to the road and then to that fence way over there. Do you notice something strange about that new house over there?"

"Yes, it's in the center of the property line. I wonder why?"

Doyle asked Ned for the deed and noticed that there was a revision whereby Mr. Lancole sold one piece of property, twenty-five feet by two hundred feet, to Mrs. Edanback. Dated two months ago, the deed had Lancole's signature and that of a notary public.

Doyle took out the property description that Lancole's lawyer had given him. "We have a problem. Ned, look at these two and tell me what you notice."

Ned studied the pages for several minutes. Doyle then asked, "Well, enough time, what did you notice?"

"The deed we got from the lawyer doesn't show the sale of the small piece of property, and Harold Lancole's signature on the new deed doesn't match the signature on these papers. I think the new deed is a forgery."

"Bingo, Ned wins the prize!" Doyle exclaimed.

"What was the prize, Doyle?" Ned asked.

"Just a figure of speech, Ned. I wasn't serious about a prize."

"That's disappointing," Ned chuckled. "Now what do we do? Confront Mrs. Edanback?"

"No, let's go home and search for her son. Something tells me he's up to his armpits in this murder."

Copper Smells A Killer

Doyle pulled into his garage, and Ned parked in the driveway next to Sandy's car. Sandy and Doyle walked out of the garage and approached Ned.

Sandy turned to Doyle and whispered, "Al, I need to go home. I had an exciting time today, but I can't take much more. Call tonight to let me know what happened, and please be careful." She gave him a hug and a kiss.

"Thank you for the help, Sandy. I'll call this evening, and Ned and I will be careful," Doyle promised.

The two men walked to the side door. Copper was in his outdoor room watching their every move and ran through his doggy door when they entered the house. Doyle opened the refrigerator and removed a bottle of water. He asked Ned, and he requested water, too.

Doyle placed two bottles of cold water on the counter and asked, "Any idea where Jeffery would be?"

"No, but Chad might know. I believe they attended school together, and they might still be friends." Ned took his cell phone and called Chad.

"Chad, any idea where Jeffery Edanback is today? Doyle and I want to talk to him about his mother's property."

Ned put the speakerphone on so Doyle could hear Chad. "Yes, he works on a dairy farm north of Pigeon. I often see him at the bar in Bay Port, and we used to go fishing together. Do you want me to call him?"

"I take it you have his number?" Doyle asked.

Chad asked, "Ned, is that Doyle?"

"Yes, he's listening to us. Chad, would Jeffery be at work now, or at home?"

"He gets out of work in an hour. Why do you want to talk to him?"

Chad asked. He didn't understand why Doyle was looking for his friend, and Doyle sensed Chad was questioning their motives.

Doyle said, "Chad, I'll be honest with you. Jeffery may be Lancole's killer. I'm sorry, but all the evidence points to him, and we need to bring him in for questioning. I don't want anyone to get hurt... so... do you have any ideas?"

"Mr. Doyle, I'm in your driveway. I was only two miles away when you called, so let me come in and we can talk," Chad said.

The three men sat at Doyle's counter thinking of ways they could approach Jeffery. Copper was watching them, hoping someone would throw him a treat. Doyle stood and Copper ran to him, expecting a Bacon Treat... but nothing.

Doyle sat back down and spoke, "Enough of this nonsense, we have to bring him in for questioning. We could try to come up with some fancy way to lure him here, or trick him into surrendering, or whatever. I say, the two of you deputies do what you always do when you have to bring a suspect in. Go to where he works, ask to talk to him, throw the handcuffs on, and drag his ass to Bad Axe. I'll meet you there! Agreed?"

Chad thought for a moment and asked, "What if he tries to run?"

"Chase him until you catch him. Just do your job, Chad. I'm sure you've arrested your friends before. I mean, it's a small county, and you know almost everyone around. Just do your job and get it over with." Doyle was firm. He walked to the door and opened it. Copper almost ran out, but Ned stopped him.

Ned said, "Stay Copper. Doyle, we'll meet you at the sheriff's office in less than an hour."

"I'll be there," Doyle promised.

After cleaning the pub kitchen, Doyle put his coat on and headed for the door. He took one look at Copper's sad face and went back to give him a treat. "Copper, this is your case too, so come on, let's go catch our killer."

When he pulled into the county parking lot, he saw Ned and Chad escorting a young man into the sheriff's office. Doyle and Copper followed them, and Doyle asked Ned if they had had any problems.

"He tried to run, but Chad stopped him. He hasn't said a word since."

"Is there an interview room here?" Doyle asked.

Before Ned could answer, Sheriff McNabb walked into the reception area. "Doyle, what is this? An arrest? It's about time you worked on this case. Come in my office and tell me what you got."

Doyle told Ned to get Jeffery ready for an interview. "Be sure we have a recorder, audio and video. I don't want someone to imagine we pressured him into confessing."

As Ned and Jeffery walked by, Copper's nose twitched and he barked. "Copper, what's the matter?" Doyle asked.

McNabb stuck his head out of his office and yelled, "What's wrong with your dog, Doyle?"

"I believe he smells a killer, Sir," Doyle yelled back.

Chapter 24

He Said Awful Things

Doyle led Copper away from Jeffery Edanback's scent and into Sheriff McNabb's office. The sheriff tried to bend down and pet Copper, but could only pat him on the head.

"Who is your suspect? I haven't seen him in here before, so he isn't a hardened criminal."

"He's Jeffery Edanback; he lives with his mother a couple of miles south of Bay Port. We identified him as the man who had argued with Lancole before his death. I believe they built his mother's home on land that Lancole owned, and someone forged Lancole's signature on the deed to show he sold the land to her. I think Jeffery did that, and I suspect he killed the old man."

"So why the hell are you standing here? Get in there and do your job," the sheriff insisted.

"Can I leave Copper in your office?" asked Doyle.

"No problem. He's a wonderful dog. So Copper found the dead man and identified the killer?" Sheriff McNabb asked.

"Yes, Sir. He's an amazing bloodhound," Doyle opened the door and headed toward the interview room.

Jeffery was sitting on one side of a small black table with three bottles of water and notepads. There were two chairs on the other side, and Ned was sitting in one. Both men looked up when Doyle walked into the room. "We can get started now, Ned. Is everything ready?"

"Yes, Sir. I have read Jeffery his rights, and he refused a lawyer. The recorder is still running."

Doyle sat down and opened the folder containing the paperwork for the murder case. "Jeffery, did you forge the deed to your mother's home?"

"Yes, but it's a long story. Mr. Lancole killed my dad by cheating him. He caused my dad to have a massive stroke from all the stress," Jeffery looked emotional with tears running down his cheeks. Doyle realized that asking questions would be difficult.

"In that case, Jeffery, why don't you tell us everything that happened, in your own words."

Jeffery took a deep breath and a sip of water. "I grew up next door to the Lancole property. We farmed two-hundred-forty acres, one-hundred-twenty of those we leased from the Lancole estate. Do you know about the murder in 1919?"

"Yes, we know all about it," Doyle replied.

"Well... my grandfather leased the land from Mrs. Lancole. She gave him a one-hundred-year lease, and all Grandpa had to do was pay the property tax and take care of the land. They left the house where her husband had killed her family *to rot on the land*. Grandpa told me all about Mr. Lancole, the killer. He was crazy — I mean off-the-wall crazy."

Jeffery took another sip of water. Doyle could see that talking about his ordeal was making him feel calmer, so he allowed him to continue uninterrupted.

"My dad took over the farm when Grandpa died. Years ago a farmer could make a good living with a small farm, but when dad farmed those two-hundred-forty acres, he could only afford old equipment that broke down, and he soon had to take on a job during the winter, just to make ends meet."

"Mom worked part time at the big clothing store in Pigeon, but when they closed she couldn't find work, because she couldn't stand for long periods. Now she's in a wheelchair, and I have nurses helping her."

Doyle suggested Jeffery stick to what happened. "You're getting off track here. Tell us why you forged the will."

Jeffery continued, "Well... Dad was getting older, and he wanted to retire. He sold the farm, except where our house stood. It was on the corner of the hundred-twenty acres Dad owned. The land sold for over a million dollars, and then Dad put half the money into tearing down our old house and building a new one. Mom and Dad bought a motor home, and they went to Florida that winter. While in Florida, he had a new house built. When they got home, Dad discovered that the map he gave the builders was wrong, and they built the house over the property line."

"Dad got upset, and he called Mr. Lancole to see if he could buy a small section of his land. Lancole told him there was no problem. He said, 'Finish the house and when the lease is up, I'll give you the land.' Lancole said he didn't want the land anymore."

"Last year, Lancole met with my dad, and he told him to either move the house or to burn it down because the hundred year lease was up and he wanted his land back. Dad got upset, and that night he had a stroke and died."

Jeffery stopped to wipe tears from his eyes. "It still hurts, you know?"

"We understand, but can you continue?" asked Ned.

"Yes, Mom became depressed and talked about killing herself if anyone tore down the house Dad built for her. Her mind wasn't clear, and that scared me. I drove to Sand Point and talked with Mr. Lancole. He was a nasty bastard. He said things that were awful and he refused to sell me any of the land. Mr. Doyle, I got down on my knees and begged. I would have done anything to help my mom... anything."

Doyle told Ned to stop the recorder for a minute. "Let's take a break so I can use the bathroom. Ned, could you escort Jeffery to the men's room? And take those handcuffs off. We don't need him chained to the table anymore. You won't try to run, will you, Jeffery?"

"No. I'm too tired to run, but I have more to tell you."

"I know; but we all need a break," Doyle said.

Yes, I Killed Him

Doyle stopped at the sheriff's office on his way to the restroom. He poked his head in and said, "McNabb, would you ask the District Attorney to come down. I need to talk to him; it's very important."

"I'll try, but if he's in court, you'll have to wait."

Doyle used the restroom, and on his return, the Sheriff was in the hallway. "Doyle, you're in luck. Mark Bagley, the D.A. is on his way down. I told him who you were interviewing, and he's interested in hearing what the boy has to say."

"Good, I may need his help with Jeffery."

Doyle stood outside the interview room to wait for Mr. Bagley. The tall, graying man walked up to Doyle and said, "I take it you're Albert Doyle?"

Doyle put his hand out and responded, "Yes, and your Mark Bagley. I'm glad to meet you. We have Jeffery Edanback in the interview room. He told us that Mr. Lancole cheated Jeffery's dad and caused him to suffer a deadly stroke. We stopped the interview before he could tell us about Lancole's death. I think you need to hear what happened since you will prosecute the case."

"Thank you for your professionalism; it's refreshing, Mr. Doyle."

"Just call me Doyle; let's finish this interview."

The two men walked into the room. Doyle asked Ned to get another chair. When Ned returned, Doyle said, Jeffery, this man is the District Attorney, Mr. Bagley. He will listen to the rest of your story with us. What happened after that visit with Mr. Lancole?"

Jeffery seemed a little nervous and began with, "That meeting with Mr. Lancole was about six months ago, just after Dad died. He wouldn't help, so I forged a deed. I got on the internet and studied what I had to do to show that he gave us enough property so Mom's house would be on her own land. Then I paid a friend, who is a notary public, to witness the deed. I knew that was wrong, but I didn't know what else to do."

"Mr. Lancole knew I forged the deed, and when he saw me in The Blue Water Inn, he told me he was going to the police unless I helped him. He asked if I knew where the axe was that his grandfather used to kill his mother and children. I had the axe in my room, and I told him how I had found it when I was a kid. It was under the front porch. My grandpa told me to get rid of it because it was evil; I lied and told him I got rid of it, but I hid it under my bed, instead."

"Lancole told me he would give Mom the land if I gave him the axe. I went to his home and was ready to give him the axe, and he showed me the new deed he had to give Mom her home back. I took the axe into his hellhole house, and he grabbed it and laughed. 'Now I have both the axe and my land.' He pushed me out of his house, but I grabbed the axe and ran. No way in hell was he going to screw my family again."

Jeffery stopped talking and looked at Doyle. "I broke into his house about a month ago to get the deed he had, but I couldn't find it. Then, I tried to break into your home when I heard you had taken Lancole's papers to your office. I had to see if it was there."

"My bloodhound greeted you, didn't he?" asked Doyle.

"Yes, he kept me out of the house," Jeffery added.

"Jeffery, you seem to have skipped how Mr. Lancole ended up dead. You must tell us what happened."

"Mr. Lancole's car was outside the bar, and I wanted to talk to him one more time. I figured he knew I had broken into his house, but I also knew he wanted the axe. In my mind, I hoped he would give me the deed in trade for the axe. I followed Larry, the cook at Blue Water, and when he dropped him off at Sand Point, I followed The Old Man. He saw my truck and ran in front of me, screaming. I was going so slow that he bumped me and fell down. When he got up, he had blood on his face, but I didn't care. I told him I had the axe and would trade it for the deed. He said OK, so I gave the axe to him. Lancole ran down to the beach, and I chased him. He tried to kill me with the axe, and I knocked him down, took the axe and... I didn't realize it... but... I hit him on the head. When I saw what I had done, I got scared and ran, leaving the axe on the beach. Mr. Doyle, I didn't want to kill him; I wanted him to do what was right by my mom."

Jeffery had his face in his hands and was sobbing. Ned tried to comfort him, but he couldn't.

Doyle stood and asked Mr. Bagley to step out of the room with him. "Ned, get Jeffery another water or perhaps some coffee, and get him more Kleenex tissues."

Mr. Bagley joined Doyle in the hallway. "I need to do one more thing, Mark." He dialed Richard Ketlinger, the CSI inspector in Bridgeport. "Richard, Doyle here. Can you tell me if Mr. Lancole handled the axe?"

"Just a minute, Doyle."

While Richard was getting his notes, Doyle asked Mr. Bagley what he thought about the case? Before the D.A. could answer, Richard was back.

"Yes, his were the only prints on the axe. I assumed the killer wore gloves; however, the victim handled the axe. Do you have a suspect?"

"I think we've found our man," Doyle said with a hint of sadness.

Mr. Bagley asked, "Well? Are you going to share with me?"

"Yes, the evidence matches what Jeffery told us. How are you going to handle this?"

Mark took a deep breath. "I have to consider all the evidence and ramifications to the community, but it's not premeditated and there were extenuating circumstances."

"Enough to call it self-defense?"

"I'll consider it, but he needs to get a lawyer first. Tell him I'll talk to his lawyer, but I won't charge him with first degree murder."

Doyle felt relieved, and he shook Mark's hand. Mark walked into the sheriff's office, and Doyle returned to the interview room. He told Jeffery what Mr. Bagley said and asked if he had a lawyer. Jeffery said he knew a lawyer whom he trusted, so Ned gave him his phone, and together they found the telephone number.

Doyle walked out of the room to retrieve Copper, who was eager to get out of McNabb's office. The two of them walked back to the interview room, and Ned told Doyle that Jeffery's lawyer would arrive in a few minutes. "I'll take care of the paperwork, Doyle. Jeffery was lucky you were here to handle this case. I don't think he would have been so lucky if the State Police had investigated."

Chapter 25

Party! Party! Party!

Doyle couldn't wait to get home to talk to Sandy, so he connected the phone to his car's Bluetooth and said, "Call Sandy."

The phone rang, and there she was. He told her what had happened in Bad Axe, and it relieved her to hear Jeffery would get a fair deal from the district attorney. Doyle asked if she wanted to come over for dinner, and she told him she had to go with her sister to Bay City.

"Al, the Huron County Historical Society is having a Christmas party in Bad Axe, and I was wondering if you would like to come with me. You don't have to, but it would make me happy."

"I will do anything to make you happy, Sandy. When is the party?"

"The first Saturday in December."

Doyle thought for a moment. "OK. I'll escort you to that party provided you come with me to the Caseville Chamber Christmas party on the second Friday of December at my place, and then on the third Saturday afternoon we're having a birthday party for our friend Trudy. The next party is at your home for the family Christmas."

"That sounds correct. Are there any other parties we are forgetting?" Sandy asked.

"Yes, will you accompany me to a New Year's Eve party at my place? Just a few friends?"

"We'll see, but I'm sure I can fit you in. Can I bring my cat?"

"Any time; any time at all," Dole said.

Sandy had to run, so they ended the call with an air-hug and kiss.

Copper was having trouble figuring out where Sandy was. He kept looking at the speakers, both front and back; he concluded it was magic and laid down on the front seat.

"Copper, we will be busy for the next month, so you can't find another body... understood?"

Doyle passed many windmills and farms. He took the scenic route and watched the ice forming on Lake Huron as he drove along M-25. West of Port Austin, he stopped at a small roadside park and walked with Copper along the snow covered beach. Doyle cleaned up after Copper and hurried back to the warm Buick.

When he passed a party store that was still open, he wanted a hot cappuccino. To his dismay, they turn it off after Labor Day, so he bought a cold bottle of Starbucks Ice Coffee and a small bag of turkey jerky for Copper. The girl behind the counter was working on her knitting, and Doyle asked what she was making.

"It's a coat for my cat. She gets cold in the winter. I also make them to sell at the craft shows in town."

Doyle took her business card and said he would call if he needed one for his girlfriend's cat.

Back in the car, he asked Copper if he wanted a coat for winter. Copper looked out the window as snow fell on the brown leaves along the side of the road, and Doyle decided his answer was no.

As Doyle drove, he considered how finding one dead body on the beach had changed his life in Huron County. *It started as a simple retirement;* he thought. *Now that I'm a detective again, I have new friends, and everyone wants to have their parties in my man cave. Strange how things happen... Is it destiny or just good luck?*

He looked down at Copper; he was fast asleep.

Driving through Caseville, Doyle noticed Barry was still in the

Caseville Chamber office. At first he thought about sneaking past the office, but he stopped.

"Barry, it's good to see you at work. Anything new happening in town?" Doyle knew Barry always had the latest news.

"I have no news to share, but I understand you found Lancole's killer? Can you talk about it?"

Barry learned Doyle doesn't share the same way many in the community do. Doyle smiled and said, "Sure can, Barry. We arrested Jeffery Edanback." Doyle told Barry everything that happened, and how Jeffery wasn't guilty of premeditated murder. "It was more of an accident or self-defense than murder," he said.

Barry didn't realize it, but Doyle was using him to spread the word. If Barry tells his grapevine what happened, then perhaps they won't pester Doyle for information. Besides, Doyle liked Barry, even though he asks too many questions.

At home, Doyle contacted Mr. Lancole's nephew, his lawyer and daughter, Linda. He told them what had happened, and they understood that the Old Man's anger and bitterness had caused his death. Kenneth Lancole put it best when he said, "That axe was evil, but I am convinced my uncle had the same sickness that his grandfather had."

Linda asked if Doyle knew of a place she could stay when she came up to see the cottage. Doyle gave her information about the motels in Bad Axe and one year-round motel in Caseville. "I will call the Caseville motel and reserve a room," she said. "You can expect me in the second week of December. I'm still not adjusted to having money, but I want to get away from the city, and I've always wanted to live up north. Will you be around to show me the house?"

"Yes, but once you see the house, you might decide to tear it down and build a new home," Doyle advised.

Doyle and Copper watched a beautiful sunset, and then they spent the evening watching television. Doyle enjoyed a British Mystery and Copper ended the evening watching Planet Earth.

Party Time In Huron County

Doyle and Sandy enjoyed the Huron County Historical Society Christmas party in Bad Axe. It took place at the Franklin Inn, a banquet hall with a nice buffet. The buffet was for everyone, not just their party, but it was nice. Sandy introduced Doyle to the other Historical Society members, from Pigeon and around the County.

Barry and Barbara represented the Caseville Museum. Doyle mentioned having them join their table, but Sandra was waiting for the rest of the Pigeon Members to arrive. "I promised to save them a place at our table."

The party was enjoyable, and only a few guests asked Doyle about the murder he helped solve. Doyle tried to give Copper all the credit by saying, "My bloodhound discovered the old man's body and, in the last moments of the case, he identified the person responsible. I'm just glad the young man isn't being charged with murder. It was a sad situation that ended as well as expected."

That statement became a mantra that Doyle used many times. Sandra tired of hearing it and suggested he come up with something new. He couldn't think of anything, so he used it only when she wasn't around.

The following Saturday, at Trudy's birthday party, Doyle decided on a simple lunch of footlong hot dogs, chili cheese fries, fried mushrooms, or onion rings, and coleslaw. Trudy's favorite meal at Lefty's Diner. He also made a birthday cake decorated in shades of pink, dark green, and white. Angie helped with the cake, and Alex cooked the food. Doyle was setting the couple up in their own catering business, and he told them they could use his kitchen until he found a suitable place for them in Caseville.

Guests at the party included Colton and Lacie and their friends and family. Seth and Beth arrived a little late. Doyle enjoyed talking to all of Trudy's friends. It saddened him that none of her family came to the party even though Doyle and Sandy had sent handwritten invitations to them. They didn't tell Trudy about the invitations, though.

Doyle took Colton aside and asked about his injury. "I heard what happened, but I was busy with the Lancole murder. Are you healed now?"

Colton laughed, "I can sit down again, but it still hurts, and I'm now the butt of many jokes. Are you aware I'm not delivering the Metro newspapers?"

"Yes, they sent me a letter, and the new guy drives an old beat up station wagon with smoke pouring out the windows. My paper smells like an ashtray."

"Sorry. I know who the driver is. At least he will get you the paper, no matter what the weather is like."

"Are you dedicating more time to your business?"

"Yes, and also to Lacie. We can now date like normal people."

The two friends returned to Trudy's birthday party. Instead of giving a gift, they all made donations to the food bank in her name. She loved having her friends share her joy.

The Caseville Chamber of Commerce Christmas party was not as easy as the first two. Doyle and Alex planned a meal for twenty couples. The chamber hired Angie and Alex as their caterers and, with Doyle's help, Alex ordered the food. He was nervous because if this party is a success, word will spread and their business will start on a firm footing.

Roger insisted on prime rib, potatoes, a vegetable, salad, and two deserts. Doyle showed Alex how to cook the dishes using the professional kitchen. When the guests arrived, Angie helped with the bar as Doyle and Alex finished the food. Sandra played hostess and welcomed the chamber members. When the guests passed by the buffet, it pleased Alex to hear all the compliments. "Wow, this looks great." "Look at that prime rib. It's done just the way I like it!" "I'm so hungry I could eat a horse; this isn't a horse, is it? I'm just joking, Alex... everything looks great."

Doyle and Sandy filled their plates after the rest of the guests went through the line. Sandy pointed out who was who. "That's the banker and his latest girlfriend. He's been single for almost six months. He divorced his third wife, and now he's looking for his fourth."

Barry was sitting at Doyle's table, and Barb was helping Sandy describe the members Sandy didn't recognize. She pointed out an elderly woman and her young escort. "That's Mrs. Stuffel. Her husband owned a chain of supermarkets in Detroit, which he sold to Kroger. Then he up and died four years ago. Now she has a thing for young men, or should I say, boys?"

"Barbara, you're so catty. She's on the Pigeon Library Board, and she's delightful. For her age, she looks remarkable."

Barbara laughed. "She should be in good condition; those boys keep her active."

The two girls were having fun, but Sandy realized they were getting out of hand. "I'm sorry, Doyle, we're not always making fun of people, but sometimes... we... " Sandy had no excuse. She and Barbara returned to eating their food.

Barry whispered to Doyle, "See that enormous guy over there? He's the judge."

Doyle laughed out loud. "So, he finally got his meal, didn't he?"

"What you you mean?" asked Barry.

"I owed him one or two dinners, that's all."

Harold Lancole's daughter called Doyle the following Monday and said, "I'm at the hotel and I wonder if I could meet you at your place. Are you still willing to show me my house in Sand Point?"

Doyle agreed, but he wanted to call Sandy first. "You can come here after lunch, about one o'clock. Be sure to dress warm, I'm not sure the heat is on in the house."

After ending the call, Doyle spoke to Sandy. She was eager to meet Linda Shepherd. "Do you know what her plans are for the house?"

"No, that's why I wanted you here."

Sandy and Linda arrived at the same time. They parked in the

Doyles's driveway. Sandy introduced herself, and by the time Doyle greeted them, they sounded like old friends. Linda agreed with Sandy that they should preserve the historical home, and Doyle reminded her she may change her mind after she looked inside the house.

Linda was not shocked when she saw the house. She talked about how beautiful it will be when she's done remodeling the house. Sandy suggested having a contractor clean the house, and Doyle gave her Richard Waters' phone number. Doyle assured her she would love his work.

A Family Christmas and New Years

The party season was almost over, and Sand Point looked like a Christmas card with beautiful snow sparking like glitter. Doyle and Sandy had already purchased their gifts and didn't need to do more shopping. Doyle picked out a beautiful pair of diamond earrings and a handmade silk scarf in Sandy's favorite colors. He wasn't sure what Sandy bought him; he hoped it wasn't clothing because he is fussy and hates to tell people when he doesn't like their gift.

Family Christmas at Sandy's always took place on Christmas Eve. They spent Christmas Day in church and relaxing in front of the fireplace. Doyle arrived at her home at five in the afternoon. He brought several bottles of wine and a large box of gourmet chocolates direct from the maker in Grand Haven. It was Doyle's favorite when he was in Detroit, and he always orders several boxes every year.

Doyle had met both of Sandy's sons and daughter in-laws, but he hadn't met the grandchildren... there were three, aged five, twelve and sixteen. He met Matthew, the sixteen-year-old, in December when he stopped at his place to sell nuts for the Future Farmers of America group in Pigeon. Matthew knew Doyle would place a big order, and two hundred dollars later, Matthew thanked him and shook his hand. He was a nice boy, with his father's good looks.

Copper and Casey chased each other around the house, and

Copper couldn't understand what Casey was doing in the little box in the corner. After he put his nose in the sand, he knew better than to do that again. Sandy and her daughters-in-law wouldn't let Doyle help with the food. "You go into the family room and visit. We're the chefs tonight."

Doyle discussed farming, football, and baseball with Sandy's sons. He suggested they all go to the Tigers' opening game next spring, and the kids got excited at the prospect. "We'll see," said Ronald, Sandy's eldest son. "It's just hard to get away in the spring. Lots of work to do."

The girls came out and announced, "Dinner is served." The kids ran into the kitchen, and the adults followed. Doyle could tell there was tension between Sandy's sons, but he tried to ignore it.

A feast of beef, baked potatoes, and assorted vegetables and salads covered the table. On the counter, there were several homemade pies ready to eat.

Sandy asked Doyle if he would say a blessing. He said the Lord's Prayer and added, "Lord, thank you for guiding me to this wonderful community where I have found so much to be thankful for. Please keep us all in good health and let us help those around us whenever we can. Bless this food and those who prepared it for us. Amen."

Copper stayed in the living room because Doyle warned him, but Casey came in and Sandy gave him treats under the table. After dinner, Sandy's sons helped with the dishes while the kids sat around the Christmas tree trying to figure out what was in their gifts.

The first gifts opened were the children's. It was an electronic festival of gifts mixed with clothing and a new pickup truck for young Matthew. Matthew's dad gave him the keys and told him to go into the garage. The truck wasn't new, but to Matthew it was the best gift ever.

Doyle and Sandy put both of their names on one gift for each of the kids. Doyle let her pick them out since she knew their tastes better than he did. They loved their gifts. The adults exchanged a few gifts. Sandy told Doyle Her sons and their wives saved their gifts for a personal time at home.

When Sandy opened Doyle's two gifts, she exploded with happiness. The diamond earrings were perfect, and she put the silk scarf on. Doyle opened one gift from Sandy, and it was an arctic style overcoat with a removable hood and face mask. "You'll need it this winter when you judge the fishing contest," Sandy advised him. "It gets cold on the ice, and even colder if you fall through the ice."

Doyle shivered at the thought. The second gift was a large envelope. Inside there was a flyer about Ireland and two tickets for a guided tour, including airline tickets. The note said, *'So we can find family and enjoy our golden years. Love Sandy.'*

It surprised Doyle, and he gave her a hug and asked, "What about your family?"

We can plan something. "Two of the girls from Pigeon are also going on this tour, and I thought it would be fun to share with you."

The last two gifts were for Copper and Casey. Doyle handed Sandy a small gift bag decorated with cats wearing Santa caps. Sandy pulled out the tissue, and there was a beautiful reddish brown sweater for Casey. In light peach letters, the artist wrote the name Casey on each side.

"Casey, come here. Look what Doyle got you," Sandy said.

"Meow," Casey said as he walked away.

Sandy gave Copper's gift box to the bloodhound. Copper chomped on it and pulled the paper off, revealing Bacon Treats, a shearling coat like Doyle's, and a tweed jacket and cap. Sandy explained, "It's a Sherlock Holmes outfit. I could have gotten the pipe with it, but Copper doesn't smoke."

Copper ate the treats and left the coat laying on the floor. Doyle said, "He loves it, Sandy."

Everyone agreed it was a wonderful Christmas in Sand Point. The kids loved the snow. There were over five inches on the ground, and the forecast called for five more before the New Year.

At the end of a long evening, Doyle picked up his gifts and put Copper's leash on his collar. At the door he thanked Sandy, and she gave him a loving kiss. "I'll see you on New Year's Eve. Bye."

Chapter 26

Happy New Years

Sandy drove to Doyle's on New Year's Eve. His party was to start at nine p.m. with a light dinner and would end with dancing, billiards, darts, cards, or whatever activity the guests wanted to take part in. They limited the guest list to five couples: Sandy and Doyle, Angie and Alex, Ned and Alice, Sandy's sister Kathy and her husband Sam, and Barry and Barbara.

Sandy and Barbara helped with the decorations, and Barbara picked out romantic background music. Dinner was a seafood feast with lobster, salmon, shrimp, fried potatoes, a cucumber salad, and cheese biscuits.

Everyone enjoyed the meal, and after dinner the music volume increased and some guests, including Doyle and Sandy, danced. Several of the guys wanted to play pool, but their wives and girlfriends outnumbered them. Doyle turned the television on at eleven thirty so they could watch the New York Celebration.

Barry suggested that next year they all go to New York to celebrate. After consideration, everyone declined. "Too cold," they agreed.

"It's nice and warm right here," Barbara said as she cuddled up to Barry. Ned and Alice made themselves comfortable on the leather sofa, and Doyle and Sandy sat on the rug in front of the fireplace, chatting. A few minutes before the ball dropped, Alex and Angie brought around a bottle of champagne and filled their glasses. At midnight they broke into song and cheers. It was a new year with new friends.

Even Copper and Casey looked like they were celebrating because someone put little party hats on their heads.

After Angie and Alex cleaned the pub and kitchen, Doyle gave them a cash tip and thanked them for helping. They told Doyle that he made them happy by including them in his life. They headed home to relieve their baby sitter and Sandy and Doyle led the animals up the stairs to his living quarters.

Doyle smiled and gave her a big kiss. If you had an overnight case, I'd suggest staying with me tonight. Sandy walked to the front closet and pulled her case out. "I was expecting you to ask, so yes, I would love to spend the first night of the new year with you."

Copper and Casey watched as Sandy shut Doyle's bedroom door. The two animals, Copper and Casey, laid down on Copper's rug and fell asleep. It was a happy New Year in Sand Point, with many more to come.

The author's other novels.

In Search Of Elysium

Kevin Carpenter is learning disabled. In a touching adventure he leads his friends on a search for God, taking them deep into space, in search of a planet called Elysium.

Death on the Point

The Blackwell Series - 1

Colton Blackwell, a football star and teenage detective, stars in this fast moving mystery series; a humorous and romantic novel filled with action and adventure

Blood Bath

The Blackwell Series - 2

Colton Blackwell is faced with another murder. The humor, romance, and adventure continues.

Deadly Sixteen & A Killer With

The Spirit Walker Series - 1 & 2

Psychological thrillers with emotional weight. They feel like a blend of Shutter Island, The Sixth Sense, and small-town Americana horror. The pacing and character dynamics are powerful.

Doyle Mysteries

No. 1 - The Scent Of Murder

Doyle, a retired police detective and master chef, and his Bloodhound (Copper) face a life filled with luxury and murder. A cozy mystery for all ages.

www.duanewurst.com

duanewurst.com@gmail.com

Share your opinion and do a review.

COMING SOON

Deadly Guilt and Shame

A Halocaust story you will never forget.

The Spirit Walker Series

Book 4

www.duanewurst.com

duanewurst.com@gmail.com

Deadly Dance

The Spirit Walker Series

Book 3

The big bands are playing your favorite tunes,
but a killer is on the loose. Can Tianna and Charlie help
stop a killer from Detroit's 1930s?

Duane Wurst

www.ingramcontent.com/pod-product-compliance
Lightning Source LLC
Chambersburg PA
CBHW060316260626
47160CB00007B/2632